"A twisted love story." —Hamptons.com

"Koontz has covered a multitude of fiction genres during his long and successful writing career, but when he turns his attention to suspense thrillers there are few authors who can match him for sheer page-turning power. His plots are compelling and unpredictable, the characters engaging, and the wording as sleek and on-target as a guided missile. Anything can happen, and not just within the usual confines of natural law and order. . . . Masterful economy of words . . . Koontz takes readers down the twisted and torturous path of paranoia . . . [and] keeps readers guessing every step of the way, building the suspense until the plot seems ready to burst and then, in a brilliant finale, [he] ties all the threads together. . . . Another gem from a master of suspense that raises a number of profound questions while letting readers discover the answers for themselves, both in the plot and in their lives."

—Toledo *Blade*

"A thriller ripped from the pages of our nightmares."

—BarnesandNoble.com

ALSO BY DEAN KOONTZ

Relentless • *Odd Hours* • *The Darkest Evening of the Year*
The Good Guy • *Brother Odd* • *The Husband*
Forever Odd • *Velocity* • *Life Expectancy* • *The Taking*
Odd Thomas • *The Face* • *By the Light of the Moon*
One Door Away From Heaven • *From the Corner of His Eye*
False Memory • *Seize the Night* • *Fear Nothing*
Mr. Murder • *Dragon Tears* • *Hideaway* • *Cold Fire*
The Bad Place • *Midnight* • *Lightning Watchers*
Strangers • *Twilight Eyes* • *Darkfall* • *Phantoms*
Whispers • *The Mask* • *The Vision* • *The Face of Fear*
Night Chills • *Shattered* • *The Voice of the Night*
The Servants of Twilight • *The House of Thunder*
The Key to Midnight • *The Eyes of Darkness*
Shadowfires • *Winter Moon* • *The Door to December*
Dark Rivers of the Heart • *Icebound* • *Strange Highways*
Intensity • *Sole Survivor* • *Ticktock*
The Funhouse • *Demon Seed*

DEAN KOONTZ'S FRANKENSTEIN
Book One: Prodigal Son
Book Two: City of Night

DEAN
KOONTZ

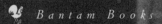 *Bantam Books*

YOUR HEART
BELONGS *to* ME

A Novel

2009 Bantam Books Mass Market Export Edition

Copyright © 2008 by Dean Koontz

Published in the United States by Bantam Books, an imprint of The Random House Publishing Group, a division of Random House, Inc., New York.

BANTAM BOOKS and the rooster colophon are registered trademarks of Random House, Inc.

Originally published in hardcover in the United States by Bantam Books, an imprint of The Random House Publishing Group, a division of Random House, Inc., in 2008.
A signed, limited edition has been privately published by Charnel House.
charnelhouse.com

Title page photograph © Fletcher Buckley

ISBN: 978-0-553-84144-2

Cover design by Jac Song: jsong@optonline.net
Cover image from Trevillion images

Printed in the United States of America

www.bantamdell.com

9 8 7 6 5 4 3 2 1

This book is dedicated to Tim and Serena Powers
for reasons obvious to anyone who knows them

Things fall apart; the centre cannot hold;

Mere anarchy is loosed upon the world,

The blood-dimmed tide is loosed, and everywhere

The ceremony of innocence is drowned . . .

—*W. B. Yeats*, "The Second Coming"

YOUR HEART
BELONGS *to* ME

P
A
R
T

1

The houses are all gone under the sea.
The dancers are all gone under the hill.

—*T. S. Eliot,* "East Coker"

ONE

Ryan Perry did not know that something in him was broken.

At thirty-four, he appeared to be more physically fit than he had been at *twenty*-four. His home gym was well equipped. A personal trainer came to his house three times a week.

On that Wednesday morning in September, in his bedroom, when he drew open the draperies and saw blue sky as polished as a plate, and the sea blue with the celestial reflection, he wanted surf and sand more than he wanted breakfast.

He went on-line, consulted a surfcast site, and called Samantha.

She must have glanced at the caller-ID readout, because she said, "Good morning, Winky."

She occasionally called him Winky because on the

afternoon that she met him, thirteen months previously, he had been afflicted with a stubborn case of myokymia, uncontrollable twitching of an eyelid.

Sometimes, when Ryan became so obsessed with writing software that he went thirty-six hours without sleep, a sudden-onset tic in his right eye forced him to leave the keyboard and made him appear to be blinking out a frantic distress signal in Morse code.

In that myokymic moment, Samantha had come to his office to interview him for an article that she had been writing for *Vanity Fair*. For a moment, she had thought he was flirting with her—and flirting clumsily.

During that first meeting, Ryan wanted to ask for a date, but he perceived in her a seriousness of purpose that would cause her to reject him as long as she was writing about him. He called her only after he knew that she had delivered the article.

"When *Vanity Fair* appears, what if I've savaged you?" she had asked.

"You haven't."

"How do you know?"

"I don't deserve to be savaged, and you're a fair person."

"You don't know me well enough to be sure of that."

"From your interviewing style," he said, "I know you're smart, clear-thinking, free of political dogma, and without envy. If I'm not safe with you, then I'm safe nowhere except alone in a room."

He had not sought to flatter her. He merely spoke his mind.

Having an ear for deception, Samantha recognized his sincerity.

Of the qualities that draw a bright woman to a man, truthfulness is equaled only by kindness, courage, and a sense of humor. She had accepted his invitation to dinner, and the months since then had been the happiest of his life.

Now, on this Wednesday morning, he said, "Pumping six-footers, glassy and epic, sunshine that feels its way deep into your bones."

"I've got a deadline to meet."

"You're too young for all this talk about death."

"Are you riding another train of manic insomnia?"

"Slept like a baby. And I don't mean in a wet diaper."

"When you're sleep-deprived, you're treacherous on a board."

"I may be radical, but never treacherous."

"Totally insane, like with the shark."

"That again. That was nothing."

"Just a great white."

"Well, the bastard bit a huge chunk out of my board."

"And—what?—you were determined to get it back?"

"I wiped out," Ryan said, "I'm under the wave, in the murk, grabbin' for air, my hand closes around what I think is the skeg."

The skeg, a fixed fin on the bottom of a surfboard, holds the stern of the board in the wave and allows the rider to steer.

What Ryan actually grabbed was the shark's dorsal fin.

Samantha said, "What kind of kamikaze rides a shark?"

"I wasn't riding. I was *taken* for a ride."

"He surfaced, tried to shake you off, you rode him back down."

"Afraid to let go. Anyway, it lasted like only twenty seconds."

"Insomnia makes most people sluggish. It makes you hyper."

"I *hibernated* last night. I'm as rested as a bear in spring."

She said, "In a circus once, I saw a bear riding a tricycle."

"What's that got to do with anything?"

"It was funnier than watching an idiot ride a shark."

"I'm Pooh Bear. I'm rested and cuddly. If a shark knocked on the door right now, asked me to go for a ride, I'd say no."

"I had nightmares about you wrestling that shark."

"Not wrestling. It was more like ballet. Meet you at the place?"

"I'll never finish writing this book."

"Leave the computer on when you go to bed each night. The elves will finish it for you. At the place?"

She sighed in happy resignation. "Half an hour."

"Wear the red one," he said, and hung up.

The water would be warm, the day warmer. He wouldn't need a wet suit.

He pulled on a pair of baggies with a palm-tree motif.

His collection included a pair with a shark pattern. If he wore them, she would kick his ass. Figuratively speaking.

For later, he took a change of clothes on a hanger, and a pair of loafers.

Of the five vehicles in his garage, the customized '51 Ford Woodie Wagon—anthracite-black with bird's-eye maple panels—seemed to be best suited to the day. Already stowed in the back, his board protruded past the lifted tailgate windows, skeg up.

At the end of the cobblestone driveway, as he turned left into the street, he paused to look back at the house: gracefully sloping roofs of red barrel tile, limestone-clad walls, bronze windows with panes of beveled glass refracting the sun as if they were jewels.

A maid in a crisp white uniform opened a pair of second-floor balcony doors to air the master bedroom.

One of the landscapers trimmed the jasmine vines that were espaliered on the walls flanking the carved-limestone surround at the main entrance.

In less than a decade, Ryan had gone from a cramped apartment in Anaheim to the hills of Newport Coast, high above the Pacific.

Samantha could take the day off on a whim because she was a writer who, though struggling, could set her own hours. Ryan could take it off because he was rich.

Quick wits and hard work had brought him from nothing to the pinnacle. Sometimes when he considered his origins from his current perch, the distance dizzied him.

As he drove out of the gate-guarded community and descended the hills toward Newport Harbor, where thousands of pleasure boats were docked and moored in the glimmering sun-gilded water, he placed a few business calls.

A year previously, he had stepped down as the chief executive officer of Be2Do, which he had built into the most successful social-networking site on the Internet. As the principal stockholder, he remained on the board of directors but declined to be the chairman.

These days, he devoted himself largely to creative development, envisioning and designing new services to be provided by the company. And he tried to persuade Samantha to marry him.

He knew that she loved him, yet something constrained her from committing to marriage. He suspected pride.

The shadow of his wealth was deep, and she did not want to be lost in it. Although she had not expressed this concern, he knew that she hoped to be able to count herself a success as a writer, as a novelist, so that she could enter the marriage as a creative—if not a financial—equal.

Ryan was patient. And persistent.

Phone calls completed, he transitioned from Pacific Coast Highway by bridge to Balboa Peninsula, which separated the harbor from the sea. Cruising toward the peninsula point, he listened to classic doo-wop, music younger than the Woodie Wagon but a quarter of a century older than he was.

He parked on a tree-lined street of charming homes and carried his board half a block to Newport's main beach.

The sea poured rhythmic thunder onto the shore.

She waited at "the place," which was where they had first surfed together, midway between the harbor entrance and the pier.

Her above-garage apartment was a three-minute walk from here. She had come with her board, a beach towel, and a small cooler.

Although he had asked her to wear the red bikini, Samantha wore yellow. He had hoped for the yellow, but if he had asked for it, she would have worn red or blue, or green.

She was as perfect as a mirage, blond hair and golden form, a quiver of light, an alluring oasis on the wide slope of sun-seared sand.

"What're those sandals?" she asked.

"Stylin', huh?"

"Are they made from old tires?"

"Yeah. But they're premium gear."

"Did you also buy a hat made from a hubcap?"

"You don't like these?"

"If you have a blowout, does the auto club bring you a new shoe?"

Kicking off the sandals, he said, "Well, *I* like them."

"How often do they need to be aligned and balanced?"

Soft and hot, the sand shifted underfoot, but then was compacted and cool where the purling surf worked it like a screed.

As they waded into the sea, he said, "I'll ditch the sandals if next time you'll wear the red bikini."

"You actually wanted this yellow one."

He repressed his surprise at her perspicacity. "Then why would I ask for the red?"

"Because you only *think* you can read me."

"But I'm an open book, huh?"

"Winky, compared to you, Dr. Seuss's simplest tale is as complex as Dostoyevsky."

They launched their boards and, prone upon them, paddled out toward the break.

Raising his voice above the swash of the surf, he called to her: "Was that Seuss thing an insult?"

Her silvery laughter stirred in Ryan memories of mermaid tales awash with the mysteries of the deep.

She said, "Not an insult, sweetie. That was a thirteen-word kiss."

Ryan did not bother to recall and count her words from *Winky* to *Dostoyevsky*. Samantha noticed everything, forgot nothing, and was able to recall entire conversations that had occurred months previously.

Sometimes he found her as daunting as she was appealing, which seemed to be a good thing. Samantha would never be predictable or boring.

The consistently spaced waves came like boxcars, four or five at a time. Between these sets were periods of relative calm.

While the sea was slacking, Ryan and Samantha paddled out to the lineup. There, they straddled their boards and watched the first swell of a new set roll toward the break.

From this more intimate perspective, the sea was not as placid and blue as it had appeared from his house in the hills, but as dark as jade and challenging. The approaching swell might have been the arching back of some scaly leviathan, larger than a thousand sharks, born in the deep but rising now to feed upon the sunlit world.

Sam looked at Ryan and grinned. The sun searched her eyes and revealed in them the blue of sky, the green of sea, the delight of being in harmony with millions of tons of water pushed shoreward by storms three thousand miles away and by the moon now looming on the dark side of the earth.

Sam caught the second swell: on two knees, one knee, now standing, swift and clean, away. She rode the crest, then did a floater off the curling lip.

As she slid out of view, down the face of the wave, Ryan thought that the breaker—much bigger than anything in previous sets—had the size and the energy to hollow out and put her in a tube. Good as it gets, Sam would ride it out as smoothly as oil surging through a pipeline.

Ryan looked seaward, timing the next swell, eager to rise and walk the board.

Something happened to his heart. Already quick with anticipation of the ride, the beat suddenly accelerated and began to pound with a force more suited to a moment of high terror than to one of pleasant excitement.

He could feel his pulse throbbing in his ankles, wrists, throat, temples. The tide of blood within his arteries seemed to crescendo in sympathy with the sea that swelled toward him, under him.

The sibilant voice of the water became insistent, sinister.

Clutching the board, abandoning the attempt to

rise and ride, Ryan saw the day dim, losing brightness at the periphery. Along the horizon, the sky remained clear yet faded to gray.

Inky clouds spread through the jade sea, as though the Pacific would soon be as black in the morning light as it was on any moonless night.

He was breathing fast and shallow. The very atmosphere seemed to be changing, as if half the oxygen content had been bled out of it, perhaps explaining the graying of the sky.

Never previously had he been afraid of the sea. He was afraid of it now.

The water rose as though with conscious intention, with malice. Clinging to his board, Ryan slid down the hunchbacked swell into the wide trough between waves.

Irrationally, he worried that the trough would become a trench, the trench a vortex. He feared that he would be whirled down into drowning depths.

The board wallowed, bobbed, and Ryan almost rolled off. His strength had left him. His grip had grown weak, as tremulous as that of an old man.

Something bristled in the water, alarming him.

When he realized that those spiky forms were neither shark fins nor grasping tentacles, but were the conceptacles of a knotted mass of seaweed, he was not relieved. If a shark were to appear now, Ryan would be at the mercy of it, unable to evade it or resist.

TWO

As suddenly as the attack came, it passed. Ryan's storming heart quieted. Blue reclaimed the graying sky. The encroaching darkness in the water receded. His strength returned to him.

He did not realize how long the episode had lasted until he saw that Samantha had ridden her wave to shore and, in the relative calm between sets, had paddled out to him once more.

As she came closer, the concern that creased her brow was also evident in her voice: "Ryan?"

"Just enjoying the moment," he lied, remaining prone on his board. "I'll catch one in the next set."

"Since when are you a mallard?" she asked, by which she meant that he was floating around in the lineup like a duck, like one of those gutless wannabes who soaked all day in the swells just beyond the break point and called it surfing.

"The last two in that set were bigger," he said. "I have a hunch the next batch might be double over-head, worth waiting for."

Sam straddled her board and looked out to sea, scanning for the first swell of the new set.

If Ryan read her correctly, she sensed that he was shining her on, and she wondered why.

With his heart steady and his strength recovered, he stopped hugging the board, straddled it, getting ready.

Waiting for the next wave train, he told himself that he had not experienced a physical seizure, but instead merely an anxiety attack. At self-deception, he was as skilled as anyone.

He had no reason to be anxious. His life was sweet, buttered, and sliced for easy consumption.

Focused on far water, Samantha said, "Winky."

"I see it."

The sea rose to the morning sun, dark jade and silver, a great shoulder of water shrugging up and rolling smoothly toward the break.

Ryan smelled brine, smelled the iodine of bleed-ing seaweed, and tasted salt.

"Epic," Sam called out, sizing the swell.

"Monster," he agreed.

Instead of rising into a control position, she left

the wave to him, her butt on the board, her feet in the water, bait for sharks.

A squadron of gulls streaked landward, shrieking as if to warn those on shore that a behemoth was coming to smash sand castles and swamp picnic hampers.

As the moment of commitment neared, apprehension rose in Ryan, concern that the thrill of the ride might trigger another ... episode.

He paddled to catch the wave, got to his feet on the pivot point, arms reaching for balance, fingers spread, palms down, and he caught the break, a perfect peeler that didn't section on him but instead poured pavement as slick as ice. The moving wave displaced air, and a cool wind rose up the curved wall, pressing against his flattened palms.

Then he was in a tube, a glasshouse, behind the curtain of the breaking wave, shooting the curl, and his apprehension burst like a bubble and was no more.

Using every trick to goose momentum, he emerged from the tube before it collapsed, into the sparkle of sun on water filigreed with foam. The day was so real, so right. He admonished himself, *No fear*, which was the only way to live.

All morning, into the afternoon, the swells were monoliths. The offshore breeze strengthened, blowing liquid smoke off the lips of the waves.

The beach blanket was not a place to tan. It was for rehab, for massaging the quivers out of overtaxed muscles, for draining sinuses flooded with seawater, for combing bits of kelp and crusted salt out of your hair, for psyching each other into the next session.

Usually, Ryan would want to stay until late afternoon, when the offshore breeze died and the waves stopped hollowing out, when the yearning for eternity—which the ocean represented—became a yearning for burritos and tacos.

By two-thirty, however, during a retreat to the blanket, a pleasant weariness, the kind that follows work well done, overcame him. There was something delicious about this fatigue, a sweetness that made him want to close his eyes and let the sun melt him into sleep. . . .

As he was swimming effortlessly in an abyss vaguely illuminated by clouds of luminescent plankton, a voice spoke to him out of the deep: "Ryan?"

"Hmmmm?"

"Were you asleep?"

He felt as though he were *still* asleep when he opened his eyes and saw her face looming over him: beauty of a degree that seemed mythological, radiant eyes the precise shade of a green sea patinaed by the blue of a summer sky, golden hair crowned with a corona of sunlight, goddess on a holiday from Olympus.

"You *were* asleep," Samantha said.

"Too much big surf. I'm quashed."

"You? When have you ever been quashed?"

Sitting up on the blanket, he said, "Had to be a first time."

"You really want to pack out?"

"I skipped breakfast. We surfed through lunch."

"There's chocolate-cherry granola bars in the cooler."

"Nothing but a slab of beef will revive me."

They carried the cooler, the blanket, and their boards to the station wagon, stowed everything in back.

Still sodden with sunshine and loose-limbed from being so long in the water, Ryan almost asked Samantha to drive.

More than once, however, she glanced at him speculatively, as if she sensed that his brief nap on the beach blanket was related to the episode at the beginning of the day, when he floated like a mallard in the lineup, his heart exploding. He didn't want to worry her. Besides, there was no reason to worry.

Earlier, he'd had an anxiety attack. But if truth were known, most people probably had them these days, considering the events and the pessimistic predictions that constituted the evening news.

Instead of passing the car keys to Sam, Ryan drove the two blocks to her apartment.

Samantha showered first while Ryan brewed a pitcher of fresh iced tea and sliced two lemons to marinate in it.

Her cozy kitchen had a single large window beyond which stood a massive California pepper tree. The elegant limbs, festooned with weeping fernlike leaves divided into many glossy leaflets, appeared to fill the entire world, creating the illusion that her apartment was a tree house.

The pleasant weariness that had flooded through Ryan on the beach now drained away, and a new vitality welled in him.

He began to think of making love to Samantha. Once the urge arose, it swelled into full-blooded desire.

Hair toweled but damp, she returned to the kitchen, wearing turquoise slacks, a crisp white blouse, and white tennies.

If she had been in the mood, she would have been barefoot, wearing only a silk robe.

For weeks at a time, her libido matched his, and she wanted him frequently. He had noticed that her desire was greater during those periods when she was busiest with her writing and the least inclined to consider his proposal of marriage.

A sudden spell of virtuous restraint was a sign that she was brooding about accepting the engagement ring, as though the prospect of matrimony required that sex be regarded as something too serious, perhaps too sacred, to be indulged in lightly.

Ryan happily accepted each turn toward abstinence when it seemed to indicate that she was on the brink of making a commitment to him. At twenty-eight, she was six years younger than he was, and they had a life of lovemaking ahead.

He poured a glass of iced tea for her, and then he went to take a shower. He started with water nearly as cold as the tea.

In the westering sun, the strawberry trees shed elongated leaf shadows on the flagstone floor of the restaurant patio.

Ryan and Samantha shared a caprese salad and lingered over their first glasses of wine, not in a hurry to order entrees.

The smooth peeling bark of the trees was red, especially so in the condensed light of the slowly declining sun.

"Teresa loved the flowers," Sam said, referring to her sister.

"What flowers?"

"On these trees. They get panicles of little urn-shaped flowers in the late spring."

"White and pink," Ryan remembered.

"Teresa said they look like cascades of tiny bells, wind chimes hung out by fairies."

Six years previously, Teresa had suffered serious head trauma in a traffic accident. Eventually she had died.

Samantha seldom mentioned her sister. When she spoke of Teresa, she tended to turn inward before much had been said, mummifying her memories in long windings of silence.

Now, as she gazed into the overhanging tree, the expression in her eyes was reminiscent of that look of longing when, straddling her surfboard in the lineup, she studied far water for the first sign of a new set of swells.

Ryan was comfortable with Sam's occasional silences, which he suspected were always related to thoughts of her sister, even when she had not mentioned Teresa.

They had been identical twins.

To better understand Sam, Ryan had read about twins who had been separated by tragedy. Apparently the survivor's grief was often mixed with unjustified guilt.

Some said the intense bond between identicals, especially between sisters, could not be broken even by death. A few insisted they still felt the presence of the other, akin to how an amputee often feels sensations in his phantom leg.

Samantha's contemplative silence gave Ryan an opportunity to study and admire her with a forthrightness that was not possible when she was aware of his stare.

Watching her, he was nailed motionless by admiration, unable to lift his wineglass, or at least disinterested in it, his eyes alone in motion, traveling the contours of her face and the graceful line of her throat.

His life was a pursuit of perfection, of which perhaps the world held none.

Sometimes he imagined that he came close to it when writing lines of code for software. An exquisite digital creation, however, was as cold as a mathematical equation. The most fastidious software architecture was an object of mere precision, not of perfection, for it could not evoke an intense emotional response.

In Samantha Reach, he'd found a beauty so close to perfection that he could convince himself this was his quest fulfilled.

Gazing into the tree but focused on something far beyond the red geometry of those branches, Sam said, "After the accident, she was in a coma for a month. When she came out of it . . . she wasn't the same."

Ryan was kept silent by the smoothness of her skin. This was the first he had heard of Teresa's coma. Yet the radiance of Sam's face, in the caress of the late sun, rendered him incapable of comment.

"She still had to be fed through a tube in her stomach."

The only leaf shadows that touched Samantha's face were braided across her golden hair and brow, as though she wore the wreath of Nature's approval.

"The doctors said she was in a permanent vegetative state."

Her gaze lowered through the branches and fixed on a cruciform of sunlight that, shimmering on the table, was projected by a beam passing through her wineglass.

"I never believed the doctors," she said. "Teresa was still complete inside her body, trapped but still Teresa. I didn't want them to take out the feeding tube."

She raised her eyes to meet his, and he had to make of this a conversation.

"But they took it out anyway?" he asked.

"And starved her to death. They said she wouldn't feel anything. Supposedly the brain damage assured that she'd have no pain."

"But you think she suffered."

"I know she did. During the last day, the last night, I sat with her, holding her hand, and I could feel her looking at me even though she never opened her eyes."

He did not know what to say to that.

Samantha picked up her glass of wine, causing the cross of light to morph into an arrow that briefly quivered like a compass needle seeking true north in Ryan's eyes.

"I've forgiven my mother for a lot of things, but I'll never forgive her for what she did to Teresa."

As Samantha took a sip of wine, Ryan said, "But I thought . . . your mother was in the same accident."

"She was."

"I was under the impression she died in the crash, too. Rebecca. Was that her name?"

"She is dead. To me. Rebecca's buried in an apartment in Las Vegas. She walks and talks and breathes, but she's dead all right."

Samantha's father had abandoned the family before the twins were two. She had no memory of him.

Feeling that Sam should hold fast to what little family she had, Ryan almost encouraged her to give her mother a chance to earn redemption. But he kept silent on the issue, because Sam had his sympathy and his understanding.

His grandparents and hers—all long dead—were of the generation that defeated Hitler and won the Cold War. Their fortitude and their rectitude had been passed along, if at all, in a diluted form to the next generation.

Ryan's parents, no less than Sam's, were of that portion of the post-war generation that rejected the responsibilities of tradition and embraced entitlement. Sometimes it seemed to him that he was the parent, that his mother and father were the children.

Regardless of the consequences of their behavior and decisions, they would see no need for redemption. Giving them the chance to earn it would only offend them. Sam's mother was most likely of that same mind-set.

Samantha put down her glass, but the sun made nothing of it this time.

After a hesitation, as Ryan poured more wine for both of them, he said, "Funny how something as lovely as strawberry-tree flowers can peel the scab off a bad memory."

"Sorry."

"No need to be."

"Such a nice day. I didn't mean to bring it down. Are you as ferociously hungry as I am?"

"Bring me the whole steer," he said.

In fact, they ordered just the filet mignon, no horns or hooves.

As the descending sun set fire to the western sky, strings of miniature white lights came on in the strawberry trees. On all the tables were candles in amber cups of faceted glass, and busboys lit them.

The ordinary patio had become a magical place, and Samantha was the centerpiece of the enchantment.

By the time the waiter served the steaks, Sam had found the lighter mood that had characterized the rest of the day, and Ryan joined her there.

After the first bite of beef, she raised her wineglass in a toast. "Hey, Dotcom, this one's to you."

Dotcom was another nickname that she had for him, used mostly when she wanted to poke fun at his public image as a business genius and tech wizard.

"Why to me?" he asked.

"Today you finally stepped down from the pantheon and revealed that you're at best a demigod."

Pretending indignation, he said, "I haven't done any such thing. I'm still turning the wheel that makes the sun rise in the morning and the moon at night."

"You used to take the waves until they surrendered and turned mushy. Today you're beached on a blanket by two-thirty."

"Did you consider that it might have been boredom, that the swells just weren't challenging enough for me?"

"I considered it for like two seconds, but you were snoring as if you'd been plenty challenged."

"I wasn't sleeping. I was meditating."

"You and Rip Van Winkle." After they had assured the attentive waiter that their steaks were excellent, Samantha said, "Seriously, you were okay out there today, weren't you?"

"I'm thirty-four, Sam. I guess I can't always thrash the waves like a kid anymore."

"It's just—you looked a little gray there."

He raised a hand to his hair. "Gray where?"

"Your pretty face."

He grinned. "You think it's pretty?"

"You can't keep pulling those thirty-six-hour sessions at the keyboard and then go right out and rip the ocean like you're the Big Kahuna."

"I'm not dying, Sam. I'm just aging gracefully."

▪

He woke in absolute darkness, with the undulant motion of the sea beneath him. Disoriented, he thought for a moment that he was lying faceup on a surfboard, beyond the break, under a sky in which every star had been extinguished.

The hard rapid knocking of his heart alarmed him.

When Ryan felt the surface under him, he realized that it was a bed, not a board. The undulations were not real, merely perceived, a yawing dizziness.

"Sam," he said, but then remembered that she was not with him, that he was home, alone in his bedroom.

He tried to reach the lamp on the nightstand... but could not lift his arm.

When he tried to sit up, pain bloomed in his chest.

THREE

Ryan felt as though concrete blocks were stacked on his chest. Although mild, the pain frightened him. His heart raced so fast that the beats could not be counted.

He counseled himself to remain calm, to be still, to let the seizure pass, as it had passed when he had been floating on his surfboard.

The difference between then and now was the pain. The racing heart, the weakness, and the dizziness were as disturbing as before, but the added element of pain denied him the delusion that this was nothing more than an anxiety attack.

Even as a small child, Ryan had not been afraid of the dark. Now darkness itself seemed to be the weight on his chest. The black infinity of the universe, the thick atmosphere of the earthly night, the blinding gloom in the bedroom pressed each upon the next, and all upon him, relentlessly bending his breastbone inward until his heart knocked against it as if seeking to be let out of him and into eternity.

He grew desperate for light.

When he tried to sit up, he could not. The pressure held him down.

He discovered that he could push against the mattress with his heels and elbows, gradually hitching backward, three feather pillows compacting into a ramp that elevated his head and shoulders. His skull rapped against the headboard.

The weight on his chest forced him to take shallow inhalations. Each time he exhaled, a sound thinner than a whimper also escaped him, offending the black room like a nail drawn down a chalkboard.

After he had hitched into a reclining position, not sitting up but more than halfway there, some strength returned to him. He could lift his arms.

With his left hand, he reached blindly for the bedside lamp. He located the bronze base, and his fingers slid along a cast-bronze column with a bamboo motif.

Before he found the switch, the ache in his chest intensified and swiftly spread to his throat, as if the agony were ink and his flesh an absorbent blotter.

The pain seemed to be something that he had swallowed or was regurgitating intact. It blocked his airway, restricted breathing, and pinched his cry of shock into a half note followed by a hiss.

He fell from bed. He did not know how it happened. The bed became the floor, leaving him with no awareness of the fall, with only a recognition that mattress had been replaced by carpet.

He was not alone in the house; but he might as well have been. At this hour, Lee and Kay Ting, the couple who managed the estate, were asleep in their quarters, on the lowest of the three floors, in the wing of the house farthest from the one that contained Ryan's third-floor master suite.

In the same way that he had fallen unawares from bed, he came to the realization that he was dragging himself across the floor, his torso raised on his forearms, legs twitching as feebly as the broken appendages of a half-crushed beetle.

Rapidly intensifying, the pain had spread from his throat into his jaw. He seemed to have bitten on a nail so hard that the point had penetrated between two teeth and into the mandible.

Suddenly he remembered that the house intercom was part of the telephone system. He could buzz Lee and Kay by pressing 1-1-1. They could be here in a minute or two.

He did not know in which direction lay the bed,

the nightstand, the phone. He had become disoriented.

The room was large but not vast. He should have been able to find his way in the dark.

But pain seared, vertigo spun, weakness drained, fear twisted his thoughts until he had no capacity for calculation. Although the fall from bed to floor was only a couple of feet, he seemed to have been cast down from a great height, all grace pulverized on impact, and all hope.

His eyes were stung by hot tears, and his throat burned with refluxed stomach acid, and the balefire in his jaw would surely consume the bone and collapse his face.

The darkness spun and tilted. He could not crawl farther, but could only clutch the carpet as though gravity might be repealed and he might be whirled away, weightless, into a void.

His heart hammered faster than he could count its blows, at least two hundred a minute.

Pain spread from his throat into his left arm, radiated across his shoulder and down his back.

A prince of the Internet, richer than most kings, he lay now as prostrate as any commoner abashed in the presence of royalty, at the mercy of his body, mere clay.

The black ocean swelled under him, and he had nothing to which he could hold, neither a surfboard nor the dorsal fin of a shark. The sea was infinite, and he was as insignificant as a tracery of foam on a single wave. A great mass of water shouldered up, and he slid down its back into a trough, and the trough became an abyss, the abyss a vortex that swallowed him.

FOUR

The alarm-clock feature on the TV had been set for seven in the morning. The volume remained low, and Ryan woke slowly to murmuring voices, to music scored for drama.

The glow from the screen did not fully relieve the darkness. As the value of light changed in a scene and as figures moved, phantoms throbbed and flickered through the bedroom.

Ryan lay on the floor, in the fetal position, facing the screen. William Holden, many years after *Sunset Boulevard*, was in an intense conversation with a lovely young woman.

In thirty-four years, Ryan had experienced only two hangovers, but he seemed to be suffering a third. Headache. Eyes crusted shut, vision blurry. Dry, sour mouth.

Initially he could not recall the events of the previous evening or remember what possessed him to go to sleep on the floor.

Curiously, the mystery of his circumstances intrigued him less than the events on the television: the older man, the younger woman, worried talk of war. . . .

The once-sharp edges of his mind were worn, his thoughts a shapeless stream of quicksilver. Even when his vision cleared, he couldn't follow the movie or grasp the character relationships.

Yet he felt compelled to watch, haunted by the feeling that he had awakened to this movie not by accident but by the design of Fate. Here to be deciphered was a warning about his future that he must understand if he were to save himself.

This extraordinary conviction grew until he was impelled to rise to his knees, to his feet. He moved closer to the large TV.

As the fine hairs prickled on the nape of his neck, his heart quickened. The thudding in his breast knocked into memory the much more furious pounding to which he had awakened in the night, and abruptly he recalled every detail of the terrifying seizure.

He turned away from the TV, switched on a lamp. He stared at his trembling hands, closed them into fists, opened them once more, half expecting some degree of paralysis, but finding none.

In his bathroom, black granite, gold onyx, and stainless steel were reflected in a wilderness of mirrors. An infinite line of Ryan Perrys faced him, all of them gray and haggard and grim with dread.

As never before, he was aware of the skull beneath the skin, each curve and plane and hollow of bone, the perpetual death's-head grin concealed behind every expression that his face assumed.

■

Shaved, showered, and dressed, Ryan found his estate manager, Lee Ting, in the garage.

This large subterranean space provided eighteen parking stalls. The ceiling was ten feet high, to accommodate delivery trucks and—if he should ever want one—a motor home.

Golden ceramic tile, a kind used in automobile showrooms, paved the floor. Glossy white tile covered the walls. The brightwork on the Woodie and other classic vehicles sparkled in the beams of pin spots.

Ryan had always before thought the garage was beautiful, even elegant. Now the cold tile reminded him of a mausoleum.

In the corner workshop, Lee Ting was polishing a custom-made license-plate frame for one of the cars.

He was a small man but strong. He appeared to be

cast from bronze not yet patinaed, and prominent veins swelled in his hands.

At fifty, his life was defined by parenthood denied, his hope of family thwarted. Kay Ting twice conceived, but a subsequent uterine infection left her sterile.

Their first child had been a daughter. At the age of two, she died of influenza. Their second, a son, was also gone.

The sight of certain young children elicited from them the most tender smiles, even as their eyes glistened with the memory of loss.

When the power buffer clicked off, Ryan said, "Lee, do you have a staff meeting this morning or appointments with anyone?"

Surprised, Lee turned. His face brightened, his chin lifted, and a cheerful expectation came into him, as though nothing pleased him more than the opportunity to be of good service.

Ryan suspected this was in fact the case. All the strivings and the particular satisfactions of raising a family, denied to Lee, were now expressed in his job.

Putting aside the license-plate frame, Lee said, "Good morning, Mr. Perry. I have nothing scheduled that Kay can't cover for me. What do you need?"

"I was hoping you could drive me to a doctor's appointment."

Concern diminished the arc of Lee's smile. "Is something wrong, sir?"

"Nothing much. I just feel off, a little nauseous. I'd prefer not to drive myself."

Most men of Ryan's wealth employed a chauffeur. He loved cars too much to delegate his driving.

Lee Ting clearly knew this need for a driver was proof of more than mild nausea. He at once snared a key from the key safe and went with Ryan to the Mercedes S600.

A tenderness in Lee's manner and a wounded expression in his eyes suggested that he regarded his boss as more than an employer. He was, after all, just old enough to have been Ryan's father.

The twelve-cylinder Mercedes seemed to float on a cushion of air, and little road noise reached them. Although the sedan rode like a dream, Ryan knew that it carried him toward a nightmare.

FIVE

Ryan's internist had a concierge practice limited to three hundred patients. He guaranteed an appointment within one day of a request, but he saw Ryan only three hours after receiving his call.

From an examination room on the fourteenth floor, Ryan could see Newport Harbor, the Pacific Ocean, distant ships bound for unknown shores.

His doctor, Forest Stafford, had already examined him, and a med tech had administered an electrocardiogram. Then Ryan had gone down to a medical imaging company on the third floor, where they had conducted an echocardiogram.

At the fourteenth-floor window, he waited now for Dr. Stafford to return with an interpretation of the tests.

An armada of large white clouds sailed slowly

north, but their shadows were iron-black upon the sea, pressing the surf flat.

The door opened behind Ryan. Feeling as weightless as a cloud, and half afraid that in an angled light he would cast *no* shadow, he turned away from the window.

Forest Stafford's powerful square body was in contrast to his rectangular countenance, in which his features were elongated, as if affected by a face-specific gravity that had not distorted the rest of him. Because he was a sensitive man, the deforming force, at work for years, might have been the pain of his patients.

Leaning against the counter that contained the hand sink, the physician said, "I imagine you want me to cut to the chase."

Ryan made no move to a chair, but stood with his back to the window and to the sea that he loved. "You know me, Forry."

"It wasn't a heart attack."

"Nothing that simple," Ryan guessed.

"Your heart is hypertrophic. Enlarged."

Ryan at once argued his case, as if Forry were a judge who, properly persuaded, could declare him healthy. "But . . . I've always kept fit, eaten right."

"A vitamin B_1 deficiency can sometimes be involved, but in your case I doubt this is related to diet or exercise."

"Then what?"

"Could be a congenital condition only now expressing itself. Or excessive alcohol consumption, but that's not you."

The room had not suddenly gone cold, nor had the temperature plunged in the day beyond the window. Nevertheless, a set of chills rose at the back of Ryan's neck and broke along the shoals of his spine.

The physician counted off possible causes: "Scarring of the endocardium, amyloidosis, poisoning, abnormal cell metabolism—"

"Poisoning? Who would want to poison me?"

"No one. It's not poisoning. But to get an accurate diagnosis, I want you to have a myocardial biopsy."

"That doesn't sound like fun."

"It's uncomfortable but not painful. I've spoken with Samar Gupta, an excellent cardiologist. He can see you for a preliminary exam this afternoon—and perform the biopsy in the morning."

"That doesn't give me much time to think," Ryan said.

"What is there to think about?"

"Life . . . death . . . I don't know."

"We can't decide on treatment without a definitive diagnosis."

Ryan hesitated. Then: "Is it treatable?"

"It may be," said Forry.

"I wish you'd just said yes."

"Believe me, Dotcom, I wish I could just say it."

Before Forest Stafford was Ryan's internist, they

had met at a classic-car rally and had struck up a friendship. Jane Stafford, Forry's wife, bonded to Samantha as if she were a daughter; and *Dotcom* had since been more widely used.

"Samantha," Ryan whispered.

Only upon speaking her name did he realize that the preliminary diagnosis had pinned his thoughts entirely on the pivot point of this twist of fate, on just the sharp fact of his mortality.

Now his mind slipped loose of the pin. His thoughts raced.

The prospect of impending death had at first been an abstraction that inspired an icy anxiety. But when he thought of what he would lose *with* his life, when he considered the specific losses—Samantha, the sea, the blush of dawn, the purple twilight—anxiety quickened into dread.

Ryan said, "Don't tell Sam."

"Of course not."

"Or even Jane. I know she wouldn't mean to tell Sam. But Sam would sense something wrong, and get it out of her."

Like wax retreating from a flame, the mournful lines of Forry Stafford's face softened into sorrow. "When will you tell her?"

"After the biopsy. When I have all the facts."

With a sigh, Forry said, "Some days I wish I'd gone into dentistry."

"Tooth decay is seldom fatal."

"Or even gingivitis."

Forry sat down on the wheeled stool, where he usually perched to listen to a patient's complaints and to make notes in his files.

Ryan settled into the only chair. After a while he said, "You made a decision on the '40 Mercury convertible?"

"Yeah. Just now. I'm gonna buy it."

"Edelbrock two-carb manifold? That right?"

"Yeah. You should hear it."

"What's it stand on?" Ryan asked.

"Nineteen-sixty Imperials. Fifteen-inch."

"Chopped?"

"Four inches."

"That must give it a cool windshield profile."

"Very cool," Forry confirmed.

"You gonna work on it?"

"I've got some ideas."

"I think I'd like to have a '32 deuce coupe," Ryan said.

"Five-window?"

"Maybe a three-window highboy."

"I'll help you find it. We'll scout some shows."

"I'd like that."

"Me too."

They sat in silence for a moment.

The examination room had a white acoustic-tile ceiling, pale-blue walls, a gray vinyl-tile floor.

On one wall hung a print of a painting by Childe

Hassam. Titled *The White Dory, Gloucester*, it was dated 1895.

On pale water, in a white boat sat a fair woman. She wore a long white skirt, a pleated and ruffled pink blouse, and a straw boater.

Delicate, desirable, she would have been a handsome wife in those days when marriages lasted a lifetime. Ryan was overcome with a strange yearning to have known her, to have heard her voice, to have tasted her kiss, but she was lost somewhere in time, as he might soon be, as well.

"Shit," he said.

Forry said, "Ditto."

SIX

D r. Samar Gupta had a round brown face and eyes the color of molasses. His voice was lilting, his diction precise, his slender hands impeccably manicured.

After reviewing the echocardiogram and examining Ryan, Gupta explained how a myocardial biopsy was performed. He made use of a large poster of the cardiovascular system.

Confronted with a colorful depiction of the interior of the human heart, Ryan found his mind escaping to the painting of the woman in the white dory, in Forry Stafford's examination room.

Dr. Gupta seemed unnaturally calm, every movement efficient, every gesture economical. His resting pulse was probably a measured fifty beats per minute. Ryan envied the physician's serenity and his health.

"Please be at the hospital admissions desk at six o'clock tomorrow morning," the cardiologist said. "Do not eat or drink anything after midnight."

Ryan said, "I don't like sedation, the loss of control."

"You'll be given a mild sedative to relax you, but you'll remain awake to follow instructions during the procedure."

"The risks . . ."

"Are as I explained. But none of my biopsies has ever involved . . . complications."

Ryan was surprised to hear himself say, "I trust your skill, Dr. Gupta, but I'm still afraid."

In business, Ryan had never expressed uncertainty, let alone fear. He allowed no one to see any weakness in him.

"From the day we're born, Ryan, we should all be afraid, but not of dying."

In the plush backseat of the Mercedes S600, on the way home, Ryan realized that he did not understand the cardiologist's last comment.

From the day we're born, Ryan, we should all be afraid, but not of dying.

In the office, in the moment, the words had seemed wise and appropriate. But Ryan's fear and his desire to quell it had led him to hear that statement as a reassurance, when in fact it was not.

Now the physician's words seemed mysterious, even cryptic, and disturbing.

Behind the wheel of the sedan, Lee Ting glanced repeatedly at the rearview mirror. Ryan pretended not to notice his houseman's concern.

Lee could not know which of the many physicians Ryan had visited in Dr. Gupta's building, and he remained too discreet to ask. Yet he was an acutely perceptive man who sensed his employer's solemnity.

In the west, the phoenix palms and the rooftops were gilded with sunlight. The attenuated shadows of those trees and buildings, of lampposts and pedestrians, reached eastward, as if the entire coast yearned for nightfall.

On those rare occasions when Lee previously served as chauffeur, he had driven sedately, as if he were decades older than his years and part of some royal procession. This time, he exceeded speed limits with the rest of the traffic and crossed intersections on the yellow light.

He seemed to know that his employer needed the comfort of home, refuge.

SEVEN

En route from Dr. Gupta's office, Ryan called Kay Ting and placed an order for dinner that would require her to go to his favorite restaurant to get takeout.

Later, using the elevator, the Tings brought a dining-service cart to the third-floor sitting room that was part of the master suite. They put up the leaves to expand the cart into a table and smoothed out the white tablecloth.

Presented for Ryan's pleasure were three dishes of homemade ice cream—dark chocolate, black cherry, and limoncello—each nestled in a larger bowl of cracked ice. There were also servings of flourless chocolate cake, a lemon tart, a peanut-butter tart, strawberries in sour cream with a pot of brown sugar, a selection of exotic cookies, and bottles of root beer in an ice bucket.

Because Ryan allowed himself dessert only once or twice a week, the Tings were curious about this uncharacteristic indulgence.

He pretended to be celebrating the conclusion of a particularly rewarding business deal, but he knew they did not believe him. The arrayed sweets suggested the last meal of a condemned man who, though thirty-four, had never finished growing up.

Eating alone, sitting at the wheeled table, Ryan sampled a series of old movies on the big-screen plasma TV. He sought comedies, but none of them struck him as funny.

Calories no longer mattered, or cholesterol, and at first this indulgence without guilt was so novel that he enjoyed himself. Soon, however, the adolescent smorgasbord grew cloying, too rich.

To thumb his nose at Death, he ate more than he wanted. The root beer began to seem like syrup.

He wheeled the cart out of the master suite, left it in the hall, and used the intercom to tell Kay that he had finished.

Earlier, the Tings turned down the bed and plumped the pillows.

When Ryan put on pajamas and slipped between the sheets, insomnia tormented him. If fear of death had not kept him awake, the tides of sugar in his blood would have made him restless.

Barefoot, hoping to walk off his anxiety, he went roaming through the house.

Beyond the large windows lay the luminous panorama of Orange County's many cities on the vast flats below. The ambient glow was sufficient to allow him to navigate the house without switching on a lamp.

Shortly before midnight, lights in a back hall led him to the large butler's pantry, where china and glassware were stored in mahogany cabinets. He heard voices in the adjacent kitchen.

Although additional members of the household staff were at work during the day, the Tings were the only live-ins. Yet Ryan could not at once identify the speakers as Lee and Kay, because they conversed quietly, almost whispering.

Usually, the Tings would be in bed at this hour. Their workday began at eight o'clock in the morning.

Although throughout his life Ryan had not once been troubled by superstition, he was now overcome by a sense of the uncanny. He felt suddenly that his house hid secrets, that within these rooms were realms unknown, and that for his well-being, he must learn all that was being concealed from him.

Putting his left ear to the crack between the jamb and the swinging door, he strained to hear what was being said.

The spacious kitchen had been designed to function for caterers when large parties required the preparation of elaborate buffets. The low voices softly reverberated off the extensive granite countertops and off the many stainless-steel appliances.

Risking discovery, he eased the door open an inch. The voices did not become recognizable, nor did the murmurs and whispers resolve from sibilant sounds into words.

Ryan did, however, additionally hear the quiet clink and ping of dishes, which seemed curious. Lee and Kay would have washed the dinnerware hours ago, and if they had wanted a late snack, they would have prepared it in the kitchenette that was part of their private suite.

He heard also a peculiar grinding noise, soft and rhythmic. This was not an everyday sound, but vaguely familiar and—for reasons he could not define—sinister.

Gradually his eavesdropping began to seem foolish. The only thing sinister in his house was his imagination, which had been dizzied and led into dark byways by the specter of his mortality.

Nevertheless, when he thought to press the swinging door inward and learn the identity of those in the kitchen, fear swelled in him. His heart abruptly clopped as hard as hooves on stone, and so fast that all Four Horsemen of the Apocalypse might have been approaching.

He eased the door shut, backed away from it.

With his right hand over his heart and his left hand against a cabinet to steady himself, he waited for another seizure to sweep his legs out from under him and leave him helpless on the floor.

The butler's pantry went dark around him.

Ryan might have thought he'd gone blind, except for the lights in the hallway, beyond the open door by which he had entered.

Past the closed swinging door, lights had been extinguished in the kitchen. A wall switch in that room also controlled the pantry.

Now the hallway fell into darkness.

The windowless pantry could not have been blacker if it had been a padded silk-lined clamshell of mortuary bronze.

Able to hear nothing above the noise of his treacherous heart, Ryan became convinced that someone approached, someone whose vision was as keen in this perfect gloom as was the vision of a cat prowling in moonlight. He waited for a hand to be laid on his shoulder, or for a stranger's cold fingers to be pressed against his lips.

The weight of his heart insisted that he sit on the floor. His knees buckled, and he slid down the face of a cabinet, the drawer pulls gouging his back.

Minutes passed during which the riot in his breast failed to accelerate into full-blown anarchy, and in fact gradually a normal beat was reestablished, a measured rhythm.

His weakness abated, and with the return of his strength, his fear soured into humiliation.

The drawer pulls became handholds by which Ryan drew himself to his feet. He felt his way through the clinging darkness to the swinging door.

There he listened to the kitchen. No murmurs, no whispers, no clink or ping, no soft but ominous grinding noise.

He passed through the door, eased it shut, and stood with his back to it.

To his right, above the primary sinks and the flanking counters, were windows facing west. The glow of the Newport Beach lowlands and the moon above the sea defined the panes.

He dared the light switch and found that he was alone.

In addition to the door to the pantry, the big kitchen had three other exits: the first to a patio, the second to the breakfast room, and the last to the back hall. The breakfast room also offered a door to the patio and another to the hallway.

Surely, the voices had been those of Lee and Kay. They had been engaged on some mundane task, unaware that he was in the butler's pantry.

But with Ryan supposedly asleep in his bedroom one floor above and at the farther end of the big house, why had the Tings been whispering?

At each end of the kitchen, as at other points throughout the house, Crestron panels were embedded in the wall. He touched one, and the screen brightened. From this, he could control the lighting, the through-house audio, the heating and cooling, and other systems.

He selected the security display and saw that according to established routine, the Tings had engaged the perimeter alarm. No intruders could have entered the house without triggering a siren and a recorded voice identifying the breach point.

Twenty exterior cameras provided views of the grounds. He cycled through them. Although the night-vision technology offered different clarity from camera to camera, depending on ambient-light conditions, he saw no prowlers on his property, no motion other than the darting paleness of an occasional moth.

He returned to the master suite, but not to bed. In an alcove, off the sitting room where he had taken dinner, stood an amboina-wood Art Deco desk, circa 1928. He sat there, but not to work.

Lee and Kay Ting had been employed here two years. They were talented, dedicated, and reliable.

Their backgrounds had been thoroughly investigated by Wilson Mott, a former homicide detective, now a security consultant, to whom Ryan turned for all matters that were not directly related to his company, Be2Do.

Yet Forry Stafford had said something that replayed in memory: *Scarring of the endocardium, amyloidosis, poisoning...*

With every repetition, Forry's remembered voice seemed to place a more ominous emphasis on the word *poisoning,* even though he had not considered it a possibility in Ryan's case.

For a man who had been healthy all his life, not just healthy but vigorous, sudden serious heart disease seemed to require an explanation beyond the genetic disposition or the malfunctioning of his body. A life of struggle and arduous competition had taught him that in this world were people whose motives were suspect and whose methods were unscrupulous.

Poison.

A soft paradiddle drew his attention to the west window. The noise ceased the moment that he turned his head to seek the source.

The steely light of the scimitar moon failed to reveal what had tapped the glass. Most likely the visitor had been only a moth or some other nocturnal insect.

He turned his attention to his hands, which were fisted on the desk. Earlier, during the seizure, his heart had felt as if it were tightly held in a cruel fist.

Again, a noise arose at the window, less a sound of something tapping, more the soft insistent rapping of knuckles sheathed in a lambskin glove.

He was on the third floor. No balcony lay beyond this window, nothing but a sheer fall to the lawn. No one could be at those moonlit panes, seeking his attention.

The condition of his heart had affected his mind, rattling his usual confidence. Even something as harmless as a moth could set a quiet fear fluttering through him.

He refused to look again at the window, for to do so seemed to invite a thousand fears to follow. His resistance was rewarded, and the faint tap turned feeble, faded into a persistent silence.

Poison.

His thoughts turned from imagined threats to real ones, to those people he had known, in business, whose greed and envy and ambition had led them to embrace immoral methods.

Ryan had earned his fortune without sharp practice, honestly. Nevertheless, he had made enemies. Some people did not like to lose, even if they lost by their own faults and miscalculations.

After much thought, he made a list of five names.

Among the phone numbers he had for Wilson Mott was a special cell to which the detective responded personally, regardless of the day or hour. Only two or three of Mott's wealthiest clients possessed the number. Ryan had never abused it.

He hesitated to place the call. But intuition told him that he was snared in an extraordinary web of deceit, and that he needed more help than physicians could supply. He keyed in the seven digits.

When Mott answered, sounding as crisp and alert as he did at any more reasonable hour of the day, Ryan identified himself but neither mentioned the five names on his list nor suggested further background research on the Tings, as he had intended. Instead, he said something that so surprised him, he rendered himself speechless after the first sentence that he spoke.

"I want you to find a woman named Rebecca Reach."

EIGHT

Rebecca Reach. Samantha's mother.

Ryan had learned only the previous evening, at dinner with Sam, that her mother was alive. For a year, she had allowed him to think that Rebecca had died.

No, that was unfair. Samantha had not misled him. He had assumed Rebecca was dead merely from what little Samantha said of her.

Evidently mother and daughter were so estranged that they did not speak and likely never would. *She is dead. To me,* Samantha had said.

He could understand why, after Rebecca had pulled the plug on disabled Teresa, Samantha had wanted to close a door on the memories of her lost twin sister and on her mother, whom she felt had betrayed them.

"Do you have anything besides the name?" asked Wilson Mott.

"Las Vegas," Ryan said. "Rebecca Reach apparently lives in an apartment in Las Vegas."

"Is that R-e-a-c-h?"

"Yes."

"What's the context, Mr. Perry?"

"I'd rather not say."

"What discovery might you be hoping for?"

"I'm hoping for nothing. Just a general background on the woman. And an address. A phone number."

"I assume you do not want us to speak to her directly."

"That's right. Discretion, please."

"Perhaps by five o'clock tomorrow," Mott said.

"Five o'clock will be fine. I'm busy in the morning and early afternoon anyway."

Ryan hung up, not sure if what he had done was intuitively brilliant or stupid. He did not know what he expected to learn that would have any application to his current crisis.

All he knew was that he had acted now as often he had done in business, trusting in hunches based on reason. His instincts had made him rich.

If Samantha learned of this, she might think he was unacceptably suspicious, even faithless. With luck, she would never have to know what he had done.

Ryan returned to bed. He tuned the TV to a classic film, *Roman Holiday,* starring Audrey Hepburn and Gregory Peck, then switched off the bedside lamp.

Reclining against a pile of feather pillows, he watched the movie without seeing it.

He had never asked Wilson Mott to run a background check on Samantha. Generally, he reserved such investigations for potential employees.

Besides, she had come to him on assignment for a major magazine, a writer of experience and some critical reputation. He had seen no reason to vet her further when her bona fides proved to be in order and when she had been likely to spend no more than a few hours with him.

Over the years, he had dealt with uncountable people in the media. They were mostly harmless, occasionally armed but then with nothing more dangerous than a bias that justified, in their minds, misquoting him.

If something about Rebecca Reach eventually raised suspicions, however, Mott might have to conduct a deep background investigation on Samantha.

Ryan was disappointed—not in Sam, for there was yet no reason to reconsider her, but in himself. He loved being with her. He loved *her*. He did not want to believe that his judgment in this instance had been poor, that he had failed to see she was someone other than who she appeared to be.

Worse, he was dismayed by how quickly his fear

led him to doubt her. Until this day, the only crises with which he had dealt were business problems— capital shortfalls, delayed product roll-outs, hostile-takeover bids. Now he faced an existential threat, and his justifiable fear of incapacitation and death had coiled into a viper-eyed paranoia that looked less to the weakness of his flesh than to the possibility of enemies with agendas.

Disconcerted if not embarrassed to be so enthralled by fear, he considered calling Wilson Mott to cancel the background workup on Rebecca Reach.

But Forry Stafford *had* raised the possibility of poisoning. If that was a potential cause of Ryan's condition, prudence required him to consider it.

He did not touch the phone.

After a while, he switched off the TV.

He could not sleep. In a few hours, the cardiologist, Samar Gupta, would pluck three tiny pieces of tissue from Ryan's heart. His life depended on what those samples revealed. If the diagnosis was not good, he would have plenty of time to sleep; he would have eternity.

Out of the darkness and morbid silence issued a faint tapping at a new window, muffled by draperies; this window or that—he could not tell which.

When he raised his head to listen, the insistent moth or the flying beetle, or the hand in the lamb-skin glove, ceased to rap.

Each time he returned his head to the pillow, silence ensued but was not sustained. Sooner or later came a *bump* and a *bump* and a *bump-bump-bump*: muffled, toneless, dull, dead, and flat.

He could have gone to the windows, one at a time, and pulled open the draperies to catch the noise-maker in the act. Instead, he told himself that the muted tapping was imagined, and he turned his mind away from it, toward the more intimate and troubling rhythms of his heart.

He recognized a certain cowardice in this denial. He sensed that on some level he knew who tapped for his attention, and knew that to pull back the draperies and confront this visitor would be the end of him.

NINE

The moon was down, the sky still dark that Friday morning when Ryan set out for the hospital. The urban glow obscured many stars, but to the west, the sea and shore were one and black and vast.

In spite of the fact that he might have a seizure while behind the wheel, he risked driving. He preferred that Lee Ting not know he was undergoing a myocardial biopsy.

He told himself that he didn't want people who worked for him or who were otherwise close to him to worry. But in fact he did not want to give an enemy, if one existed, the satisfaction—and advantage—of knowing that he was weakened and vulnerable.

As he walked alone through the hospital parking garage, where the sorcerous-sour yellow light polished the carapaces of the cars into iridescent beetle shells, he had the eerie feeling that he was home and sleeping, that this place and the test to come were all moments of a dream within a dream.

From the out-patient admitting desk, an orderly showed him the way to the cardiac diagnostics laboratory.

The head cardiology nurse, Kyra Whipset, could not have been more lean if she had eaten nothing whatsoever but celery and had run half a marathon every day. She had so little body fat that even in high-buoyancy saltwater, she would sink like a dropped anchor.

After ascertaining that Ryan had eaten nothing after midnight, Nurse Whipset provided a sedative and water in a small paper cup.

"This won't put you to sleep," she said. "It'll just relax you."

A second nurse, Ismay Clemm—an older, pleasantly plump black woman—had green eyes in which the striations were like the bevels in a pair of intricately cut emeralds. Those eyes would have been striking in any face; they were especially arresting because of the contrast with her smooth dark skin.

While Nurse Whipset sat at a corner desk to make an entry in Ryan's file, Ismay watched him take the sedative. "You okay, child?"

"Not really," he said, crushing the empty paper cup in his fist.

"This is nothin'," she assured him as he dropped the cup in a waste can. "I'm here. I'm watchin' over you. You'll be just fine."

By contrast with Nurse Whipset's ascetic tautness, Ismay's abundance, which included a musical voice that conveyed caring as effortlessly as it would a tune, comforted Ryan.

"Well, you *are* taking three pieces of my heart," he said.

"Tiny pieces, honey. I suspect you've taken far bigger pieces from the tender hearts of a few sweet girls. And they're all still livin', aren't they?"

In an adjacent prep room, he stripped to his undershorts, stepped into a pair of disposable slippers, and wrapped himself in a thin, pale-green, collarless robe with short sleeves.

Back in the diagnostics laboratory, Dr. Gupta had arrived, as had the radiologist.

The examination table was more comfortable than Ryan expected. Samar Gupta explained that comfort was necessary because during this procedure, a patient must lie on his back, very still, for at least an hour, in some cases perhaps for two hours or more.

Suspended over the table, a fluoroscope would instantly project moving x-ray images on a fluorescent screen.

As the cardiologist, assisted by Nurse Whipset,

prepared for the procedure, Ismay Clemm monitored Ryan's pulse. "You're doing fine, child."

The sedative began to take effect, and he felt calmer, although wide awake.

Kyra Whipset scrubbed Ryan's neck and painted a portion of it with iodine.

After applying a topical anesthetic to steal the sting from the needle, Dr. Gupta administered a local anesthetic by injection to the same area.

Soon Ryan could feel nothing when the physician tested the nerve response in his neck.

He closed his eyes while something with an astringent smell was swabbed on his numb flesh.

Describing his actions aloud, Dr. Gupta made a small incision in Ryan's jugular vein and introduced a thin, highly flexible catheter.

Ryan opened his eyes and watched the fluoroscope as it followed the tedious progress of the catheter, which the cardiologist threaded carefully into his heart, guided by the image on the screen.

He wondered what would happen if in the midst of this procedure he suffered a seizure as he had on the surfboard, his heart abruptly hammering two or three hundred beats a minute. He decided not to ask.

"How are you doing?" Dr. Gupta inquired.

"Fine. I don't feel anything."

"Just relax. We're making excellent progress."

Ryan realized that Ismay Clemm was quietly reporting on his heart rhythm, which evidently had become slightly unstable upon the introduction of the catheter.

Maybe this was normal, maybe not, but the instability passed.

And the beat goes on.

Once the primary catheter was in place, Dr. Gupta inserted into it a second catheter, a bioptome, with tiny jaws at its tip.

Ryan had lost all sense of time. He might have been on the table a few minutes or an hour.

His legs ached. In spite of the sedative, the muscles in his calves were tense. His right hand had tightened into a fist; he opened it, as if hoping to receive another's hand, a gift.

Long he lay there, wondering, fearing.

The jaws of the bioptome bit.

Inhaling with a hiss through clenched teeth, Ryan didn't think that he imagined the quick painful pinch, but perhaps he was reacting to the brief frantic stutter of his heart on the fluorescent screen.

Dr. Gupta retrieved the first sample of Ryan's cardiac muscle.

Nurse Clemm said, "Don't hold your breath, honey."

Exhaling, Ryan realized that he expected to die during the procedure.

TEN

In just seventy minutes the biopsy had been completed and the incision repaired with stitches.

The power of the sedative was at its peak, and because Ryan had endured a sleepless night, the drug affected him more strongly than anticipated. Dr. Gupta encouraged Ryan to lie on the narrow bed in the prep room and rest awhile, until he felt fully alert and capable of driving.

The room was windowless. The overhead fluorescent panels were off, and only a fixture in a soffit above the small sink provided light.

The dark ceiling and shadow-hung walls inspired claustrophobia. Thoughts of caskets and the conqueror worm oppressed him, but the phobic moment quickly passed.

Relief that the procedure had gone well and

exhaustion were tranquilizing. Ryan did not expect to sleep, but he slept.

To a discordant melody, he walked a dream road along a valley toward a palace high on a slope. Through the red-litten windows he could see vast forms that moved fantastically, and his heart began to pound, to boom, until it beat away that vision and harried in another.

A wild lake, bound all around with black rocks and tall pines, was lovely in its loneliness. Then the inky water rose in a series of small waves that lapped the shore where he stood, and he knew the lake was a pool of poison. Its gulf would be his grave.

Between these brief dreams and others, he half woke and always found Ismay Clemm at his bedside in the dimly lighted room, once taking his pulse, once with her hand to his forehead, sometimes just watching him, her dark face so shadowed that her oddly lit green eyes seemed to be disembodied.

A few times she spoke to him, and on the first occasion, she murmured, *"You hear him, don't you, child?"*

Ryan had insufficient strength to ask of whom she spoke.

The nurse answered her own question: *"Yes, you hear him."*

Later, between dreams, she said, *"You must not listen, child."*

And later still: *"If you hear the iron bells, you come to me."*

When he woke more than an hour after lying down, Ryan was alone.

The one light, the many shadows, and the sparely appointed prep room seemed less real to him than either the palace with windows full of red light or the black lake, or the other places in his dreams.

To confirm that he was awake and that the memory of the biopsy was real, he raised one hand to the small bandage on his neck, which covered the jugular wound, the stitches.

He rose, took off the robe, and dressed in his street clothes.

When Ryan entered the adjacent diagnostics lab, Ismay Clemm was nowhere to be seen. Dr. Gupta and the radiologist had gone, as well.

Nurse Whipset asked if he was all right.

He felt unreal, weightless and drifting, as if he were a ghost, an apparition that she mistook for flesh and blood.

Of course, she wasn't asking if he felt emotionally sound, only if the sedative had worn off. He answered in the affirmative.

She informed him that the analysis of the biopsy specimens would be expedited. In the interest of greater accuracy and the collection of more precise information, however, Dr. Gupta had ordered the most detailed analysis; he didn't expect to have the report until Tuesday.

Initially, Ryan intended to ask where he could find Ismay Clemm. He had wanted to ask her what she meant by the strange things she said to him during the brief periods when he had been half-awake.

Now, in the sterile brightness of the diagnostics lab, he was not certain that she had actually spoken to him. She might as easily have been merely a presence in his dreams.

He retrieved his Mercedes from the garage and drove home.

The clear sky presented more birds, more often, than seemed normal. Flocks were strung out in strange formations, a calligraphy of crows in which some meaning might be read if only he knew the language in which it was composed.

At a red traffic light, when he glanced at the silver Lexus in the adjacent lane, he discovered the driver staring at him: a fortysomething man, face hard and expressionless. They locked eyes, and the stranger's intensity caused Ryan to look away first.

Two blocks later, at another red light, a young man behind the wheel of a chopped and customized Ford pickup was talking on a hands-free cell phone. Fitted to the guy's ear, the phone stirred in Ryan a memory from an old science-fiction movie: an alien parasite, riding and controlling its human host.

The pickup driver glanced at Ryan, looked immediately away, but a moment later glanced furtively at him once more; and his lips moved faster, as if Ryan were the subject of his phone conversation.

Miles farther, when Ryan turned off Pacific Coast Highway onto Newport Coast Road, he glanced repeatedly in the rearview mirror, looking for the silver Lexus and the chopped Ford pickup.

At home, staircase to hallway to room after room, Ryan did not encounter Lee or Kay Ting, or Lee's assistant, Donnie, or Kay's assistant, Renata.

He heard fading footsteps on a limestone floor, a door close in another room. A distant voice and a single response were both unintelligible.

In the kitchen, he swiftly prepared an early lunch. He avoided fresh foods and containers that were already open, in favor of items in vacuum-sealed cans and jars.

A salad of button mushrooms, artichoke hearts, yellow beets, garbanzo beans, and white asparagus was enlivened with Italian dressing from a previously untapped bottle and by grated Parmesan from a new can that he opened after inspecting it for tampering.

He put the salad on a tray with a sealed package of imported panettone and utensils. After a hesitation, he added a wineglass and a half bottle of Far Niente Chardonnay.

As he carried the tray to his office in the west wing

of the main floor, he saw no one, though a vacuum cleaner started in a far chamber.

None of the rooms featured security cameras, but the hallways had them. A video record of hallway traffic was stored on DVDs to be reviewed only in the event that the house was invaded by burglars or victimized by a sneak thief.

No one monitored the hallway cameras in real time. Nevertheless, Ryan felt watched.

ELEVEN

In his home office, Ryan ate at his desk, gazing out of the big windows at the swimming pool in the foreground, at the sea in the distance.

The phone rang: his most private line, a number possessed by a handful of people. The caller-ID window told him it was Samantha.

"Hey, Winky, you still aging gracefully?"

"Well, I haven't grown any hair in my ears yet."

"That's a good sign."

"And I haven't developed man breasts."

"You paint an irresistible portrait of yourself. Listen, I'm sorry about Wednesday night."

"What about Wednesday night?"

"I brought the whole evening down, talking about Teresa, pulling her feeding tube, the starvation thing."

"You never bring me down, Sam."

"You're sweet. But I want to make it up to you. Come over for dinner tonight. I'll make saltimbocca alla romana."

"I love your saltimbocca."

"With polenta."

"This is a lot of work."

"Caponata to start."

He had no reason to distrust her.

"Why don't we eat out?" he suggested. "Then there's no cleanup."

"I'll do the cleaning up."

He loved her. She loved him. She was a good cook. He was succumbing to irrational fear.

"It's so much work," he said. "I heard about this great new restaurant."

"What's the name?"

The great new restaurant was a lie. He would have to find one. He said, "I want to surprise you."

"Is something wrong?"

"I'm just in a going-out mood. I want to try this new place."

They talked about what she should wear, what time he would pick her up.

"Love you," she said.

"Love you," he echoed, and disconnected.

He had eaten no more than a third of his lunch, but he had lost his appetite.

With a glass of Far Niente, he went outside,

crossed the patio, and stood watching satiny ribbons of sunlight shimmer through the variegated-blue Italian-glass tiles that lined the swimming pool.

He became aware that he was fingering the bandage on his neck.

As Gypsies read tea leaves and palms, some shaman would read those tissue samples and tell him his fate.

The mental image of a Gypsy by candlelight led him to think of stories in which a lock of a man's hair was used by a practitioner of black magic to cast a curse upon him.

In the hands of a voodooist, three moist pieces of a man's heart—more intimate and therefore more powerful than a few strands of hair—might be used to destroy him in ways singularly horrific.

When a centipedal chill climbed his spine, when his heart accelerated, when a thin sweat prickled along his hairline, Ryan chastised himself for surrendering to unreason. A warrantless suspicion about Sam had metastasized into superstitious nonsense.

He went back into his office and phoned Samantha. "On second thought, I'd rather have your saltimbocca."

"What changed your mind?"

"I don't want to share you with a gaggle of envious men."

"What gaggle?"

"The waiter, the busboy, and every man in the

restaurant who would be lucky enough to lay eyes on you."

"Sometimes, Winky, you walk a thin line between being a true romantic and a bullshit artist."

"I'm only speaking from the heart."

"Well, sweetie, if you're going to do more of that this evening, bring a shovel. I don't have one."

She hung up, and before Ryan could lower the handset from his ear, he heard what might have been a brief, stifled laugh.

Although Sam had disconnected, the dial tone did not return. Ryan listened to the faint hollow hiss of an open line.

"Who's there?" he asked.

No one answered.

The house phone was a digital hybrid system with ten lines, plus intercom and doorbell functions. None of the phone lines was shared, and no other phones in the house could eavesdrop on a line that was in use.

He waited for another telltale sound, like guarded breathing or a background noise in the room where the listener sat, but he was not rewarded. He had nothing more than an *impression* of someone out there in the ether, a hostile presence that might or might not be real.

At last he returned the handset to the cradle.

By four o'clock Friday afternoon, sooner than promised, Wilson Mott provided by e-mail a background report on Samantha's mother.

As soon as Ryan had a printout, he sent the e-mail to trash, and at once deleted it from trash to ensure no one could retrieve it. He sat on a lounge chair by the pool to read Mott's findings.

Rebecca Lorraine Reach, fifty-six, lived in a Las Vegas apartment complex called the Oasis. She was employed as a blackjack dealer at one of the classier casinos.

By means most likely questionable, Mott had obtained the current photo of Rebecca on file with the Nevada Gaming Control Board. She looked no older than forty—and remarkably like her daughter.

She owned a white Ford Explorer. Her driving record was clean.

She had never been a party to a criminal or civil action in Nevada. Her credit report indicated a responsible borrowing history.

According to a neighbor, Amy Crocker, Rebecca rarely socialized with other tenants at the Oasis, had a "my-poop-don't-smell attitude," never spoke of having a daughter, either dead or alive, and was in a romantic relationship with a man named Spencer Barghest.

Mott reported that Barghest had been indicted twice for murder, in Texas, and twice had been judged innocent. As a noted right-to-die activist, he had been present at scores of assisted suicides. There was reason to believe that some of those whom he had assisted were not terminally—or even chronically—ill, and that the signatures on their requests for surcease from suffering were forged.

Ryan had no idea how an assisted suicide was effectuated. Maybe Barghest supplied an overdose of sedatives, which would be a painless poison but a kind of poison nonetheless.

Mott's report included a photo of Spencer Barghest. He had an ideal face for a stand-up comic: agreeable but rubbery features, a knowing yet ingratiating grin, and a shock of white hair cut in a punkish bristle that looked amusing on a fiftysomething guy.

Because he might be critically ill, Ryan was troubled to find only three degrees of separation between himself and a man who would be pleased to grant him eternal peace whether he wanted it or not.

This, however, did not confirm his intuitive sense that Sam's mother—and perhaps Samantha herself—was linked to his sudden health problems.

Life was often marked by synchronicities, surprising connections that seemed to be meaningful. But coincidence was only coincidence.

Barghest might be a nasty piece of work, but there was nothing sinister in his relationship with Rebecca, nothing relating to Ryan.

In his current state of mind, he had to guard

against a tendency toward paranoia. Such a regrettable inclination had already led him to order Mott's report on Samantha's mother.

Rebecca had turned out to be an ordinary person leading an unremarkable existence. Ryan's suspicion had been irrational.

Now that he thought about it, the presence of Spencer Barghest in Rebecca Reach's life was not surprising. It didn't even qualify as a coincidence, let alone a suspicious one.

Six years ago, she had made the difficult decision to remove a feeding tube from her brain-damaged daughter. A weight of guilt might have settled on her—especially when Samantha strenuously disagreed with her decision.

To assuage the guilt, Rebecca might have pored through right-to-die literature, seeking philosophical justification for what she had done. She might even have joined an activist organization, and at one of its meetings might have encountered Spencer Barghest.

Because Samantha had been estranged from her mother since Teresa's death, she probably didn't even know that Barghest and Rebecca were an item.

Ashamed that he had entertained any doubts about Sam, Ryan got up from the poolside lounge chair and returned to his study.

He sat at his desk and switched on the paper

shredder. For a long moment, he listened to its motor purring, its blades scissoring.

Finally he switched off the shredder. He put the report in a wall safe behind a sliding panel in the back of a built-in cabinet.

Fear had gotten its teeth so firmly into him that he could not easily pry it loose.

TWELVE

Over the years, the immense pepper tree had conformed around the second-story deck. Consequently, the feeling of being in a tree house was even greater here than when you looked out of the apartment windows.

Samantha had draped a red-checkered cloth over the patio table and had set out white dishes, flatware, and a red bowl of white roses.

Filtered through the tree, late golden sunlight showered her with a wealth of bright coins as she poured for Ryan a Cabernet Sauvignon that was beyond her budget, while he lied to her about the reason for the bandage on his neck.

Following a crimson sunset and purple twilight, she lit red candles in clear cups and served dinner as the stars came out, with a Connie Dover CD of Celtic music turned low.

Having allowed fear to raise doubts about Sam, having ordered a background report on her mother, Ryan initially expected to feel awkward in her company. In a sense, he had betrayed her trust.

He was at once, however, at ease with her. Her singular beauty did more to improve his mood than did the wine, and a dinner superbly prepared was less nourishing than the faultless golden smoothness of her skin.

After dinner, after they stacked the dishes in the sink, and over the last of the wine, she said, "Let's go to bed, Winky."

Suddenly Ryan was concerned that impotence might prove to be a symptom of his illness. He need not have worried.

In bed, in motion, he wondered briefly if love-making would stress his heart and trigger a seizure. He survived.

Cuddling afterward, his arm around Samantha and her head upon his chest, he said, "I'm such an idiot."

She sighed. "Surely you didn't just arrive at this realization."

"No. The thought has occurred to me before."

"So what happened recently to remind you?"

If he confessed his absurd suspicions, he would

be forced to disclose his health concerns. He did not want to worry her until he had Dr. Gupta's report and knew the full extent of his problem.

Instead, he said, "I threw out those sandals."

"The pair recycled from old tires?"

"I was suckered by the planet-friendly name of the company—Green Footwear."

"You're gorgeous, Dotcom, but you're still a geek."

For a long while, they talked about nothing important, which sometimes can be the best kind of conversation.

Samantha drifted into sleep, a golden vision in the lamplight, and Ryan soon traded the soothing sight of her for dreams.

Dream changed fluidly into dream, until he was in a city in the sea, at the bottom of an abyss. Shrines and palaces and towers were lit by eerie light streaming up domes, up spires, up kingly halls, up fanes, up Babylon-like walls. He drifted through flooded streets, drowned in deep-sea silence...until he heard a bass throbbing full of melancholy menace. Although he knew the source of the sound, he dared not name it, for to name it would be to embrace it.

He woke in low light. The dread that weighed him down was not of an imminent threat but of some monumental peril he sensed coming in the weeks and months ahead, not the failure of his body but some worse and nameless jeopardy. His heart did not race, but each beat was like a heavy piston stroke in some great slow machine.

Although Samantha's alluring scent clung to the sheets, she had risen from the bed while Ryan slept. He was alone in the room.

The digital clock on the nightstand read 11:24 P.M. He had been asleep less than an hour.

The light that came through the half-open door called to mind the strange glow in the submerged city of his dream.

He pulled on his khakis and, barefoot, went in search of Sam.

In the combination dining room and living room, beside an armchair, a bronze floor lamp with a beaded-glass shade provided a brandy-colored light, dappling the floor with bead gleam and bead shadow.

The kitchen was an extension of the main room, and there the door stood open to the deck on which they had sat for dinner.

The candles were extinguished. Only faint moonlight glazed the air, and the branches of the old tree were tentacular in the gloom.

The mild air was slightly scented by the nearby sea, more generously by night-blooming jasmine.

Samantha was not on the deck. Stairs descended to the courtyard between the garage and the house.

Murmuring voices rose from below, leading Ryan away from the stairs to a railing. Looking down, he saw Samantha because a shaft of moonlight devalued her hair from gold to silver and caressed her pearl-white silk robe.

The second person stood in shadows, but from the timbre of the voice, Ryan knew this was a man.

He could not hear their words, and he could not discern their mood from the rhythms of their conversation.

As in the butler's pantry the previous night, when he tried unsuccessfully to eavesdrop on a whispered discussion in the kitchen, he was overcome by a creeping unease, by a tantalizing suggestion of hidden dimensions and secret meanings in things that had heretofore seemed simple, clear, and fully understood.

From a tonal change in the voices, Ryan inferred that the pair below had reached the end of their discussion. Indeed, the man turned away from Samantha.

As the stranger moved, shadows at first clung to him, but then relented. The lunar glow was illuminating yet at the same time misty and mystifying, veiling as much as it revealed.

Tall, slim, moving with athletic confidence, the man crossed the moonshadow-mottled lawn toward the alleyway behind the garage, his hair white and punk-cut, as though he wore a jagged crown of ice.

Spencer Barghest, reputed lover of Rebecca Reach, compassionate and eager guide to the suicidal, was visible for only a brief moment. Moonlight shrank from him, and shadows took him in; the intervening limbs and leaves of the California pepper blocked him from further view.

Below, Samantha turned toward the steps.

THIRTEEN

Ryan backed barefoot off the deck and through the open door. He turned and hurried out of the kitchen, across the front room.

In the bedroom, he stripped off his khakis. He draped them over the arm of a chair, as they had been, and returned to bed.

Under the covers, he realized that he had not thought through this retreat, but had instinctively chosen to avoid confrontation. In retrospect, he was not sure that he had taken the wisest course.

Feigning sleep, he heard Samantha enter the bedroom, and heard the silken rustle of her robe discarded.

Under the covers once more, she said softly, "Ryan?" When he did not reply, she repeated his name.

If she believed that he was faking sleep, she might

suspect that he had seen or heard something of the assignation under the pepper tree. Therefore, he said sleepily, "Hmmmm?"

She slid against him and took hold of what she wanted.

Under the circumstances, he did not believe that he could rise to the occasion. He was surprised—and dismayed—to discover desire trumped his concern that she was guilty of dissimulation if not duplicity.

The qualities he found most erotic in a woman were intelligence, wit, affection, and tenderness. Sam had all four and could not fake the first two, though Ryan now worried that her intelligence was of a kind that facilitated manipulation and fostered cunning. He wondered if in fact she loved him and wanted the best for him, or had all along been disingenuous.

Never before had he made love when his heart was a cauldron of such wretched feelings, when physical passion was detached from all of the gentler emotions. In fact, love might have had nothing to do with it.

When the moment had passed, Samantha kissed his brow, his chin, his throat. She whispered, "Good night, Winky," and turned away from him, onto her side.

Soon her open-mouthed breathing indicated that she slept. Or pretended to sleep.

Ryan pressed two fingers to his throat to time his pulse. He marveled at the slow steady throb, which seemed to be yet another deception, the most intimate one so far: his body pretending to be in good health when actually it was in the process of failing him.

For an hour, he stared at the ceiling but in fact examined, with memory's eye, a year of loving Samantha. He sought to recall any incident that, from his new perspective, suggested she had darker intentions than those he had attributed to her at the time.

Initially, none of her actions through the months seemed in the least deceitful. When Ryan considered those same moments a second time, however, shadows fell where shadows had not been before, and every memory was infused with an impression of hidden motives and of secret conspirators lurking just offstage.

No specific deceit occurred to him, no example of her possible duplicity prior to the last few days, yet a cold current of suspicion crawled along his nerves.

The tendency to paranoia that infected contemporary culture had always disquieted him. He was ashamed to be indulging in the self-delusion that troubled him in others. He had a few disturbing facts; but he was trying to manufacture others out of fevered fantasies.

Ryan rose quietly from bed, and Samantha did not stir.

A window invited moonlight, which fell so lightly in this space that he could not have perceived the positions of the furniture if he had not been familiar with the room.

More than half blind, but with a blind man's intuition, he found his clothes, dressed, and silently navigated the bedroom. Without a sound, he closed the door behind him.

Familiarity with the floor plan and dark-adapted eyes allowed him to reach the kitchen without a misstep or collision. He switched on the light above the sink.

On the notepad by the telephone, he left her a message: *Sam, manic insomnia strikes again. Too jittery to lie still. Call you tomorrow. Love, Winky.*

He drove home, where he packed a suitcase.

The great house was as silent as the vacuum between planets. Although he made only a few small noises, each seemed as loud as thunder.

He drove to a hotel, where no one on his house staff or in his private life would think to look for him.

In an anonymous room, on a too-soft bed, he slept so soundly for six hours that he did not dream. When he woke Saturday morning, he was in the fetal position in which he had gone to sleep.

His hands ached. Evidently, he had closed them into fists through most of the night.

Before ordering a room-service breakfast, Ryan made two phone calls. The first was to Wilson Mott, the detective. The second was to arrange to have one of Be2Do's corporate jets fly him to Las Vegas.

FOURTEEN

Flensing knives of desert sun stripped the air to the bone, and the shimmers of heat rising off the airport Tarmac were as dry as the breath of a dead sea.

The Learjet and crew would stand by to return Ryan to southern California the following morning.

A black Mercedes sedan and chauffeur awaited him at the private-plane terminal. The driver introduced himself as George Zane, an employee of Wilson Mott's security firm.

He wore a black suit, a white shirt, and a black tie. Instead of shoes, he wore boots, and the blunt toes looked as though they might be reinforced with steel caps.

Two knots of pale scar tissue marked his shaved head at the brink of his brow. Tall, muscular, with a thick neck, with wide nostrils and intense eyes as purple-black as plum skins, Zane looked as though his lineage included bull blood, suggesting that the scars on his skull resulted from the surgical removal of horns.

He was not only a driver but also a bodyguard, and more. After Zane stowed Ryan's suitcase in the trunk, he opened a rear door of the sedan for him and presented him with a disposable cell phone.

"While you're here," Zane said, "make any calls with this. They can never be traced to you."

Like a limousine, this customized sedan was equipped with a motorized privacy panel between the front seat and the back.

Through the tinted windows, Ryan gazed at the barren desert mountains in the distance until a maze of soaring hotels and casinos blocked the natural world from view.

At the hotel where Ryan would stay, Zane parked in a VIP zone. While Ryan waited in the car, the driver carried the suitcase inside.

When Zane returned, he opened a back door to give an electronic-key card to Ryan. "Room eleven hundred. It's a suite. It's registered to me. Your name appears nowhere, sir."

As they pulled away from the hotel, the disposable cell phone rang, and Ryan answered it.

A woman said, "Are you ready to see Rebecca's apartment?"

Rebecca Reach. Samantha's mother.

"Yes," said Ryan.

"It's number thirty-four, on the second floor. I'm already inside."

She terminated the call.

Away from the fabled Strip, Vegas was a parched suburban sprawl. Pale stucco houses reflected the bloodless Mojave sun, and many landscape schemes employed pebbles, rocks, cactuses, and succulents.

The palm fronds looked brittle. The olive trees appeared more gray than green.

Ribbons of heat, rising from vast parking lots, caused shopping malls to shimmer and shift shape like the underwater city in his troubling dream.

Sand, dry weeds, and litter choked tracts of undeveloped land.

The Oasis, an upscale two-story apartment complex, was a cream-colored structure with a roof of turquoise tiles. The privacy wall that concealed its large courtyard was inlaid with a caravan of ceramic Art Deco camels that matched the color of the roof.

Behind the apartments stood garages, as well as guest parking shaded by horizontal trellises festooned with purple bougainvillea.

Zane put down the privacy panel and both front windows before switching off the engine. "You best walk in alone. Be casual."

After stepping out of the car, Ryan considered returning at once to it and calling off this questionable operation.

The memory of Spencer Barghest standing under the pepper tree with Samantha, his thatch of hair whiter than white in the moonlight, reminded Ryan of what he needed to know and why he needed to know it.

Beyond the back gate lay a covered walkway to the courtyard, but the gate could be opened only with a tenant's key. He had to walk around to the public entrance.

The wrought-iron front gate featured a palm-tree motif and had been finished to resemble the green patina of weathered copper.

At the center of the courtyard lay a large pool and spa with turquoise-tile coping. Faint fumes of chlorine trembled in the scorched air and seemed to vibrate in Ryan's nostrils.

Sun-browned and oiled, a few residents lay on lounge chairs, courting melanoma. None looked toward him.

The deep deck that served the second-floor apartments formed the roof of a continuous veranda benefiting the first-floor units. Lush landscaping included queen palms of various heights, which did much to screen the three wings of the building from one another.

He climbed exterior stairs and found Apartment

34. The door stood ajar, and it opened wider as he approached.

Waiting for him in the foyer was an attractive brunette with a honeymoon mouth and funereal eyes the gray of gravestone granite.

She worked for Wilson Mott. Although entirely feminine, she gave the impression that she could protect whatever virtue she might still possess, and could leave any would-be assailant with impressions of her shoe heels in his face.

Closing the door behind Ryan, she said, "Rebecca is a day-shift dealer. She's at the casino for hours yet."

"Have you found anything unusual?"

"I haven't looked, sir. I don't know what you're after. I'm just here to guard the door and get you out quickly in a pinch."

"What's your name?"

"If I told you, it wouldn't be the truth."

"Why not?"

"What we're doing here's illegal. I prefer anonymity."

From her manner, he inferred that she did not approve of this mission or of him. Of course, his life, not hers, was in jeopardy.

In Rebecca Reach's absence, the air conditioner was set at seventy degrees, which suggested she did not live on a tight budget.

Ryan started his search in the kitchen, half expecting to find an array of poisons in the pantry.

FIFTEEN

Initially, roaming Rebecca Reach's apartment, Ryan felt like a burglar, although he had no intention of stealing anything. A flush burned in his face and guilt increased the tempo of his heart.

By the time he finished with the kitchen, the dining area, and the living room, he decided he couldn't afford shame or any strong emotion that might precipitate a seizure. He proceeded with clinical detachment.

From the decor, he deduced that Rebecca cared little for the pleasures of hearth and home. The minimal furnishings were in drab shades of beige and gray. Only one piece of art—an abstract nothing—hung in the living room, none in the dining area.

The lack of a single keepsake or souvenir implied that she was not a sentimental woman.

By the lack of dust, by the alphabetical arrangement of spices in the kitchen, by the precise placement of six accent pillows on the sofa, Ryan determined that Rebecca valued neatness and order. The evidence suggested she was a solemn person with an austere heart.

As Ryan stepped into the study, the disposable cell phone rang. No caller ID appeared on the screen.

When he said hello, no one replied, but after he said hello a second time, a woman began softly to hum a tune. He did not recognize the song, but her crooning was sweet, melodic.

"Who is this?" he asked.

The soft voice became softer, faded, faint but still felicitous, and faded further until it receded into silence.

With his free hand, he fingered the bandage on his neck, where a day previous the catheter had been inserted into his jugular.

Although the singer had not sung a word, perhaps subconsciously Ryan recognized the voice—or imagined that he did—because into his mind unbidden came the emerald-green eyes and the smooth dark face of Ismay Clemm, the nurse from the cardiac-diagnostics lab at the hospital.

After he had waited nearly a minute for the singer to find her voice again, he pressed END and returned the phone to a pants pocket.

In memory, he heard what Ismay had said to him

as he had dozed on and off, recovering from the sedative: *You hear him, don't you, child? Yes, you hear him. You must not listen, child.*

A deep misgiving overcame Ryan, and for a moment he almost fled the apartment. He did not belong there.

Inhaling deeply, exhaling slowly, he strove to steady his nerves.

He had come to Las Vegas to seek the truth of the threat against him, to determine if he had only nature to fear or, instead, a web of conspirators. His survival might depend on completing his inquiries.

Rebecca's study proved to be as blandly furnished and impersonal as the other rooms. The top of her desk was bare.

About a hundred hardcover books filled a set of shelves. They were all nonfiction, concerned with self-improvement and investing.

Closer consideration revealed that none of the books offered a serious program for either self-assessment or wise money management. They were about the mystical power of positive thinking, about wishing your way to success, about one arcane secret or another that guaranteed to revolutionize your finances and your life.

In essence, they were get-rich-quick books. They promised great prosperity with little work.

That Rebecca collected so many volumes of this nature suggested that she had drifted through the years on dreams of wealth. By now, at the age of fifty-six, disappointment and frustration might have left her bitter—and impatient.

None of these volumes would suggest that you marry your daughter off to a wealthy man and poison him to gain control of his fortune. Any illiterate person could conceive such a plan, without need for the inspiration of a book.

At once, Ryan regretted leaping to such an unkind conclusion. By suspecting Rebecca of such villainy, he was being unfair to Samantha.

Months ago, he proposed to Sam. If she were involved in a scheme to murder him for his money, she would have accepted his proposal on the spot. By now they would be husband and wife.

In one of the desk drawers, Ryan found eight magazines. On top of the stack was the issue of *Vanity Fair* that contained Samantha's profile of him.

Each of the other seven magazines, published over a period of two years, contained an article by Samantha.

Sam might be estranged from her mother, but Rebecca apparently followed her daughter's career with interest.

He paged through all the publications, searching for a letter, a note, a Post-it, anything that might prove that Sam had sent the magazines to her mother. His search was fruitless.

In the well-appointed bathroom and the large

bedroom, he found nothing of interest. As regarded Rebecca if not her daughter, Ryan had already discovered enough to sharpen his distrust into mistrust.

Wilson Mott's nameless operative waited in the foyer. After setting the door to latch behind them, she left the apartment with Ryan.

She surprised him by taking his hand and smiling as if they were lovers setting off for lunch and an afternoon adventure. Perhaps on the theory that no one would suspect them if they called attention to themselves, she chattered brightly about a movie she'd recently seen.

As they followed the public balcony that served the second floor and descended the open stairs to the courtyard, Ryan twice muttered a response. Both times she laughed with delight, as though he were the wittiest of conversationalists.

Both her voice and her laugh were musical, her eyes sparkling with an elfin sense of fun.

When they stepped through the copper-green front gate, out of the courtyard onto the public sidewalk in front of the Oasis, her voice lost all its music. The arc of humor in her ripe mouth went flatline, and her eyes were gravestone-gray once more.

She let go of him and blotted her palm on her skirt.

With chagrin, Ryan realized that his hand had

been damp with sweat when she had taken hold of it.

"I'm parked in the next block," she said. "George will take you back to your hotel."

"What about Spencer Barghest?"

"He's at home right now. We have reason to believe he's going out tonight. We'll take you into his place then."

As Ryan watched her walk away from him, he wondered who she was when she wasn't on the job for Wilson Mott. Might the cold gray gaze be most indicative of the real woman—or might the musical laugh and elfin eyes be the truth of her?

He was no longer confident that he could discover the essential truth of anyone.

He returned to the Mercedes sedan, where George Zane waited.

On the way back to the hotel, seen through the tinted windows, the world seemed to change subtly but continuously before Ryan's weary eyes—flattened by sunlight, bent by shadow, every surface harder than he remembered it, every edge sharper—until it seemed that this was not the Earth to which he had been born.

SIXTEEN

From the hotel, using his cell rather than the disposable phone, Ryan Perry called Samantha because he had promised to do so in the few lines he had written on her kitchen notepad the previous night.

He was relieved to get her voice mail. He claimed to have flown to Denver on unexpected business and said he would be home Tuesday.

He also said he loved her, and it sounded like the truth to him.

Although he rarely drank wine before dinner, he ordered a half bottle of Lancaster Cabernet Sauvignon with his room-service lunch.

He had intended to visit the casino where Rebecca Reach worked as a blackjack dealer. He wanted to get a look at her in the flesh.

Although he hadn't intended to play at her table, it now seemed unwise even to observe her from a distance. If she had read her daughter's article in *Vanity Fair*, she had seen photos of Ryan.

Perhaps Rebecca remained in contact with her daughter, contrary to what Samantha had said, in which case she must not catch a glimpse of Ryan here when he claimed to be in Denver.

After lunch, he hung the DO NOT DISTURB sign on the door. Relaxed by the wine, he stretched out fully clothed on the bed.

Hard desert light pressed at the edges of the closed draperies, but the room was cool, shadowy, narcoleptic.

He dreamed of the city under the sea. Lurid light streamed through the abyss, projecting tormented shadows across shrines, towers, palaces, up bowers of sculptured ivy and stone flowers.

Drifting along strangely lit yet dark streets, he moved less like a swimmer than like a ghost. Soon he realized he was following a spectral figure, a pale something or someone.

When his quarry glanced back, she was Ismay Clemm; the paleness was her nurse's uniform. Ryan had an urgent question, though he could not remember it. Throughout his dream, he never drew close enough to Ismay for his voice to carry to her through the drowned streets.

Daylight was waning beyond the draperies when

he woke. In a lake of darkness, the suite's furniture loomed like gray islands.

Whether or not the soft insistent rapping had awakened him, Ryan heard it now. The disorientation that accompanied the sudden disembarkation from a dream slowly ebbed, until he identified the adjoining chamber as the source of the sound.

In the living room, he switched on a lamp, and the rapping drew him to the door. He put one eye to the lens that gave him a wide view of the public corridor, but no one stood out there.

Now that Ryan was fully awake, the *tap-tap-tap* seemed to come from a living-room window that offered an expansive view of the Las Vegas Strip.

At the horizon, the blood-drop sun pressed on jagged mountains, swelled, burst, and streamed red across the western heavens.

Here on the eleventh floor, nothing cast itself against the window except the blinking lights and throbbing neon of the casinos that, with nightfall, used luminous titillation and sham glamour to lure the moneyed herd in the street toward penury.

Turning from the window, Ryan heard the soft knock coming from a different direction. He followed it to the bathroom door, which he had left closed.

The door could only be latched from the inside. No one would be in there, knocking to be let out.

Hesitantly, with an increasing sense that he was in

jeopardy, he stepped into the bathroom, switched on the light, and blinked in the dazzle of bright reflections.

A new hollow, sonorous quality to the sound suggested that it might be issuing from a drainpipe. After he opened the shower door and then bent to each of the two sinks, he still could not identify the source.

Drawn back into the bedroom, Ryan now thought the *tap-tap-tap* came from the big plasma-screen TV, although he had never switched it on.

You must not listen, child.

The sudden deterioration of his health had left him emotionally vulnerable. He began to wonder about his mental stability.

On the nightstand, the disposable cell phone rang.

When Ryan answered it, George Zane said, "The way is clear for your second visit. I'll be out front in half an hour with the car."

Ryan pressed END, put down the phone, and waited for the rapping sound to begin again.

The persistent silence didn't quell his unfocused anxiety. He had not let anyone into the suite, yet he felt that he was no longer alone.

Resisting the irrational urge to search every corner and closet, he took a quick shower. When steam clouded the glass door, he wiped it away to maintain a clear view of the bathroom.

Dressed and ready for the night, he felt neither refreshed nor less concerned about the possible presence of another in the suite. Surrendering to paranoia, he searched closets, behind furniture.

He tried the sliding door to the balcony. Locked. No one was out there anyway.

In the spacious foyer, he glanced at his reflection in the mirror above the console. Although he half expected someone to appear in the suite behind him, no one did.

SEVENTEEN

Spencer Barghest, indicted twice for murder in Texas and twice found innocent, lived in a middle-class neighborhood of single-story ranch houses.

After George Zane drove past the address to park half a block away and across the street from the Barghest residence, Ryan walked back to the house.

The warm night air was so dry that it would not support the fragrances of trees and flowering shrubs, only the generic alkaline scent of the desert upon which the city had encroached but over which it had not triumphed.

Landscape spotlights, fixed high in lacy melaleucas, cast on the front walkway leaf shadows so crisp they ought to have crunched underfoot.

Light glowed behind the curtained windows, and

the nameless brunette with the soft mouth and the stony eyes greeted him before he could ring the bell.

Inside, as the woman closed the door behind them, Ryan said, "How long do I have?"

"Three or four hours at least. He's out to dinner with Rebecca Reach."

"They take that long for dinner?"

"Dinner and horizontal dancing at her place. According to our sources, Barghest is a Viagra cowboy. There's not a day he doesn't take a dose and ride."

"Dr. Death is a Don Juan?"

"You're giving him too much credit. He's a slut."

"What if they come back here?"

"They won't. Maybe a few nut-case women find this decor arousing, but most don't. Rebecca's one who doesn't."

In the living room, she showed him what she meant. In addition to the expected furniture, there were two dead men, one dead woman, all naked.

Having read a newspaper story about exhibitions of cadaver art touring fine museums and galleries and universities nationwide, Ryan knew at once that these were not sculptures, not mere representations of dead people. They were painstakingly preserved corpses.

These dead had been treated with antibacterial solutions, drying agents, and numerous preservatives. Thereafter they were submerged in polyurethane, which sealed them in an airtight glaze that prevented decomposition, and were strapped to armatures supporting them in various postures.

One of the men apparently had died of a wasting disease; he was emaciated. His narrow lips were pinched tight. One eye closed, the other open, he appeared to have lacked the courage to turn his full gaze on approaching Death.

The second man looked healthy; the cause of his death was not evident. He seemed to be alive, except that the polyurethane made him glisten head to foot like a well-basted holiday turkey.

Evidently the middle-aged woman had died soon after a single mastectomy, because the lurid scars had not yet healed before she passed. As was true also of the men, her head had been shaved.

Her blue eyes fixed Ryan with a look of mortification and horror, as though she were aware of the atrocities to which she had been subjected after death.

When he could speak, Ryan asked: "The authorities know he has these?"

"Each...person in the collection either signed over his body to Barghest before death—or the family did so. He's displayed them at various events."

"Health hazard?"

"The experts say no, none."

"Certainly isn't good for anyone's *mental* health."

"It's all been adjudicated. Courts believe it's legitimate art, a political statement, cultural anthropology, educational, hip, cool, fun."

Squeamish not because he stood in the company of the dead but because he felt that their exploitation was an affront to human dignity, Ryan looked away from the three specimens.

"When do we start feeding Christians to the lions?" he wondered.

"Tickets go on sale next Wednesday."

She returned to the foyer to allow him to tour the house alone.

A hallway led off the living room, and a fourth glistening cadaver stood at the end, bathed in light from an art spot.

This man must have perished in an accident or possibly as the consequence of a brutal beating. The left eye was swollen shut in his battered face, and the right was red with blood. A cheekbone had been crushed. The frontal bone of his skull had fractured into two plates, and one had slightly dislocated from the other.

Ryan wondered if the brain remained in the skull or if it had been removed. Likewise, the internal organs. He didn't know every step taken in the preservation process.

Already, he had begun to adjust to this barbaric "art," finding it no less offensive than before, but nevertheless letting curiosity and a kind of dark wonder armor him against pity and outrage.

He told himself that his response to these abominations was not apathy, not even indifference, but necessary stoicism. If he did not repress his sympathy for these men and women and his disgust at what had been done to their remains, he would not be able to continue with the necessary search that he had come here to conduct.

In the bedroom, an armature supported a dead woman in a seated position. Her suggestive posture and the intensity of her dead stare so disturbed Ryan that he made only the most cursory inspection of the room and the adjacent closet.

Barghest's home office contained the sole significant discovery related to Ryan's personal situation.

On a bookshelf, among more ordinary volumes, were two ring binders of high-quality eight-by-ten color photographs. Faces.

Every face was expressionless, and not a single pair of eyes regarded the camera or appeared to be focused on anything. These were the faces of dead people.

A clear-plastic sleeve protected each photo. Affixed to each sleeve, a small label offered what might have been a file number neatly printed by hand.

Ryan assumed that these people had requested Barghest—or their families had requested him—to assist their departure from this world by suicide or, in the case of the mentally incapacitated, by the ad-

ministration of some lethal but untraceable sub-
stance.

The absence of names and dates of death suggested that Barghest thought the photographs might
be incriminating in spite of society's current tolerance for the kind of compassion that he so enjoyed
administering.

Relieved that the room lacked an observing cadaver, Ryan sat at the desk with both ring binders.
He did not know why he should force himself to
study so many faces of corpses, but intuition suggested that this ordeal would reward him.

Barghest's trophies were of both sexes, young and
old, and of all races. The word *trophies* surprised
Ryan when it occurred to him, but after a dozen
faces, no other term seemed as accurate.

In some instances, the subjects' eyes appeared to
have frozen open at the moment of death. Sometimes, however, small pieces of Scotch tape fixed the
eyelids to the brows.

Ryan tried not to consider why open eyes were so
important to Barghest. In a moment of uncanny per-
ception, however, he *knew* the euthanasia activist
savored each dead gaze with the insistence of a
rapist compelling his victim to meet his stare, that
every photo had a quasi-pornographic purpose.

The album suddenly felt greasy, and he put it
down.

He rolled the office chair back from the desk,

leaned forward, and hung his head. Breathing through his mouth, he struggled to quell a rush of nausea.

His heart did not race, but each beat felt like a wave, a great swell breaking in his chest. The floor seemed to rise and fall, as if he were afloat, and a thin *scree* sounded like gulls crying in the distance, although he realized that he was listening to the faint whistle of his pinched breathing.

The internal waves rose in sets, in the way that real waves formed upon the sea, some larger than others, with pauses between. He knew that strokes of uneven force and the loss of rhythm could be a prelude to cardiac arrest.

He placed one hand on his chest, as though he could press calm upon his heart.

If Ryan died in this place, Wilson Mott's agents might leave his body behind rather than risk explaining why he and they had been here. Found by Dr. Death, he might wind up as one more exhibit in the gallery of cadavers. Stripped naked, preserved, and glazed after being bent into a humiliating posture, he would ornament a currently vacant corner of the house, thereafter subject to Spencer Barghest's attention and unholy touch.

EIGHTEEN

Whether by an act of sheer will or by the grace of Fate, Ryan survived the episode and, after a couple of minutes, felt his heart reestablish rhythmic beats and measured force.

The dry, cool air in Barghest's house was odorless but had a faint metallic taste. Counseling himself not to contemplate the source of that flavor, Ryan stopped breathing through his mouth.

He sat up straight in the office chair and rolled it to the desk once more. After a hesitation, he opened the first ring binder to the photograph that he'd been studying when nausea had overcome him.

Still operating on a hunch, he paged with grim determination through the first book of photos. His patience was at last rewarded when he saw the third face in the second binder.

Samantha. Her eyes were taped open, her full lips slightly parted, as if she had let out a sigh of satisfaction as the shutter of the camera caught her.

This was not Samantha, of course, but Teresa, her identical twin. Prior to death, she lingered in a vegetative state, abed for months following the auto accident, and the experience diminished her beauty. So pale, Teresa nevertheless remained lovely, and in fact her suffering gave her the ethereal radiance, the fragile otherworldly beauty of a martyr ascending to sainthood in an old-master painting.

Evidently, Barghest had known Rebecca six years ago. He must have been present at Teresa's death.

By her own account, Samantha also had been at her sister's bedside during those final hours. Yet she never mentioned Barghest.

She rarely spoke of her lost twin. But that was understandable and in no way suspicious. Surely the loss still hurt.

She had revealed the length of Teresa's ordeal only a few nights earlier, under the strawberry trees. Previously she had allowed Ryan to think that her sister died either in the accident or shortly thereafter.

Again, Sam's reticence was proof of nothing more than the pain that Teresa's death still caused her.

In the photo, the dead woman's head rested on a pillow. With care that suggested tenderness, her golden hair had been brushed and arranged flatteringly around her face.

In contrast to the hair, the tape holding open the sightless eyes was an affront, even a violation.

As loud and irregular as Ryan's heart had been recently, so now it was to a similar degree quiet and steady, and the house was also quiet, and the night beyond the house, as if every soul in Las Vegas in the same instant fell into a deep sleep or turned to dust, as if every wheel stopped rotating and every noisy machine lost power, as if nocturnal birds could not use their wings or find their songs, as if all crawling things were seized by paralysis between creep and slither, and an absolute stillness befell the air, allowing no breeze or draft or eddy. Time froze in tickless clocks.

Whether the hush was real or imagined, so extraordinary was the moment that Ryan had the urge to shout and shatter the silence before the world permanently petrified.

He did not cry out, however, because he sensed meaning in this unmitigated muffle, a truth insisting on discovery.

The silence seemed to well from the photo in front of Ryan, to pool up from it and flood the world, as though dead Teresa's face had the power to still Creation and to compel Ryan's attention. His subconscious commanded: *Observe, see, discover.* In this image was something of terrible importance to him, a shocking revelation that he had thus far overlooked and that might save him.

He studied her dead stare, wondering if the twists of light and shadow reflected on her eyes would reveal the room in which she had died and the people in attendance at her passing, or something else that would explain his current, mortal circumstances.

Those reflections were too small. No amount of squinting could force them to resolve into intelligible images.

His gaze traveled down her lovely cheeks, along the exquisite slopes and curves of her nose, to her generous and perfectly formed mouth.

Her parted lips issued no breath, only silence, but he half expected to hear, with his mind's ear, a few words that would explain his hypertrophic heart and reveal his future.

At the periphery of Ryan's vision, movement startled him.

He looked up, expecting that one of the glazed cadavers had pulled free of its armature and had come for him.

The nameless brunette stepped into the study from the hallway, and her voice broke the spell of silence. "I don't get creeped-out easily, but this place is getting to me."

"Me too," he said.

He slipped Teresa's photo out of the plastic sleeve, set it aside, and closed the ring binder.

"He'll miss it," the brunette warned.

"Maybe he will. I don't care. Let him wonder."

Ryan returned both ring binders to the bookshelf where he had found them.

In the doorway, leaning against the jamb, arms folded across her breasts, she said, "We have a tail on them. They finished dinner. Now they're back at her apartment."

She must have been between thirty and thirty-five, but she had the air of someone older. She radiated a self-confidence that seemed to be wisdom more than pride.

"Would you let him?" Ryan wondered.

"Let him what?"

"Touch you."

Her eyes were not gravestone granite, after all, but castle ramparts, and only a fool would try to storm her.

She said, "I'd shoot off his pecker."

"I believe you would."

"It'd be a service to humanity."

Ryan wondered, "Why does Rebecca let him?"

"Something's wrong with her."

"What?"

"And not just her. Half the world is in love with death."

"Not me."

As if in quiet accusation, the brunette glanced at the photo of Teresa on the desk.

Ryan said, "That's just evidence."

"Of what?"

"I don't know yet."

Earlier, he had searched the desk. He returned to the drawer that contained stationery and selected a nine-by-twelve envelope, into which he slipped the photograph.

"I'm done here," he said.

They walked the house together, turning off lights, pretending not to listen for the footfalls of corpses in their wake.

In the foyer, at the security-system panel, she said, "The alarm was engaged when I got here. I have to reset it."

As she keyed in a code that she had somehow learned, Ryan asked, "How did you disarm it without setting it off?"

"A few small tools and years of practice."

The tools were evidently sufficiently compact to fit in her purse, for she carried no other bag.

Outside, she said, "Stay with me," and after passing under the weeping boughs of the melaleucas, she headed south on the public sidewalk. "I'm parked a block and a half away."

He knew that she didn't need him at her side for protection any more than did the hulking George Zane.

In the absence of streetlamps and in the weakness of the moon, they cast no shadows.

Here, miles from the flash of the casinos, the sky offered a desolation of stars.

Like all Mojave settlements, regardless of size and history, this one seemed to have a tenuous existence. An ancient ocean had withdrawn millennia ago, leaving a vast sea of sand, but the desert was no more eternal than the waters before it, and the city markedly more ephemeral than the desert.

"Whatever's wrong in your life," she said, "it's none of my business."

Ryan did not disagree.

"The way Wilson Mott runs his operation, I'd be fired for saying one word more than I've just said."

Curious about where this might be leading, Ryan assured her, "I've no reason to tell him anything you say."

After a silence, she said, "You're a haunted man."

"I don't believe in ghosts."

"I'm not surprised by that."

Across the street, Zane sat behind the wheel of the Mercedes. They passed him and kept going.

She said, "Not ghosts. You're haunted by your own death."

"What does that mean?"

"It means, you're waiting for the ax to fall."

"If I were paranoid," he said, "I'd wonder if Wilson Mott has been investigating *me*."

"I'm just good at reading people."

With a thrum, a presence passed overhead. Looking up at broad pale wings, Ryan thought it might have been an owl.

"The way I read you," she continued, "you can't figure out who."

"Who what?"

"Who's going to kill you."

Across the night, the monotonous song of cicadas sounded like razor blades stropping razor blades.

As they walked, she said, "When you're trying to figure out who...you've got to keep in mind the roots of violence."

He wondered if she had been a cop before she had gone to work for Mott.

"There are only five," she said. "Lust, envy, anger, avarice, and vengeance."

"Motives, you mean."

Arriving at her car, she said, "It's best to think of them as failings, not motives."

Parking lights and the lazy engine noise of a coasting car rose behind them.

"More important than the roots," she said, "is the taproot."

She opened the driver's door of the Honda and turned to stare solemnly at him.

"The taproot," she said, "is always the killer's ultimate and truest motivation."

Among the numerous strange moments of the past four days, this conversation had begun to seem the strangest.

"And what is the taproot of violence?" Ryan asked.

"The hatred of truth."

The coasting car behind them proved to be the Mercedes sedan. George Zane brought it to a stop in the street, parallel to but slightly forward of the Honda, leaving Ryan and the woman in moon haze and shadows.

She said, "In case you ever need to talk, I'm... Cathy Sienna." She spelled the surname.

"Just this morning, you said you'd never tell me your true name."

"I was wrong. One more thing, Mr. Perry..."

He waited.

"The hatred of truth is a vice," she said. "From it comes pride and an enthusiasm for disorder."

The moonlight made silver coins of her gray eyes.

She said, "Moments ago, we were in the house of a man who has a *fierce* enthusiasm for disorder. Be careful. It can be contagious."

Although Cathy reached for his hand, she did not shake it, but pressed it in both of her hands, more the affectionate gesture of a friend than the good-bye of a business associate.

Before he could think of anything to say, she got into her car, closed the door, and started the engine.

Ryan stood in the street, watching her drive away. Then he got into the backseat of the Mercedes.

"Return to the hotel, sir?" Zane asked.

"Yes, please."

In Ryan's hands was the manila envelope that

contained the photo of Teresa Reach, which he suspected might hold a clue that would save him.

To further study the photo, he needed to have it scanned at high resolution and examine it with the best image-enhancement software. He could do nothing more with it this night.

During the ride, Ryan's thoughts repeatedly returned to Cathy Sienna, to the question of whether her concern was genuine.

In light of recent events, he wondered if her advice and further counsel would have been offered if he had not been a wealthy man.

NINETEEN

In the Mercedes, Ryan made a few phone calls. By the time he reached his hotel, he felt comfortable about trusting the manila envelope to George Zane.

Although Wilson Mott's primary offices were in New York, Los Angeles, and Seattle, he had relationships with security firms in other cities, including Las Vegas. He had been able to arrange for the digital processing of Teresa's photograph by reliable locals and for the acquisition of the software and hardware that would allow Ryan to study it better.

By 6:30 in the morning, when the corporate Learjet flew Ryan out of Vegas, Mott's people would have delivered the Teresa package to his hotel suite in Denver.

Having told Samantha that he had been called to

Denver on business, he now intended to go there. He did not know why.

This trip would not atone for the lie that he had told her or even make it less of a lie. And at this point, he had no intention of revealing his investigation of her mother and of Spencer Barghest, which was an omission—a calculated concealment—that counted as a far greater betrayal than the lie about his destination.

Returning to his home in Newport Coast well in advance of his appointment with Dr. Samar Gupta on Tuesday was not an option. Following Lee and Kay Ting's whispering in the kitchen, he had felt—and still would feel—under surveillance in his own house.

Las Vegas offered him nothing more than games of chance. Already he was in a game with the highest possible stakes, and neither craps nor blackjack, nor baccarat, could distract him from the knowledge that his life was on the line.

So Denver in the early morning.

As he had taken lunch in his hotel room, so he took dinner. He had no appetite, but he ate.

Not surprisingly, that night he dreamed. He might have expected cadavers, preserved or not, in his dreams, but they did not appear.

His nightmares were not of people or other bogeymen, but of landscapes and architecture, including but not limited to that city in the sea.

He walked a valley road toward a palace on a slope. The valley had once been green. Now seared grass, withered flowers, and blighted trees flanked a river in which flowed a turgid mass of black water, ashes, and debris. Palace windows once filled with golden light were strangely red, alive with capering shadows, and the closer he drew to the open door, the more terrified he became of what hideous throng might rush out of it and fall upon him.

After the valley, he appeared on the shore of a wild lake bound with black rock and trees that towered all around. The grinning moon in the black sky was a snarling moon on the black water. Poisonous waves lapped at the stones on which he stood, and something rose in the center of the lake, some behemoth beyond measuring, from which sloughed the inky water and with it the wriggling moon.

In the morning, while he showered, while he breakfasted, while he flew to Denver in the corporate jet, images from the nightmares rose frequently in his mind. He felt as though these were places he had visited years before, not in sleep but when awake, for they were too real to be figments of a dream, too detailed, too evocative, too intimately felt.

He wondered again if not only his body was failing him but also his mind. Perhaps the inadequate function of his heart resulted in diminished circulation, with detrimental consequences to the brain.

TWENTY

The hotel rated five stars. The windows of the presidential suite—the only accommodations available on short notice—looked out across a serrated skyline of glass-and-steel towers.

In the west, great forested mountains thrust toward greater clouds: Andes of cumulus congestus, on which ascended Himalayas of cumulonimbus, so the weight of the celestial architecture, if it should collapse, appeared great enough to sunder the earth below.

Waiting for Ryan in the suite's cozy library were a computer and sufficient linked equipment to allow him to conduct an exhaustive study of the photo of dead Teresa. Beside the keyboard stood a box of cookies from Denver's best bakery. Wilson Mott always delivered.

The photographic-analysis software included a well-executed tutorial. Although Ryan had made a fortune from the Internet and had a gift for both software comprehension and design, he experimented most of the morning before he was comfortable with the program.

By noon, he needed a break. Having feasted on cookies, he wanted no lunch. But a pleasure drive appealed to him, and he wished he had his Ford Woodie Wagon or one of his other customized classics.

Perhaps his heart condition warranted a chauffeur, but he wanted to cruise alone. En route from Vegas, his pilot had called ahead to have the hotel book for Ryan a rental SUV to be available 24/7.

The black Cadillac Escalade had every comfort and convenience. He could cruise randomly through the city and not worry about getting hopelessly lost, because when he was ready to return to the hotel, the vehicle's navigation system would tell him the way.

Although he had been to Denver twice before, he never ventured farther than the convention center and immediate environs. Now he wanted to see more of the city.

Sunday traffic was light. Within half an hour, he came upon a small park that occupied two or three acres at the most. It lay adjacent to an old brick church.

What inspired him to curb the Escalade and go

exploring on foot were the aspens—or so he thought. In their autumn dress, the trees were a golden spectacle made more flamboyant by their contrast with the mantled sky.

The park offered no playground or war memorial, only winding brick paths strewn with fallen leaves and an occasional bench on which to sit and contemplate the glory of nature.

On this mild afternoon, the first snowfall seemed still weeks away.

While galleons of clouds sailed eastward at high altitude, the world was becalmed at ground level. Yet even in this stillness, the aspens trembled, as they always did.

Walking, he paused frequently to listen to the whisper of the trees, a sound he had always loved. The aspens were so sensitive to air movement because their leafstalks were only narrow ribbons and were set at right angles to the hanging leaf-blades.

As he rested on a bench, he realized that he could not recall when he had ever before heard aspens whispering or how he knew the design of their leafstalks was what gave them an unceasing voice.

His initial sight of the park had strummed a sympathetic chord in him. Upon first walking among the trees, he had felt an affection for them that was entirely familiar.

Now, on this bench under a canopy of shiny yellow leaves, the affection ripened into a more intense sentiment, into a tender-hearted yearning that was nostalgic in character. Inexplicably, though he had never been here before, he felt that he had sat beneath these very trees many times, in all seasons and weather.

Wood warblers, soon to migrate south, sang in the whispering trees, sweet high clear notes: *swee-swee-swee-ti-ti-ti-swee*.

Ryan did not know where he had learned these birds were wood warblers, but suddenly their song moved him from a curious nostalgic yearning to full-blown deja vu. Today was not his first experience of this park.

The certainty that he had been here before, not just once but often, became so electrifying that it brought him off the bench, to his feet, so pierced by a sense of unnatural forces at work that his scalp prickled and the hairs quivered on the nape of his neck, and a chill traced the contours of his spinal column with the specificity of a diligent physiology professor using a laser pointer.

Although the church had interested him only as backdrop, Ryan turned toward it with the conviction that, on some occasion now forgotten, he had been inside of the place. Earlier, he had not been near enough to the church to see its name, but somehow he knew that the denomination was Roman Catholic.

The day remained mild, yet he grew steadily

colder. He slipped his hands into his jacket pockets as he crossed the park to the church.

Because they had been swept clean for the morning services, the concrete steps of St. Gemma's were brightened by only a few aspen leaves. The last Mass of the day had been offered, and the church stood quiet now.

Hesitating at the bottom of the steps, Ryan knew the crucifix above the altar would be of carved wood, that the crown of thorns on Christ's head would be gilded, likewise the nails in His hands and feet. Behind the cross, a gilded oval. And radiating from the oval, carved and gilded rays of holy light.

He climbed the steps.

At the door, he almost turned away.

Shadows gathered in the narthex, fewer in the nave, where daylight pressed colorfully through the stained-glass windows and where some altar lights remained aglow.

In every detail, the impressive crucifix proved to be as he had foreseen it.

Alone in the church, he stood in the center aisle, transfixed, trembling like the quaking aspens in the park.

Ryan remained certain that he had never been here before, and he was not a Catholic. Yet he was overcome by the sense of comfort that one feels in well-loved places.

This comfort did not warm him, however, and did not calm him, but compelled him to retreat.

Outside, on the steps, he needed a minute to regain control of his ragged breathing.

In the park once more, on a bench to which his wobbly legs had barely carried him, he used his cell phone to call Wilson Mott's most private number.

After speaking with Mott, he expected to sit there for a while, because he was not yet calm or fit to drive. But the brilliance of the aspens, the black iron lampposts with crackle-glass panes, the wrought-iron bench painted glossy black, and the herringbone brick walkway filled him with yearning for a past he could not recall, indeed for a past that he had never lived.

The weirdness of it all became too much for him, and he left the park at something less than a run but more than a walk.

After Ryan entered the name of his hotel in the Escalade's navigator, the mellifluous voice of a patient young woman guided him successfully through Denver in spite of a few missed turns.

TWENTY-ONE

In the library of the presidential suite, high above Denver, Ryan Perry worked obsessively on the digitized photo of dead Teresa.

The photographic-analysis package provided numerous tools with which he could enhance the cadaver's eyes, enlarging and clarifying the scene reflected in those glassy surfaces. Some of the techniques could be used in combination. And when the zone of interest was so enlarged that it lost resolution, the computer was able to clone the pixels until density and definition had been restored to the image.

Nevertheless, by 7:05 Sunday evening, when Wilson Mott's agent arrived, Ryan had not been able to make anything of the patterns of light and shadow in those optic reflections.

Earlier, just before leaving the park, when he had called Mott to request the services of a trusted and discreet phlebotomist, he had been told that the nearest such medical technician that could be tapped for the job was George Zane, who had not yet returned from Las Vegas to the security company's offices in Los Angeles. Before signing on with Mott, Zane had been a U.S. Army Medical Corpsman, administering first aid on the battlefields of Iraq.

Now, Ryan stretched out on a bed in the master bedroom, with a towel under his arm, while Zane performed a venesection and drew 40 milliliters of blood into eight 5-milliliter vials.

"I want to be tested for every known poison," Ryan said.

"Yes, sir."

"Not just those that are known to cause cardiac hypertrophy."

"We've located a cooperative lab right here in Denver and two blood specialists who'll work through the night on it. You don't want to know their fee."

"I don't care about their fee," Ryan assured Zane.

One of the best things about having serious wealth was that if you knew the right service providers—like Wilson Mott—you could get what you wanted, when you wanted it. And no matter how eccentric the request, no one raised an eyebrow, and everyone treated you with the utmost respect, at least to your face.

"I want to be tested for drugs, too. Including—no, especially—for hallucinogenics and for drugs that might cause hallucinations or delusions as a side effect."

"Yes, sir," said Zane, setting aside the fourth vial, "Mr. Mott has informed me of all that."

With the knots of scar tissue on his bald head, with his intense purple-black eyes, with his wide nostrils flaring wider as though the scent of blood excited him, George Zane should have been a disturbing figure. Instead, he was a calming presence.

"You're very good with the needle, George."

"Thank you, sir."

"Didn't sting at all. And you have a good bedside manner."

"Because of the army."

"I didn't realize they taught bedside manner in the army."

"The battlefield teaches it. The suffering you see. You want to be gentle."

"I never served in the military."

"Well, in the military or not, we all go to war every day. Two more syringes, sir."

As Zane removed the blood-filled barrel from the cannula and attached an empty one, Ryan said, "You probably think I'm some kind of paranoid."

"No, sir. There's evil in the world, all right. Being aware of it makes you a realist, not a paranoid."

"The idea that someone's poisoning me or drugging me..."

"You wouldn't be the first. The enemy isn't always on the other end of a gun or a bomb. Sometimes he's very close. Sometimes he looks like us, which makes him almost invisible, and that's when he's most dangerous."

▧

Ryan had also instructed Wilson Mott to obtain a prescription sleeping drug and send it along with Zane. He wanted a medication of sufficient strength not merely to prevent the wide-eyed, twitchy-legged, mind-racing, fully-wired insomnia that made him manic enough to try to ride a shark, but one also potent enough to submerge him so deep in sleep that he would not dream.

After Zane left with the blood, Ryan ordered a room-service dinner so heavy that the consumption of it should have sedated him as effectively as a cocktail of barbiturates.

Following dinner, he consulted the dosage instructions on the pill bottle, took two capsules instead of the one recommended, and washed them down with a glass of milk.

In bed, he used the remote to surf the ocean of entertainment options offered by the satellite-TV service to which the hotel subscribed. On a classic-movie channel, he found a women-in-prison movie so magnificently tedious that perhaps he would not have needed the prescription sedative.

He slept.

A silent dark, a vague awareness of a tangled sheet, and then a quiet dark, only the rhythmic interior sounds of heart contractions and arterial rush, as black as a moonless lake, as a raven's wings, darkness there and nothing more, merely this and nothing more...

And then a flickering dream framed in a rectangle, surrounded by blackness.

A man and woman spoke, the male voice familiar, and there was music and a sense of urgency, and gunfire.

The dream flickered because Ryan blinked his eyes, and it was framed in a rectangle because it was not a dream, not the women-in-prison movie, either, but whatever the classic-movie channel deemed classic at this hour.

Glowing numerals on the bedside clock read 2:36. He had been asleep four hours, maybe five.

He wanted more, needed more, fumbled for the remote, found it, extinguished the rectangle of colorful images, silenced the guns, silenced the music, silenced the woman, silenced William Holden.

As the remote slipped out of his slackening hand, as he sank into the solace of oblivion, he realized that the movie he had just switched off was the same one to which he had regained consciousness on Thursday morning, after the terrible attack Wednesday night that had driven him to his internist, Forry Stafford.

Waking Thursday morning on his bedroom floor, curled in the fetal position, eyes crusted shut, mouth dry and sour, he had become convinced that the unknown William Holden film on the TV had special meaning for him, that in it was a message to be deciphered, a warning about his future.

That feeling had passed as he came fully awake and recalled the seizures and the spike-sharp pain that had racked him in the night.

But now, almost four days later, the sense of pending revelation swelled once more, and Ryan thought he should struggle against the gravity that pulled him down into sleep, should rise, switch on the TV, identify the film and wring its scenes to squeeze from the story any bitter omen that it might contain.

A heavy dinner, a powerful drug, a weight of exhaustion, and a kind of cowardice influenced him, instead, to let the remaining sand grains of consciousness sift through his grasp.

He slept over ten hours and woke Monday morning with a headache that a drunk might have earned after a three-day bender.

In the shower, water pelted his skull as if every drop were a hailstone. Even low light stung his eyes, and every odor offended.

He fought this hangover with pots of coffee. He drank the first pot black, the second with cream but without sugar.

Later he ordered dry toast. Later still, a buttered English muffin. In the afternoon, he wanted a dish of vanilla ice cream.

Room service brought him one thing at a time, as he asked for it, as though he were an ill child making requests of a doting mother.

Without surcease, he worked on the computer, striving to enhance the reflections on Teresa Reach's dead eyes and discover the meaning that he thought he would find in them. Hours after he knew that no meaning existed to be identified, he labored on those twin images.

Without this task to occupy him, he might have called the valet to have the Escalade brought from the hotel garage, and he might have driven again to the park with the aspens, if he could find it. Once in the park, he would not be able to resist St. Gemma's, and he worried that a second visit to the church might contribute not to any resolution of this mystery, not even to any degree of clarification, but only to greater disorientation.

The many strangenesses of the past few days had initially led to bewilderment that stoked his curiosity. Bewilderment had given way to a muddy confusion that, in its persistence, was mentally and emotionally debilitating.

Monday afternoon, he finally acknowledged that nothing in Teresa's eyes would enlighten him either as to the identity of the people who might be conspiring against him or as to their motives.

Nevertheless, he continued to feel that *something* about this last photograph of her was important. Spencer Barghest had no doubt held the camera; therefore, Barghest had assisted Rebecca Reach in ending Teresa's life.

Samantha claimed to be estranged from her mother.

She is dead. To me. Rebecca's buried in an apartment in Las Vegas. She walks and talks and breathes, but she's dead all right.

Yet on Friday night, hardly more than forty-eight hours after making that angry declaration, she had slipped out of her apartment while Ryan napped, to meet with Barghest under the moonlit pepper tree.

Spencer Barghest was part of this, and because he seemed to be at best disturbed and at worst depraved, he was not involved because he was concerned for Ryan's welfare. Barghest terminated

Teresa, and he might be part of a scheme to terminate Ryan, which argued that Ryan's intuitive reaction to the photograph—that it contained a key to unlocking this mystery—should not be lightly dismissed.

If the answer was not in her eyes, it might be found in another part of the photo.

His attention turned next to her mouth, which hung open. Her full lips were parted, as if the breath of life had pressed them apart to escape her.

The darkness past her lips, within her mouth, was not uniform in shade and texture, as it appeared upon a cursory look. He saw now that Teresa seemed to have something lodged in her mouth, an object just beyond her teeth, a subtle shadowy shape too geometric to be her tongue.

He enlarged her lips to fill the screen. He cloned pixels to restore definition at the greater scale.

The woman's shapely mouth seemed to cry out to him, but the silence was unbroken, and the stillness gave no token of the final words she may have spoken as Barghest had finished her by whatever means.

Ryan bent to this new work as obsessively as he had studied the reflections in her eyes.

At 8:40 Monday evening, as Ryan ate a Stilton-cheese sandwich with cornichons and worked at the computer, George Zane called with the results of the blood tests.

In an exhaustive analysis, the two blood specialists and their lab assistants had discovered no traces of poisons, drugs, or other problematic chemicals in the 40 milliliters that Zane had drawn from Ryan.

"They could have missed it," Ryan said. "No one's so good, they don't screw up now and then."

"Do you want me to take additional samples," Zane asked, "and find someone new to analyze them?"

"No. Whatever it is, it's too subtle to be detected by the standard tests. You could drain me of every drop, employ a thousand hematologists, and I'd learn nothing more than I know now."

Ryan flushed the sedatives down the toilet and ordered a pot of coffee from room service.

He felt that time was running out for him, and not primarily because his appointment with Dr. Samar Gupta, to receive the results of the myocardial biopsy, was little more than eighteen hours away.

As the evening waned and then on past midnight, the contours of Teresa Reach's lips and teeth and oral cavity became his universe, so seductive and all-consuming that he never went to bed, but fell asleep in the office chair, in front of the computer, sometime after three o'clock in the morning, his search for truth still unrewarded.

■

From Denver to John Wayne Airport in Orange County, California, cosseted in the corporate Learjet, Ryan from time to time studied the photograph without benefit of computer enhancement, wondering if the clue that he sought might be hidden in Teresa's hair, in the delicate shell of her one revealed ear, or even in the folds of the pillow that was visible to one side of her face....

The plane touched down and taxied to the terminal less than an hour before Ryan's appointment with the cardiologist.

Rather than compromise his secrets by having Lee Ting meet him at the airport with a car, Ryan had arranged for a limousine company to provide transport. They sent a superstretch white Cadillac and a courteous driver who did not feel that conversation was part of his job description.

In the limo, all the way to Dr. Gupta's office, Ryan stared at Teresa's dead face.

He had slid into a state of mind that was not characteristic of him. The confusion that had overcome him in Denver had thickened to such a degree that he was no longer merely confused but confounded, his mental faculties overwhelmed by what he had learned, by what he had experienced, and by his failure to make sense of any of it.

Being confounded for the first time in his life would have been sufficient to sap his spirit, but he felt as well a quiet resignation building in him, which was worse because he had not thought himself capable of any form or degree of surrender.

His parents' selfishness and their indifference to him had only inspired him to achieve, not only later in life but also as a child, when he had determined never to be like them.

In business, he had seen every setback as an opportunity, had viewed every triumph as a challenge to achieve even more. He never surrendered, never capitulated, never so much as yielded except when he ceded his position on one issue in order to gain a much greater advantage on another.

He would have liked to believe that this growing resignation harbored in it an element of fortitude that would stave off despair. But fortitude was endurance animated by courage, and with every turn of the limousine's wheels, he felt more isolated from his previous sources of strength and less able to summon courage.

He began to wonder if his every act these past five days—the entire investigation into Rebecca Reach and Barghest, all of it—had been only a desperate attempt to distract himself from considering the news that he was likely to receive at the appointment with the cardiologist this afternoon. Loath to accept a mortal diagnosis about which he could do nothing, perhaps he had busied himself seeking a bogeyman whom he could more readily engage in battle.

When they arrived at the medical building in which Dr. Gupta had his offices, the limo curbed in a no-parking zone.

Ryan slid Teresa's photograph into the manila envelope.

The chauffeur got out from behind the wheel and stepped to the rear of the car to open Ryan's door.

In the grip of unreason, Ryan took the dead woman's photograph with him, not to show it to the cardiologist, merely to be able to hold it, as if it were a talisman, the power of which might prevent him from descending the final steep step between resignation and despair.

TWENTY-TWO

"Cardiomyopathy," said Dr. Gupta.

He sat with Ryan not in an examination room but in his private office, as though he felt the need to deliver this news in a less clinical, more reassuring environment.

On a shelf behind the desk, in silver frames, were photos of the physician's family. His wife was lovely. They had two daughters and a son, all good-looking kids, and a golden retriever.

Also on the shelf stood a model of a sailboat, and two photos of the Gupta family—dog included—taken aboard the real vessel.

Listening to his diagnosis, Ryan Perry envied the cardiologist for his family and for the evident richness of his life, which was a blessing quite different from—and superior to—riches.

"A disease of the heart muscle," said Samar Gupta. "It causes a reduction in the force of contractions, a decrease in the efficiency of circulation."

Ryan wanted to ask about cause, the possibility of poisoning that Forry Stafford had mentioned, but he waited.

Dr. Gupta's diction was as precise as ever, but the musicality of his voice was tempered now by a compassion that imposed on him a measured solemnity: "Cardiomyopathies fall into three main groups—restrictive cardiomyopathy, dilated, and hypertrophic."

"Hypertrophic. That's the kind I've got."

"Yes. An abnormality of heart-muscle fibers. The heart cells themselves do not function properly."

"And the cause?"

"Usually it's an inherited disorder."

"My parents don't have it."

"Perhaps a grandparent. Sometimes there are no symptoms, just sudden death, and it's simply labeled a heart attack."

Ryan's paternal grandfather had died of a sudden heart attack at forty-six.

"What's the treatment?"

The cardiologist seemed embarrassed to say, "It is incurable," as if medical science's failure to identify a cure was his personal failure.

Ryan focused on the golden retriever in the family portrait. He had long wanted a dog. He'd been too busy to make room for one in his life. There had always seemed to be plenty of time for a dog in the years to come.

"We can only treat the symptoms with diuretic drugs to control heart failure," said Dr. Gupta, "and antiarrhythmic drugs to control abnormal rhythms."

"I surf. I lead a fairly vigorous life. What restrictions are there going to be, how will things change?"

The cardiologist's hesitation caused Ryan to look away from the golden retriever.

"The primary issue," said Dr. Gupta, "is not how restricted your life will be . . . but how long."

In the physician's gentle eyes, as in a fortune-teller's sphere, Ryan saw his future.

"Your condition is not static, Ryan. The symptoms . . . they can be ameliorated, but the underlying disease is not arrestable. Heart function will steadily deteriorate."

"How long?"

Dr. Gupta looked away from Ryan, at another photo of his family that stood on his desk. "I think . . . no more than a year."

Wednesday night, writhing in pain on the floor of his bedroom, Ryan had expected to die right there, right then. In the days since, he had anticipated being felled at any moment.

A year should, therefore, have seemed like a gift, but instead the prognosis was a psychic guillotine that cut through him, and his anguish was so intense that he could not speak.

"I could tell you about advances in adult stem-cell research," said Dr. Gupta, "but there's nothing coming within a year, perhaps nothing ever, and you aren't a man who would take comfort in such wishful thinking. So there is only a transplant."

Ryan looked up from the envelope containing Teresa's photograph, which he gripped with both hands, as if it were a buoy keeping him afloat. "Heart transplant?"

"We'll register you with UNOS immediately."

"UNOS?"

"The United Network for Organ Sharing. They ensure equitable allocation of organs."

"Then . . . there's a chance."

"Frequently the results of a heart transplant are quite good. I have a patient who has lived the fullest life for fifteen years with a new heart, and she's still going strong."

Instead of ameliorating Ryan's anguish, the possibility that he might escape death through a transplant rendered him even more emotional.

He did not want to be reduced to tears in front of Samar Gupta, and in searching for something to say that would help him stave off that embarrassment, he returned to the central theme of the past few days: "Could I have been poisoned?"

Dr. Gupta frowned. "Surely not."

"Dr. Stafford did mention it as a possible cause of an enlarged heart. Though he also did . . . dismiss it."

"But in studying the biopsied tissue," the cardiologist said, "I feel quite sure your case is familial."

"Familial?"

"Inherited. The cell characteristics are classic for a familial attribution."

"You're quite sure," Ryan said, "but not certain?"

"Perhaps nothing in life is certain, Ryan."

Having successfully repressed his tears, Ryan smiled thinly and said, "Except death and taxes."

Dr. Gupta received Ryan's smile with gratitude, and smiled himself. "Although at least the IRS will give you your day in court."

TWENTY-THREE

In the days following his appointment with Dr. Gupta, Ryan surrendered to fits of denial during which he spent hours obsessively searching medical sites on the Internet for the latest developments in the treatment of cardiomyopathy.

When he found no scientific news dramatic enough to lift his spirits, he switched to alternative-medicine sites. Eagerly he sought stories about patients cured with the bark of an exotic Brazilian tree or with a tea brewed from the leaves of a plant found only deep in the jungles of Thailand.

Again and again, he read a thick packet of material about heart transplants, provided by Dr. Gupta. On each reading, his admiration for the skill of contemporary surgeons gave way to frustration over the imbalance between the number of patients in need of transplants and the number of organ donors, and to impatience with the system established by the health-care bureaucracy that was authorized to address that imbalance.

As he struggled to adjust to his radically altered future—or lack of one—Ryan avoided Samantha by pretending still to be in Denver on business.

Before seeing her, he wanted to live with his diagnosis long enough to begin to accept it. He intended to be in control of himself when he shared the news with her, because regardless of what happened between them, the meeting would be perhaps the most important of his life. He needed to be sufficiently composed to remain alert to every nuance of what she said, to every subtlety of her expressions and her body language.

The photo of Teresa continued to intrigue Ryan.

On the flight home from Colorado, he had brought the photo-analysis workstation that Wilson Mott established for him in the Denver hotel. It now stood on the desk in the retreat off the master bedroom.

When he could not ascertain if in fact a foreign object was lodged in the dead woman's mouth, he next divided the photograph into eighty one-inch squares, enhanced them one by one, and analyzed them exhaustively. Some revelatory item might be snagged in her lustrous golden hair or half folded in a pillow crease. Or perhaps in a way impossible to fully imagine, a faint mark on her face might provide a clue that linked Teresa's death to Ryan's current crisis.

After he had studied twenty squares over two days, however, he began to feel that he was engaged in a foolish quest, that the photo had electrified him solely because Teresa was Samantha's twin, which made seeing her in this condition seem like a clairvoyant glimpse of Sam's death, therefore a profound shock.

Eventually he switched off the computer, intending to abandon his analysis of the portrait.

Although the digitized photo on the monitor no longer held any fascination for him, though he was weary of it, the original eight-by-ten glossy still riveted him when he extracted it once more from the manila envelope. He was pierced again, as he had been pierced in Spencer Barghest's study, by the conviction that with this photograph he was trembling on the brink of a discovery that would do more than explain all of the recent weirdness, that would also and literally *save* him.

In business, over the years, every hunch proved worth pursuing. But his recent moments of irrational speculation, his newly developed tendency to paranoia, might be the consequences of the compromised efficiency of his heart, the diminished oxygenation of his blood. In that case, his intuition could no longer be trusted, nor could he be sure that his thinking would always remain as clear as it had once been.

He did not for a moment dwell on the unfairness of receiving a death sentence at thirty-four. In this case, as with any negative turn in life, you could whine or you could act. Action offered the only hope.

Unlike in business, where courses of action in an emergency were constrained only by the sharpness of your wits and your willingness to work hard, options in a health crisis were more limited. But Ryan refused to be a victim. If a way existed to escape the grim prognosis that bound him, he would discover how to slip the knot and cast off the ropes.

While he adjusted to his condition and rapidly educated himself about organ-sharing protocols and transplant-surgery techniques, he expected to be felled momentarily by another sudden seizure, but he wasn't stricken. Dr. Gupta had prescribed three medications that apparently, for the time being, were repressing the symptoms that had recently plagued him.

Through Thursday, he remained in the master suite and did not once venture elsewhere in the house. He didn't want to see anyone, because he worried that during even innocent conversation, he might imply—or someone might infer—that he had a serious health problem. He did not want a hint of his condition to reach Samantha before he was ready to break the news to her.

On Kay Ting's voice mail, he recited a list of meals and snacks that he would prefer and the times at which he would like to receive them. These deliveries were made by food-service cart and left in the elevator alcove outside the master suite.

Sometimes, when he fell into a hypercreative flow state while writing a piece of software, Ryan passed days like a hermit, living in his pajamas and shaving only when his beard stubble began to itch. Therefore, this regimen would not strike the household staff as peculiar.

He didn't worry much that what he ate and drank might be laced with poison or with hallucinogenic drugs. Since suspicion had led him to Rebecca Reach and then to Spencer Barghest in the house of the modern-day mummies, the Tings and other household employees seemed to be the least likely of the people in his life to be conspiring against him.

Besides, the damage to his heart had already been done. The poisoner, if one existed, would achieve nothing by administering superfluous doses but would risk revealing his identity.

The dreams of sunken cities, lonely lakes, and demon-populated palaces no longer troubled Ryan's sleep. He heard no unexplainable tapping, no moth or bird or gloved hand rapping at any window, wall, or chamber door.

Perhaps receiving a precise diagnosis and a sobering prognosis had focused him so entirely on a *real* threat that his mind no longer needed to expend nervous energy on imaginary menaces, and in fact could not afford to do so if he were to concentrate on surviving until a heart became available for transplantation.

By Friday, he was prepared to share his dire news with Samantha. He called her to say that he was home from Denver, and that he hoped to see her for dinner.

"What if we try that new restaurant you were so hot about last week," she suggested.

"These have been a busy few days, Sam. I'd rather we had a quiet evening, just us. Is your place okay?"

"I'm all cooked out, Dotcom. You bring deli, and it's a deal."

"See you at five-thirty," he said, and hung up.

He considered bringing as well the death photo of Teresa, in case the evening took a turn that required cold questions and hard answers.

After looking once more at the dead woman's portrait, Ryan decided that even if reason arose to be more suspicious of Samantha than he had yet allowed himself to be, using this picture to shake her confidence would constitute a cruelty of which he was not capable.

He returned the photo to the envelope, which he stowed in a desk drawer.

TWENTY-FOUR

In silk slippers and a blue-and-gold kimono, Samantha was so much lovelier than Ryan remembered her that he felt at once disarmed, and knifed by desire.

He had recently spent so much time staring at her lost twin, whose looks were weathered by suffering, that his memory of her exceptional face had been clouded.

As soon as Ryan put the deli bags on the kitchen counter, Sam came into his arms. She would have kissed him straightaway into the bedroom; and he almost allowed himself to be led there.

Crazily, in memory, he heard the voice of the young woman who spoke for the navigation system in the Cadillac Escalade, leading him back to his Denver hotel and away from the park full of aspens.

This bizarre association lowered the flame of his desire, and he regained control of himself.

"I'm starving," he said.

"You're kidding."

"Totally starving."

"You must be."

"Look," he said, "corned beef sandwiches."

"I really thought this kimono made me irresistible."

"With that cheese you like and the special mustard."

"Next time I'll wear corned beef and cheese."

"And the special mustard," he said.

"With pickles for earrings."

"That's one fashion risk too many. Look, pepper slaw and potato salad and that three-bean-and-peppers-and-celery dish, whatever they call it."

"Pepper slaw would have been enough. What's this—custard cake?"

"And then, here, those fabulous cookies."

"What're you fattening me up for?"

"I just can't control myself in that deli. I shouldn't be allowed to go in there without a chaperone."

They transferred everything from bags and plastic containers to dishes and bowls, and then carried the feast to the table on the deck.

"I'm surprised you didn't bring a keg of beer," she said.

"You don't drink beer."

"I don't eat eight pounds of deli at one sitting, either, but that didn't stop you."

"I brought wine," he said, pointing to the bottle that he had left on the table on arrival, before he'd gone into the kitchen. "An excellent Meritage."

"I'll get glasses."

After he poured, before they sat at the table, they clinked wineglasses, and a note as sweet as that from a silver bell rang through the surrounding pepper tree.

They sipped, they kissed, they sat, and Ryan was so instantly comfortable with her that he knew, whether this Sam was a lie or not, he loved her, and he would continue to love her even if there was another Sam who was a conniving bitch.

"It's been a whole week," she said.

If it turned out that he had been diagnosed with a bad ticker *and* this night discovered he was in love with Ms. Jekyll in spite of Ms. Hyde, it would perhaps be the most eventful week of his life.

A web of shadows and late sunshine seemed not to overlay them but instead to entwine them, as if they were embedded in it and it in them, a matrix of light and dark, known and unknown, a warp and woof of mystery from which their future would take shape.

"Why did we let a whole week go by?" she wondered.

He said, "The novel's going especially well, isn't it?"

"Good. I've had several good days in a row. How did you know?"

Ryan had no intention of telling her that when she was swept up in her writing, she thought less about his proposal of marriage, and that when marriage was not on her mind, she was less chaste than when it was.

Instead, he said, "Your eyes are shining with excitement, and your voice is full of delight."

"Maybe that's because you're here."

"No. If you were that glad to see me, you'd be wearing corned beef and cheese."

"Okay, the book. Hard to explain. But text and subtext are coming together in ways I never could have anticipated."

"That *is* exciting."

"Well, it is for me."

"How are you doing with the past participles?"

"I've got them under control."

"And the semicolons, the gerunds, the whole who-whom thing?"

"If this wine weren't so good, I'd pour it over your head."

"Which is why I buy only the best. Self-defense."

Quick footsteps ascended the stairs from the courtyard.

Ryan turned in time to see the ice-crown of white

hair that, in the moonlight one week previous, had identified the tall man in the yard, conferring with Samantha, as Spencer Barghest.

Without the moon, the identification did not hold. This man was Barghest's body type, but he was a decade younger than Dr. Death, in his forties, and he lacked the rubbery facial features of a stand-up comic behind which Barghest hid.

"Oh," he said upon seeing them at the table, halting one step below the deck. "I'm sorry. I don't mean to interrupt."

"Kevin," she said, "please join us. I'll get another glass."

"No, no. Really. I only have a moment anyway. I've got to be off to the hospital, evening visiting hours."

As Ryan rose from his chair, Samantha said, "Have you guys met?"

When Ryan regretted that they had not, Samantha introduced him to Kevin Spurlock, the son of Miriam Spurlock, who owned the house that came with the garage above which Sam lived.

"How is your mom?" Samantha asked.

"She's doing well. Really well."

For Ryan's benefit, Samantha said, "Miriam had a very bad attack of angina a week ago—in fact a week ago this evening."

"She was in a restaurant," Kevin said. "Paramedics rushed her to a hospital. The worst for her was making a scene in a public place. She was mortified."

"Heart attack?" Ryan asked.

"No, thank God. But tests revealed blocked arteries."

"Critically blocked," Samantha said. "The next morning, she had a quadruple bypass."

"She loved your flowers," Kevin told Samantha. "Calla lilies—they're her favorite."

"I'll fill her bedroom with them when she gets home."

After Kevin had gone, Samantha told a few stories about Miriam, one of which Ryan had heard before. The landlady was something of an eccentric, although unfailingly sweet and kind.

A week earlier, when Ryan thought he'd caught Samantha in a furtive conversation with Spencer Barghest, she evidently had been receiving the news about Miriam Spurlock's hospitalization.

Seeing a light in the apartment, Kevin must have come to the door. The knock failed to stir Ryan from a postcoital nap. To avoid waking him, Sam had gone outside to talk with her landlady's son.

Inspired by a paranoid interpretation of this innocent meeting, Ryan had flown to Las Vegas the following morning, seeking proof of a nonexistent conspiracy.

Now Rebecca Reach's get-rich-quick books seemed to be evidence of nothing worse than her gullibility and wishful thinking.

The collection of magazines containing articles

by Sam proved only that, estranged from her daughter, Rebecca nonetheless remained proud of her.

Spencer Barghest might be perverse, even depraved, and Rebecca might be a terrible judge of men, less than intellectually keen, and morally adrift—but neither she nor her corpse-infatuated lover was scheming against Ryan.

Samantha had never mentioned either that she had met Barghest or that he had been present when her sister, Teresa, had been forced on from this world.

In retrospect, however, her silence on the subject most likely indicated only embarrassment. No one would be quick to reveal that her mother slept with a creepy nihilist who lived with cadavers that he claimed were art.

Following the episode on the surfboard and then the terrifying seizure that same night, which had sent him to Forry Stafford, Ryan had obsessed on one word uttered by the internist—*poisoning*—to avoid confronting the truth that his body was failing him. He needed instead to identify an external enemy that would be easier to defeat than a disease or a genetic abnormality.

In his desperation, he had retreated from the logic with which he had previously coped with every problem of business and of life. He abandoned reason for unreason.

Forced by Kevin Spurlock's visit to acknowledge

his weakness and his error, Ryan was mortified. Hopeful that the wine would smooth the edges off his humiliation, he poured a second glass.

He was grateful for the pepper-tree patterns of fading sunlight and swelling shadow because they partially masked him. He hoped that at least this once, Sam might find his face more difficult to read than Dr. Seuss.

After a third little story about Miriam, Samantha fetched four votive candles from the kitchen. She arranged them on the table.

As her face brightened in the glow of the butane match and her gaze traveled wick to wick, Ryan said, "I love you," and felt like a weasel, although like a weasel in rehab.

TWENTY-FIVE

With the moon still tethered to the eastern horizon but straining higher, with the giant pepper tree occluding most of the eternally receding stars, the time to talk of death had come.

After dinner, with the table clear except for wine and candles, Ryan held Samantha's left hand and said, "I've been happy every moment we've been together."

"Sounds like the next word is going to be *but*, in which case these slippers aren't adequate ass-kicking shoes."

He would not mention his delusional adventure, his fear that he had been poisoned. If he died within a year, he wanted Sam to remember him as a better man than he actually had been.

Because Sam took life the same way that she took

the sea when surfing—on her terms but with respect for its unpredictable nature, boldly and without fear—Ryan explained his situation succinctly and directly. He neither made a tragic opera of his news nor pretended that it was a light opera certain to end in flags and flourishes and sparkling arpeggios of harp strings.

Her hand tightened around his, as if she would hold him to this world. Tears pooled in her eyes, shimmered with her effort to retain them, and the shimmering caused the candle flames to quiver more in reflection than they did in the cut-glass cups that held them.

She understood that delivering this news was as hard for him as hearing it was devastating to her. Two things they admired in each other were self-sufficiency and a clear-eyed recognition that life was a struggle requiring optimism and confidence.

Grateful that she did not lose control and weep, pleased that she remained attentive instead of interrupting him with questions, Ryan was also *moved* by Samantha's effort to repress her tears and to stay strong.

The intensity of her heart's response could not be mistaken, for her pulse so strengthened that it grew visible in her slender throat, and quickened. The kimono did not conceal the tremors that shook her body, but instead, even in candlelight, the bells of the sleeves and every slack fold of the lustrous silk made visible her shivering as clearly as the air conveyed his voice.

When Ryan finished, Sam breathed deeply twice, shifted her gaze from his eyes to their entwined hands, and chose to confront the essence of the terror with her first question.

"What's the likelihood you'll get a new heart?"

"Four thousand Americans a year need a transplant. Only about two thousand donor hearts become available."

"Fifty-fifty then," she said.

"Not that good. The donor's heart has to be compatible with my immune system. There has to be a match to minimize the chance my body will reject it."

"What's the likelihood of a match?"

"I have the most common blood type. That's good. But there are other criteria. And even if they're all met, the heart will go to someone higher on the waiting list if he's a match as well."

"Are you already on the list?"

"Provisionally. Next week I'll undergo psychological testing. It all depends on that."

"Why?"

"They try to detect social and behavioral factors that would interfere with recovery."

"You mean . . . like alcoholism?"

"Alcoholism, smoking, attitudinal problems that would make me less likely than some other patient to comply with medications and make lifestyle changes."

Looking up from their hands, avoiding his eyes, Sam stared at the four candles as if the future might be read in the configurations of their flames. "Intelligence must be something they're looking for. A smart patient should be a better patient."

"Maybe."

"That's in your favor. What else? What's the bright side?"

"I'm young and otherwise in good health. If I had multiple organ problems, if I had diabetes, I wouldn't be an ideal candidate."

Drawing one candle close, Samantha first gave the flame a breath to grow on, then blew it out. "What else? I want more bright side."

"I don't need insurance-company approval. I can pay out of pocket."

As a pale ribbon of smoke unraveled from the briefly sputtering black wick, Samantha drew a second candle close to her and breathed darkness upon it, as well.

Ryan said, "Sometimes there's a distance problem. Once a donor is certified brain-dead and surgeons remove his heart, they can keep it cooled to forty degrees in saline solution—but only six hours."

"So the surgical team—what?—looks for a recipient within a certain radius?"

"In my case, they don't have to bring it to me. I can

go to them by Learjet, while they keep the donor alive on machines."

She dipped a thumb and forefinger in the last of her wine and pinched out the flame on the third candle.

"The five-year-survival rate for a transplant is slowly but surely creeping toward seventy percent," he said.

Without wetting her fingers again, Sam extinguished the final flame with a pinch, and hissed as if she felt its heat, but also as if she wanted to feel it.

The kitchen door was closed, and the curtained window poured no light onto the deck.

"If I make five years, then my chances of making five more are good. And so much is happening in medicine. Each year. So much."

Although the night was not absolutely black, it should have given cover to Samantha. Yet on her face, the quiet grief that she could no longer repress glistered faintly, as though her tears contained a phosphoric salt.

Pushing her chair back from the table, rising, still holding his hand, she said, "Come lie in bed with me."

He got to his feet.

"Just lie with me," she said, "and hold me."

TWENTY-SIX

In bed, lying clothed atop the covers, Samantha rested her head on Ryan's chest, cuddled into him, his right arm around her.

Exhaustion nearly immobilized him. He felt weighed down and wrung out.

They had endured a rite of passage in their relationship, the acknowledgment that even as young as they were, Death was a presence at their dance, their life together finite.

Like him, she probably had much she wanted to say but no energy to say it and, at the moment, possessed no words adequate to express her thoughts.

They dozed but did not sleep deeply, changed positions but held fast to each other.

When at last she spoke again, Samantha's voice was small and lacked her usual spirit. "I'm afraid."

"Me too. That's okay. They'll match me to a donor. I'll get a heart."

"I know you will," she said.

"I will."

"You will if anyone will. But you've got to be careful, Ryan."

"I'll do everything the doctors say."

"You especially. You, being you, have to be careful."

"I won't try riding any sharks."

"You've got to let it happen however it will."

"It'll happen."

"I'm afraid."

"I won't just fade away," he said. "That's not me. You know that's not me."

"I'm afraid for you," she said.

"I'll handle it, Sam."

"Don't handle it. Just let it develop."

"Don't worry about me. I'm not afraid."

"Sometimes it's good to be afraid," she said. "It keeps you clear and squared away."

Much later, he said, "Marry me." She did not reply, but he was sure that she was awake. "I know you're there."

"Yeah. I'm here."

"So marry me."

"It'll look like I married you because you're dying."

"I'm not going to die."

"Everyone'll think I married you for your money."

"I don't care what they think. I never have. Why should I now?"

"I love you. I'll stay with you through this if you just let it happen. Every step of the way through all of it, but you have to do what Dr. Gupta says."

"He's my doctor. Of course I'll do what he says."

"I know you. I know you so well. I so much want you to be right ... to be all right at the end of this."

"Then marry me."

"I'll marry you when it's over, when everything is right."

"After the transplant, you'll marry me?"

"If you relax. Just relax and accept and let this thing happen like it should."

"Then you're my reward," he said.

"I didn't mean it that way."

He said, "You're all I want, Sam."

"It's got to be right."

"We are right. We're perfect together."

"We are, we really are, day to day," she agreed.

"So there you go."

"So if you'll just let this happen the way it will, just relax and go with it the way it wants to happen, then I'll know we'll also be right not just day to day, but year after year."

"Okay. I can chill out. Is that what you want?"

"You've got to be so careful, Dotcom."

"Just watch me chill."

"So very careful. I'll be there all the way, but you have to listen to me."

"Yes, dear."

"I'm serious. You listen to me."

"I will."

"You listen to me."

"I'm listening."

Clinging tightly to him, Samantha said, "Oh, God, I'm so afraid."

Dozing, they eased apart. Parting, they woke. Waking, they clung again to each other. That was the rhythm of their night.

At dawn, she woke once more to a separation, but felt for him and found him with an urgency that suggested she expected him to be gone. Stirred from sleep by her search and her touch, he held her close, but closeness was no longer quite enough.

Their lovemaking was different from any Ryan had known, rich with desire for a perfect union, yet without lust, giving without taking, receiving without wanting. Tender, selfless, almost innocent, this was a sweet celebration of life, but more than a celebration, it was a commemoration of all they had been to each other to this point in time, to this fulcrum of their lives, and it was a solemnization of a commitment to be two in one henceforth, to be as one, always one, one forever.

Even after Ryan had received a virtual death sentence from his cardiologist, such a moment of beauty and joy was possible, which not only gave him hope but also stropped a sharper edge on his determination to live.

This consummation at dawn was his high tide, his lifetime-best surf, a perfect set of double overhead swells, and it was not in his nature to imagine that what came thereafter would be not more of the same and soon a new life with a new healthy heart, but instead error, disorder, terror, anguish, and loss.

The storm.

TWENTY-SEVEN

Ryan sailed through the psychological testing and was added to the heart-recipient list of the United Network for Organ Sharing.

Following the diagnosis of cardiomyopathy and his revelation of his condition to Samantha, he was spared the dreams that had plagued him for a week. The city in the sea, the lake of black water, and the haunted palace had been deleted from his nightly itinerary.

No other dreams arose to trouble him. He slept well each night and woke rested or at least rested enough.

In lonely moments, he no longer heard the curious rapping that—at windows, at doors, in bathroom plumbing, and from a plasma TV—had insisted upon his attention.

His sense of being watched, of being the object of a sinister conspiracy, blew away with the dreams and with the phantom knocker. A fresh air came into his life, and cleared from his head the stale miasma of unreason as if he had merely been suffering from a pollen allergy.

He experienced no further episodes of deja vu. Indeed, he suspected that if he returned to Denver and located the small park with the aspens, that place—and the church adjacent to it—would not affect him as it had before.

As for knowing, before he saw it, what the crucifix would look like above the altar at St. Gemma's . . .

Over the years, he had been inside a few Catholic churches, attending weddings and funerals. He didn't remember any of those altars, but he assumed that perhaps a crucifix in one Roman church was much like that in another. Uniformity might even be required. He must have known what he would find in St. Gemma's only because he had seen the identical crucifix—or one nearly like it—at one of those weddings or funerals.

He attributed the calm and clarity that purged his paranoia to the medications that Dr. Gupta prescribed, including a diuretic to control heart failure and an antiarrhythmic drug to correct abnormal heart rhythms. His blood was better oxygenated now than it had been, and toxins once dangerously retained were being flushed from his system more efficiently.

Irrationally, he had feared that a scheming poisoner, a modern-day Medici, might be among his household employees. Ironically, the only poisoner had been the very heart within his breast, which by its diminished function had clouded his mind and fostered his delusions, or so he concluded.

Through October and November, Ryan's greatest problem proved to be impatience. As others awaiting transplants received their hearts or perished, he moved up the list, but not fast enough.

He remained acutely aware that Samar Gupta had given him at most one year to live. A sixth of that year had passed.

When he saw TV news stories about traffic accidents involving fatalities, he wondered if the deceased had signed organ-donor cards when getting their driver's licenses. Sometimes the knowledge that most people did not donate would inspire an angry rant. This was not fair to those against whom he railed, because during all the years that he'd been in good health, he never signed such a card, either.

Now enlightened, through his attorney he arranged to donate what organs, if any, might be of use to others after his body succumbed to the ravages of cardiomyopathy or, alternately, if he received a transplant but died anyway.

By December, Dr. Gupta had to adjust Ryan's drugs and add two more medications to his regimen in order to prevent the return of the frightening and debilitating symptoms.

The cardiologist used arcane medical terminology to avoid words like *deterioration*. But Ryan had no doubt that his condition was deteriorating.

He did not feel much different from the way he had felt in September, except that he tired more easily now, and he slept longer than he had in those days.

When he looked in a mirror, he noticed only small changes. A slight bloat. Sometimes a persistent unhealthy flush in his cheeks, at other times a grayblue paleness of the skin under his eyes.

He became impatient not only with his progress up the waiting list but also with Samantha. Sometimes she tested his forbearance.

For one thing, he felt that she had too much confidence in the organization that compiled the list and selected the recipients.

If Ryan had managed his business with the kind of unwarranted assumptions and the tolerance for bureaucratic inertia that he saw in this particular medical community, he would not have become a wealthy man. Since lives were at stake here, he argued that these gatekeepers should be more—not less—efficient than he had been while building a social-networking empire on the Internet.

She would listen to little complaining on the subject before reminding him that he had promised to weather this waiting period with a relaxed attitude. He had pledged not to try to handle what in truth he could not control, but to let it unfold as it would.

"Dotcom, you worry me," she told him now. "This restlessness, these spells of anger. This isn't good. It doesn't help you. You're wound too tight."

Week by week, Ryan developed more exotic strategies to survive, investigating all manner of alternative-medicine treatments that might supplement what any cardiologist could do for him, everything from rare substances obtained from the spores of rain-forest ferns to psychic healing.

With sympathy, reason, and humor, Samantha provided a reality check to each treatment scheme that he considered adopting. Although he knew she was right, sometimes her acerbic humor seemed to be cold sarcasm, her reason mere pessimism, and her sweet sympathy insincere.

Ryan suspected that his sour moods and his frequent spells of restlessness and agitation were caused by his medications. A review of the side effects listed for each drug confirmed his suspicion.

"I'm sorry, Sam," he told her more than once. "It's

these damn drugs. I'm not myself. Next thing, I'll be growing hair on my palms and howling at the moon."

He knew that he was exhausting her, that her work on the novel had come almost to a halt. He began to give her more time to herself, though she protested that she would be there for him all day, every day, until he was restored to full health, with a new heart.

On December 12, they had dinner in a restaurant where white tablecloths, Limoges china, crystal, and waiters in white jackets set both a mood and a standard.

This wasn't one of those Newport Beach high-end meat markets that layered on the style but catered to upscale singles who chose their dinner companions from the opportunities at the bar. Here the clientele was older, quieter, with at least a veneer of class, often with that old-money charm and grace that made even true class seem somewhat tacky by comparison.

Between the appetizers and the entrees, Ryan told Samantha about Dr. Dougal Hobb, a prominent cardiologist and cardiovascular surgeon with offices in Beverly Hills.

"I think I might switch to him," he said.

Surprised, she asked, "What's wrong with Dr. Gupta?"

"Nothing. He's fine. He's all right. But Dr. Hobb is so highly regarded. He's really at the top of his profession."

"Will it affect your position on the waiting list?"

"No. Not at all."

"What does Forry Stafford say?"

"I haven't discussed it with him."

"Why not? He recommended Dr. Gupta."

In any restaurant, he and Samantha usually preferred a table in a corner, to allow them greater privacy, but on this occasion they sat at the center of the establishment. The elegant room sparkled, a treat for the eyes, and it lay all around them.

"I will call Forry," Ryan said. "I just haven't yet."

"Dotcom, is this just change for the sake of change, just more restlessness?"

"No. I've given this a lot of thought."

Assisted by a busboy, their waiter arrived with the entrees and presented each dish with sufficient flourishes to confirm the excellence of the service without descending to showiness.

As they began to eat, Ryan changed the subject. "You're so lovely tonight. Everyone is taken with you, the center of attention."

"Well, we are at the center of the room, you'll notice. And I suspect most of these people know who you are, which makes me very much the supporting act."

She let him lead her down conversational byways, but in time she returned to Hobb. "Before you leave Dr. Gupta, talk to Forry."

"I will. But they don't get better than Dougal Hobb. I even had a complete background done on him."

"Background?"

"By an extremely dependable security firm. To see if he's had any malpractice suits filed against him, personal problems of any kind."

Her blue-green eyes did not darken, but her mood underwent a tidal change. "You had a private detective scope him out?"

"It's my life on the line, Sam. I want to be sure I'm in the best possible hands."

"Forry is your friend. He sent you to the best. He wants the best for you."

"Dr. Hobb has never had a complaint lodged against him, let alone a legal action."

"Has Dr. Gupta?" she asked.

"I don't know."

"I'm sure he hasn't."

"I don't know. But listen, Dr. Hobb's private life is without a stain, his finances are in perfect order, his marriage is rock-solid, his—"

Putting down her knife and fork, she said, "You're scaring me."

He raised his eyebrows. "Why?"

"Can't you hear yourself? You're trying to handle this, take charge, but it's fundamentally not yours to take charge of."

He answered her concern with a sheepish look. "Be to do. It's not just the cute name of a company. It's a life philosophy. Taking control is a hard habit to break."

"And trusting people is a difficult habit to establish, Ryan, not least of all for people like you and me, considering where we come from."

"You're right. All right. I know."

"We can shape our fates," she said, "but we can't control them. You can't control death. You need a team here. You need to make these decisions only after consultation."

"I'm consulting with you right now."

She neither broke eye contact nor replied.

"Okay," he said. "You're right. I won't do anything until I've talked to Forry and Dr. Gupta. And to you."

She drank some of the Cabernet. She put down the wineglass. She surveyed the glittering room, requiring other diners to look away from her.

Her attention on Ryan once more, she said, "Sweetie, trust the people who care for you. Trust me especially because I understand you so well, so very well, so entirely—and I love you."

Moved, he said, "I love you, too."

"If you knew me as completely as I know you," she said, "you might not love me."

"Impossible. What a thing to say."

"No, it's true. Human beings are such knotted, desperate pieces of work—it's a rare thing to know one completely, to the core, and still love him. Or her. I don't need dessert. Do you?"

She had so riveted him that her change of subject did not at first compute, and he stared at her as though she had switched from English to some obscure Russian dialect.

Then: "Oh. No. I don't need dessert."

"Maybe after the wine, a double espresso."

"That sounds good."

She said no more about Dr. Hobb or about the knotted, desperate nature of humanity, but spoke of happier things.

Over the espresso, she favored Ryan with an affectionate smile that gladdened him, and as chandelier light danced in her eyes, she said, "See, Winky, you could have taken me to the farthest corner of the room, and even in that privacy, I wouldn't have scalped you or even boxed your ears."

Little more than one day later, on December 14, at home alone, as he awaited the sleep that for hours had eluded him, comforted by the glow of a bedside lamp that he was loath to turn off these days, Ryan suffered a sudden breathing problem.

He inhaled without relief, as if the air he took in were going elsewhere than to his lungs, although his belief that he was drawing full breaths might have been a misperception. An immediate sense of suffocation overcame him, a choking anxiety, and he could not stave off panic.

When he pushed up from the mattress, he was whirled into such a dizziness that the bed seemed to be on a carousel, and he fell back onto his pillows, gasping, soaked in a copious and instant hot sweat.

In that moment, a light-year was defined as the distance between him and the telephone on the adjacent nightstand. He could see it but did not have enough knowledge of Einsteinian physics to be able to make the epic voyage.

The paroxysms lasted only a couple of minutes. But when he could again draw breath easily, air had never tasted sweeter.

For a while, he was reluctant to move, afraid that movement would trigger another event, the same or worse. When at last he sat up, swung his legs off the bed, and stood, he discovered that his ankles were badly swollen.

Although he took his medications faithfully and punctually, he was retaining water.

Standing beside the bed, for the first time in

months he heard a tapping, someone gently rapping, rapping at a window or a door.

Panic had subsided, but fear remained. The sweat that sheathed him had gone cold.

Turning, he searched for the source of the sound, cocked his head toward the insistent metronomic tap. He took a few steps in one direction, but then took a few in another, pausing repeatedly to listen.

He moved from the bedroom into the sitting room, into the bedroom once more, and then into the black granite and the gold onyx and the stainless steel and the mirrored walls of his bathroom. In that maze of reflections, the rapping continued, as loud there as everywhere else.

For a moment Ryan believed that the sound came from underfoot, that its ubiquitous nature—always the same volume, the same timbre in room after room—indicated a source beneath the floorboards, one that, incredibly, was mobile and tracking him.

But then he recalled that the floors were lightweight concrete, which had been specified for the very purpose of sound suppression. No floorboards existed to be torn up. No hollow space lay underfoot, through which the source of the sound could pursue him.

He looked at the ceiling, the only other plane universal to these third-floor rooms, and he thought of the attic overhead. He entertained the possibly lunatic, certainly antic image of a stalker above him, some phantom who had traded opera-house cellars for higher haunting grounds, electronically monitoring Ryan's position for the purpose of tormenting him with the rapping, the soft rapping, the soft rap-rap-rapping, only this and nothing more.

That absurd speculation lasted mere seconds, for abruptly Ryan realized that the sound arose from within him. Although it was not the classic *lub-dub* of the blood pump, it was associated with those rhythms. It was an ominous throb born of his heart's malfunction, not a gloved knuckle against a door, not a fat moth against a windowpane, but a blood-and-muscle sound, and if it failed to fade away this time, as it had faded before, if the rapping kept on long enough, it would be answered, not by Ryan, but by Death.

He took a shower, as hot as he could endure, hoping to chase the cold from his bones. The quiet rap came and went and came again, but he did not wipe the steam from the glass door in expectation of an intruder's grinning face.

In his closet, which was as large as a room, as he dressed, the rapping might have come from behind any cabinet door, from within any drawer, from behind any pane of the three-sided mirror, but Ryan no longer needed to search for the source.

The scheduled superstretch from the limousine service arrived at eight o'clock. The driver called himself Naraka, though Ryan didn't know if that was his first name or his last.

As they pulled away from the house, the internal knocking fell silent and never once resumed all the way from Newport Coast into distant Beverly Hills.

Two days previously, prior to dinner with Samantha, Ryan had secured an emergency appointment with Dr. Dougal Hobb. Following Sam's disapproval, he considered canceling it, but left the final decision for the last minute, for this morning.

Considering the frightening problem with his breathing in the night and the belated realization that the occasional knocking was a muffled internal sound, he believed that a conversation with Hobb would be prudent.

Ryan did not inform Dr. Gupta or Forry Stafford of his decision. He did not even tell Samantha.

His only consultation was with his instinct for survival, which told him that meeting Hobb was not merely advisable but as essential to the preservation of his life as a flame-free stairway would be indispensable to a man trapped in the inferno of a burning high-rise.

Dr. Dougal Hobb did not maintain his offices in one of the gleaming skyscrapers that lined Wilshire Boulevard, as did many other physicians. His practice occupied an entire three-story building on a quiet street on the edge of the Beverly Hills business district.

This elegant neoclassic structure—white with a black slate roof, embraced by old magnolia trees that fanned their giant spade-leaf shadows onto its walls—looked more like a private residence than like a place of business. Only a discreet brass plaque beside the front door identified the premises: D. HOBB, M.D.

Three doors opened off the foyer, and the one on the right was labeled APPOINTMENTS.

This proved to be a waiting room with a Santos mahogany floor on which floated an antique Persian carpet, a nineteenth-century Tabriz, which glowed as if woven from gold. The comfortable chairs and stylish end tables suggested that patients here were treated like guests.

Ryan could not identify the classical music that played at low volume, but he found it soothing.

The receptionist, an attractive woman in her forties, was not wearing the surgical scrubs or the shapeless exercise suits that were all but standard in most medical offices these days, but a beige knit suit of designer quality.

Both the receptionist and the nurse, Laura, who took Ryan's preliminary medical history in a small conference room, were well-spoken, professional, efficient, and warm in their manner.

Ryan felt that he had sailed out of a storm into a sunny harbor.

Laura, in her twenties, wore an oval locket suspended from an intricately braided gold chain. The enameled medallion on the front of the locket featured a stylized gold-and-red bird with spread wings, rising.

When Ryan complimented her on the beauty of the locket, the nurse said, "It's a phoenix. Early nineteenth century. Dr. Hobb gave it to me for my third anniversary." She registered his surprise, and her fair cheeks pinked as she quickly corrected the impression that she had given him. "The doctor is my father-in-law. And Andrea—Mrs. Barnett, the receptionist—she's his sister."

"You don't think of a medical practice as a family business," Ryan said.

"They're a close family," she said, "and quite wonderful. Blake, my husband, graduated Harvard Medical."

"Cardiology?"

"Cardiovascular surgery. When he finishes his residency, he'll join Dougal—Dr. Hobb—in the practice."

Given the indifference to the idea of family and tradition that characterized both of Ryan's parents, he envied the Hobb clan.

Instead of taking Ryan directly to an examination

room, Laura led him first to Dougal Hobb's study. "He'll be with you in just a minute, Mr. Perry."

Again, he felt as if he were in a private home rather than in a medical office, even though on one wall were displayed the surgeon's medical degrees and numerous honors.

Because Wilson Mott had provided a thorough file on the surgeon, Ryan did not bother to review the framed items on the wall.

Instead, when Dr. Hobb entered, Ryan stood admiring the cherry-veneer Biedermeier desk with ebony inlays.

Under six feet tall, fit and trim but not pumped, dressed in black loafers, gray wool slacks, a cranberry-red cardigan, and a white shirt without tie, Hobb did not cultivate a power look, yet Ryan felt that a force of nature had entered the study.

Although he had a clear baritone voice, Hobb spoke softly, with the trace of an ingratiating accent that might have been Carolinian. He had a full head of salt-and-pepper hair, but not a leonine silver mane; his brown eyes were direct, though not striking; his features were pleasant, though not handsome. Yet he seemed to fill the room with his presence.

They sat in armchairs that faced each other across a Biedermeier pedestal table with magnificently figured walnut veneer, in order to, as Dr. Hobb put it, "get to know each other."

Within a few minutes, Ryan understood that Dr. Hobb made such a powerful impression because he seemed, from the first encounter, to be self-effacing, even humble, although his great surgical skills and his success prepared you to expect a fulsome pride if not arrogance, and because he seemed genuinely to care about you, to be motivated by compassion that he could convey without ever sounding either as if he were selling himself or coddling his patient.

"These past three months," Ryan said, "have been frightening, of course, and dispiriting, but it's not just the fear and the bouts of depression that leave me increasingly unable to cope. It's the strangeness of these months, the downright weirdness, the sense that something's terribly wrong in my life other than just my illness. I keep thinking that someone's manipulating me, that I'm not in control of my own life anymore, that the medical care I'm being given isn't the care I should have. I understand that for a guy my age, it's easy to succumb to paranoia when you're hit with a diagnosis like this, because it's so unexpected. I mean, I'm just thirty-four years old, and I can't get my head around the idea that I'm going to die."

"We won't let that happen," said Dr. Hobb, leaning forward in his chair. "We simply will not let it happen."

Considering how the odds were stacked against Ryan, he did not think such a confident declaration as the one Hobb had made could be taken seriously, yet that was how he took it. He believed that Dougal Hobb would not let him die, and he was filled with such relief and overcome with such gratitude that his vision blurred, and for a moment he could not speak.

TWENTY-EIGHT

That day, devoting himself almost exclusively to Ryan, Dr. Hobb conducted numerous tests, though he did not put his patient through another myocardial biopsy. He made the reasonable assumption that the lab had properly analyzed the tissue samples that Dr. Gupta submitted.

As a backup procedure, he ordered a recently devised high-tech analysis of Ryan's blood, looking for the expression of key genes that would confirm abnormal cardiac-muscle function consistent with inherited cardiomyopathy. He found them.

Ryan had no illusions that Dr. Gupta's diagnosis would be overturned. What he wanted from Dougal Hobb was the hope that came with knowing he was in the care of a brilliant physician who was as committed to the aggressive practice of his specialty as

Ryan had been committed to aggressively building Be2Do.

Dr. Hobb prescribed two of the four medications that were part of Ryan's current drug regimen, dropped two others, and added three.

At seven o'clock in the evening, in his study once more, before sending Ryan back to Newport Coast, the surgeon provided him with a slim medic-alert phone. By pressing only a single button, twice, Ryan would be connected by satellite uplink with an emergency service.

"Keep it on you at all times," Hobb advised. "Make a habit of charging it on your nightstand every night. But take it out of the charger and with you when you go to the bathroom, in case anything incapacitating should happen to you there."

He gave Ryan a list of physiological crises—such as the episode of breathing difficulty—in the event of which the medic-alert phone should be used without hesitation.

"And if I'm notified that your waiting is over, that a match has been found for you," Hobb said, "I'll contact you through the same medic-alert service. Time is of the essence in these matters. I don't like to trust to ordinary phones. Unthinkingly, patients turn them off, set them to voice mail. As long as this device is charged, it's in service. There's no OFF switch. So keep it charged and keep it with you. The day may come."

After a two-hour ride in the chartered limousine with Naraka silent and solemn behind the wheel, Ryan returned home.

He had been served a light boxed lunch at Dr. Hobb's facility, but he'd had no dinner. He searched the refrigerator and put together a meal of sorts.

Lee and Kay Ting were off duty now, and were in their private quarters—doing what, he did not care. He didn't suspect them of conspiracy any longer.

Or if he did suspect them just a little, he did not worry that they could harm him further. He had taken control of his fate, and no one in his usual circles knew that he had done so.

Although Dr. Hobb might think his new patient eccentric or worse, he had agreed to honor a request not to inform Samar Gupta that Ryan was now under the care of a new cardiologist.

For seven years, Ryan had self-insured because he loathed the insurance-company and government bureaucracies, as well as the endless paperwork, of the health-care system. A $100,000 check, written as a retainer to Dougal Hobb against all future costs, had bought some relaxation of the usual protocols between physicians.

He intended to continue to keep his periodic appointments with Dr. Gupta, though he would not follow any advice given or take any medications provided by that physician.

Although Ryan didn't suspect Gupta any more than he did Lee and Kay Ting, if Gupta knew of Hobb's involvement, he would pass the news along to Forry Stafford, and Forry—or his wife, Jane—would tell Sam.

He believed that Forry was a friend. But friendships failed all the time. Brother turned against brother, since the time of Cain and Abel, and even more frequently, more savagely, in this barbarous age.

Although his heart had reached the unshakable conclusion that Samantha was faithful to him and could never betray him, and though his mind was largely in agreement with his heart, he remembered well what she had said so recently at dinner.

If you knew me as completely as I know you, you might not love me.

He loved her as he had never loved another, and he trusted her as he had allowed himself to trust no one else. But by the nature of the world, those who loved and trusted were uniquely vulnerable.

Human beings are such knotted, desperate pieces of work—it's a rare thing to know one completely, to the core, and still love him.

Perhaps that had been the most honest, the most self-revealing, and the most loving thing that anyone had ever said to him.

But in his present distress, which so easily could spiral into despair, he could not entirely dismiss the possibility that her words might have constituted a consummate act of manipulation.

He didn't like himself much right now. He might not like himself much for a long time. But he liked himself enough to want to live.

Sitting on a stool at the smaller of the two kitchen islands, preferring to dine by only the light in the cooktop hood, he ate halloumi cheese on zaatar crackers, black olives, slices of soujouk, and cold asparagus. He finished with a fresh pear and a handful of shelled pistachios.

He suspected that in the weeks and months ahead, he would be taking more meals alone than he might wish.

After consulting the labels on each of the five bottles of drugs supplied by Dr. Hobb, he took the medications as prescribed.

Upstairs, in his bedroom, he inserted the medic-alert phone in the charger and stood the charger on his nightstand, so close to his bed that he should be able to reach it regardless of his condition. As he had done the past few nights, he would go to sleep comforted by the light of a lamp. Recently, waking in darkness had felt like coming awake in a sealed casket after being prematurely buried, with too little air to long sustain him.

Lying in bed, with the TV tuned to an old

Western—John Wayne in *The Searchers*—Ryan reviewed the decisions he had made this day, and he felt good about them.

He had tremendous confidence in his new cardiologist, although even Hobb had been stumped by one thing. The doctor had not been able to explain adequately the soft insistent knocking that now and then rose within Ryan, although the physician firmly ruled out the notion that it could be some kind of blood-and-muscle problem related to the cardiomyopathy.

Hobb suggested that the sound instead might indicate a hearing problem, a malady of one ear or the other. Eventually, Ryan pretended to consider that possibility, but remained certain that the rapping had originated not in the nautilus turns of either ear, but within his chest.

Less than half his attention was with John Wayne in the post–Civil War West, because he lay waiting for the rap-rap-rapping to resume.

Eventually, as the movie drew toward an end, as wave after wave of weariness washed Ryan toward needed sleep, he thought that perhaps the knocking would not come again because he had already answered it, had opened the door.

He did not know what he meant by that. It was the kind of muddy thought that eddied through a mind half submerged in sleep's river.

And so he slept.

During the night, a landscape materialized around him, and for the first time in months, a dream returned him to one of the places that had disturbed his sleep in September.

In the beginning there was only an impression of depth. Waste and void, bottomless and terrifying.

Then the void became water, invisible without light, silent without currents, neither warm nor cold, sensed rather than felt.

A wind blew across the water, a mystic wind murmuring without melody, and in the wind was light, the pale luminosity of the moon carried like dust, which silvered every ripple, although the body of the lake remained black.

The wind breathed once, then perished, and the earth formed around the perimeter of the lake, not fertile soil but bleak rocks, and out of the rocks grew trees as colorless as shadows.

He found himself standing on the rocks, as before, but one thing had changed. He was no longer the sole visitor to the lake.

On the farther shore stood a figure. Although dark, this Other could be discerned because the landscape behind it was so much darker that contrast was achieved.

As the Other began slowly to navigate the rocks, coming around the lake, Ryan knew that it must be

Samantha, though he could see nothing of her face and little of her form.

She would have called to him, as he would have called to her. But this place had no air to carry their voices.

He began to move to meet her as she circled toward him, but he took only a few steps across the treacherous rocks before a hand on his shoulder halted him. Even in the gloom, he recognized William Holden at his side.

The long-dead actor—star of *Sabrina* and *The Bridge on the River Kwai* and so many more films, winner of the Oscar for his performance in *Stalag 17*—said, "It isn't her, pal."

Ryan was not surprised that Holden could speak in this airless realm. The rules by which others lived never applied to movie stars.

Suffering lined the actor's handsome face, as had been the case by the time that he starred in *The Wild Bunch* and *Network*.

"Listen, pal, I had a drinking problem. In Europe once, I was driving drunk, had an accident, killed a bystander."

Even if there had been air to allow speech, Ryan would not have known how to reply to the actor's non sequitur.

Still at a distance, the Other nevertheless steadily approached along the shore.

"Don't be a dope, Dotcom. That isn't her. You come with me."

Ryan followed Holden away from the relentless Other. Through the long and exhausting night, they circled the black lake together, as in movies they might have sought to avoid Indian warriors or German soldiers, and Ryan thought he should compliment the actor on his performance in *Sunset Boulevard* or ask for an autograph, but he said nothing, and Holden never spoke again.

TWENTY-NINE

With the holidays approaching, and then with the holidays upon them, Ryan found reasons to minimize the number of evenings he spent with Samantha, passing just enough time in her company to avoid raising in her the suspicion that avoidance was his intention.

Loving her more passionately than he had once thought he could love anyone, he wanted to be with her. Because she could read him so well, however, he worried that she would infer accurately from his most innocent statement or expression that he had secretly changed physicians from Gupta to Hobb.

He did not want to argue with her, but the prospect of argument dismayed him less than did the certainty of her disappointment in him if she learned what he had done. He needed her approval as the rose needs the rain.

In light of his condition, Ryan could take refuge in not only the usual seasonal excuse of prior obligations but also in complaints about reactions to his medications—nausea, headaches, insomnia, mood swings—that were even occasionally real.

And when they were together, he tried to charm, to engage, to entertain, to be Winky less than Dotcom, always with no hint of the effort behind his performance. With her, he found this easier than he would have with anyone else, because by her nature she always drew from him the best of who he was and of what he had to offer. He had always wanted to please her even before he had anything to hide from her.

Since his diagnosis in September, his disease had taken a toll from Samantha perhaps not equal to the psychological price that Ryan had paid, but serious enough that it had robbed her of the time and passion that she needed for her writing. Her novel had lost momentum. She was not blocked, but she stood high on a dry bank, far above any hope of a creative flow state.

Now, because Ryan was less often with her, she could spend more time at her work. As she became engaged with her storytelling once more, Sam's enthusiasm for the novel served Ryan's deception. When long writing sessions went well, she was exhilarated and less likely to consider how much of the time they were apart.

Every week or ten days, Ryan traveled by limo to Beverly Hills to be examined by Dr. Hobb, who insisted on monitoring closely the condition of his heart. With every visit, he became more convinced that he had made the right decision when he turned to this dedicated man.

A few unfortunate side effects of the medications gave Ryan moments of discomfort, but he suffered none of the painful seizures, spells of arrhythmia, or breathing problems that previously plagued him. This argued for the superiority of Dr. Hobb's care, but it also suggested that Ryan had been prudent when he took control of his treatment in such a way as to foil anyone who secretly might have wished him ill.

At five o'clock in the morning, on January 14, the call came. A heart match had been found.

Of all the lists on which Ryan had appeared— *Forbes* magazine's top one hundred Internet entrepreneurs, *Wired* magazine's top twenty most creative lords of the Web, *People* magazine's one hundred most eligible bachelors—he had risen to the top of the only list that mattered.

After all the months of waiting, now came the call for action, and time was of the essence to a degree that Ryan had never known before.

Having been declared brain-dead, the donor's

body would remain on life support until Ryan arrived at that hospital and was prepared for surgery. If the heart did not have to be stored for several hours in a forty-degree saline solution, if no risks had to be taken with its transport, if it could be removed from the donor by the same surgical team that without delay transplanted it into the recipient, the chances of success would be significantly increased.

Things could still go wrong. Depending on the injuries or the illness that had led to his brain death, the donor might still suffer a heart attack, severely damaging cardiac muscle and rendering his heart useless for transplant. An undetected infection of the kidneys or the liver or another internal organ, secondary to the donor's cause of death and not immediately recognized, might lead to toxemia, or in an extreme case to septic shock and widespread tissue damage. The life-support equipment could malfunction. The hospital's power supply could fail.

Ryan preferred not to dwell on what might go wrong. Considering his condition, the worst thing he could do was psych himself into high anxiety. He had lived hardly a third of the year that Dr. Gupta had predicted, but a full year had not been a guarantee, only an estimate. His heart might deal him a deathblow at any time, whereupon he would no longer be an organ recipient but a donor, his corneas and his lungs and his liver and his kidneys carved out of him for the benefit of others.

Immediately after receiving the 5:00 A.M. notification, Ryan called Samantha, desperate that she not answer the phone. He did not want to talk to her directly, to have to answer her questions, to hear the sense of disappointment in her voice or the fear for him that she would surely express.

As she labored on the final chapters of her novel, Sam often worked late into the evening and went to bed after midnight. At this hour, Ryan hoped she would have switched off the phone and that he would get her voice mail—which he did.

Even her flat sorry-I'm-not-available-to-take-your-call speech pierced him, mundane and poignant at the same time. He wondered if he would hear her voice again, or see her.

"Sam, I love you, I love you more than I can say. Listen, the call just came. A heart match. I'm flying out. I arranged with Dr. Hobb and his team to do the surgery. I didn't tell you because you would think I'm paranoid, but I don't think I am, Sam, I think what I did was what I had to do. Maybe I didn't handle the diagnosis well, maybe it made me a little crazy, and maybe paranoia is a side effect of these medications, but I don't think so. Anyway, I'll sort all that out when I'm well, when I get back, if I make it. Sam, Sam, my God, Sam, I want you with me, I wish you could be, but not if I die, and I might, it is a possibility. So it's best you stay here. What I want for you, no matter what, is that you finish the novel, that it's a huge success for you, and that you are always as happy as you so very much deserve to be. Maybe you could dedicate the book to me. No, scratch that. It's not right for me to ask. Dedicate it to anybody you want, to some idiot who doesn't deserve it, if that's what you want. But if the book is at all about love, Sam, and knowing you I think it has to be, if it's at all about love, maybe you can tell them you learned at least a little bit about the subject from me. I learned *everything* about it from you. Call you soon. See you soon. Sam. Precious Sam."

THIRTY

Ryan's suitcase had been packed for weeks. At 5:45, he rode with it in the elevator down to the main floor and carried it through the grand, silent rooms to the front door.

This was his dream house. He had devoted much time and thought to the design and the construction of every element. He loved this house. But he did not say good-bye to it or waste a moment admiring it one last time. In the end, the house didn't matter.

At this hour, neither the domestic staff nor the landscaping staff was in evidence. Outside in the predawn dark, the neighborhood lay quiet except for the hollow hoot of an owl and the idling engine of the ambulance in the driveway.

Dr. Hobb had ordered the van-style ambulance. Using Ryan's security password, he had phoned the guard gate to ensure that the vehicle would be admitted to the community.

One of the paramedics waited at the front door. He insisted on carrying the suitcase for Ryan.

After putting the bag in the back of the van and assisting Ryan inside, the paramedic said, "Would you like me to ride back here with you or up front with my partner?"

"I'll be fine here alone," Ryan assured him. "I'm not in any imminent danger."

He lay on his back on the wheeled stretcher for the trip to the airport.

Around him were storage cabinets, a bag resuscitator, a suction machine, two oxygen cylinders, and other equipment: reminders that for a while to come, his world would shrink to the dimensions of a hospital.

Not long from now, Dr. Hobb would saw through Ryan's breastbone, open his chest, remove his diseased heart while a machine maintained his circulation, and transplant into him the heart of a caring stranger.

Instead of escalating, his fear diminished. For so long, he had felt helpless, at the mercy of Fate. Now something positive could be done. We are not born to wait. We are born to do.

The driver used the array of rotating beacons on the roof to advise traffic to yield. At this hour, the freeways should not be clogged, and a siren might not be necessary.

As a driver, Ryan had a need for speed, and as a passenger, he had never before gone as fast as this—especially not while flat on his back. He liked the loud swash of the tires, which reminded him of breaking surf, and the whistle of the wind, which the ambulance created as it knifed through the early morning, a whistling that was to him neither a banshee shriek nor the keening of an alarm, but almost a lullaby.

They were nearing the airport when he realized that he had not called either his mother or his father. He had half intended to phone them.

He had never told them about his diagnosis. Bringing them up to speed would be tedious, especially at this early hour, when his mother would be set on CRANKY and his father would be set on STUPID, and neither of them would have the desire or the capacity to switch to a different mode.

Anyway, they had nothing to give him that he needed and much to give that he did not want.

If the worst happened, he had taken care of them generously in his will. They would be able to cruise through the rest of their lives with even greater self-indulgence than they had displayed to this point.

He felt no animosity toward them. They had never loved him, but they had never hit him, either. Although they were not capable of love, they were capable of hitting, so they deserved credit for their restraint in that regard. What they had done to themselves was worse than anything they had done to him.

If he wanted to take the time for a good-bye, he would receive far less emotional satisfaction from saying good-bye to his parents than he would have received if he had delayed to say good-bye to his house.

❖

Their destination was Long Beach Airport. Arranging an emergency flight out of LAX would have been too time-consuming and frustrating.

In the early light, standing on the Tarmac, the Medijet loomed larger than the corporate Learjet that Ryan had intended to use. Dr. Hobb preferred to charter this aircraft to accommodate both his team and a contingent of the patient's friends and family. In this case, Ryan's contingent consisted of the image of Samantha that he carried in his mind, which sustained him.

Furthermore, the Medijet came with medical equipment that might be required en route, and it had the capability of handling patients who were not ambulatory or otherwise had special needs.

Three ambulances, which had ferried Dr. Hobb and his team from different points in the Los Angeles area, were lined up near the jet. The last of their suitcases and other baggage was being transferred to the aircraft.

While a paramedic took his suitcase to the Medi-jet steward, Ryan stood for a moment, peering east, savoring the pink and turquoise and peach celebration of the risen sun.

Then he boarded the jet to fly to his rebirth or to his death.

THIRTY-ONE

Ryan walked in yellow radiance, and yellow crunched under his shoes, and the melting yellow warmth of an autumn sun buttered his skin.

In the yellow distance, someone called his name, and though the voice was faint, he thought he recognized it. He could not identify who summoned him, but the voice made him happy.

He seemed to walk for a long time out of yellow into yellow, untroubled by the sameness or by his lack of a destination, and then he lay supine on a black bench that he found comfortable in spite of it being iron. Overhead hung a canopy of yellow and all around him spread a yellow carpet.

When he breathed in, he discovered what yellow smelled like, and when he breathed out, he regretted expelling the yellow that he had inhaled.

Gradually he became aware that someone stood over him, holding his right wrist, timing his pulse.

Dazzling yellow sun pierced the canopy of yellow aspen leaves at a thousand points, yellow burnishing yellow into a more intense and brighter yellowness, backlighting the person who attended to him and simultaneously enveloping that presence in a misty yellow aurora through which Ryan could see no features that would allow him to identify his caregiver.

He assumed that the one taking his pulse must be the one who had called to him out of the brilliant yellow, and for a while he remained happy, for he knew this presence loved him.

Later, when he tried to express his gratitude, he discovered that he was mute, and his inability to speak reminded him of when he had been unable to reply to William Holden on the shore of the black lake.

Suddenly the looming pulse-taker seemed not to be glorified by the yellow aurora but to be hiding within the radiance, cunning and calculating, not a loving presence after all, but in fact the dark figure that had circled the shore of the lake, into the arms of whom Ryan would have delivered himself had it not been for Mr. Holden's admonition.

The thumb and two fingers on his wrist, seeking his pulse, were cold, although they had not been cold a moment ago, were *icy,* and were squeezing harder than before, were *pinching*, and the shape of a head descended toward him through the yellow aurora, a face, a face, but a face constituted entirely of a wide and hungry maw—

With a throttled cry, grasping at the safety railing, Ryan sat up in a hospital bed, in a shadowy room redolent of an astringent pine-scented cleaning solution.

The sheets smelled of bleach and fabric softener. They crackled and felt crisp, as if starched.

In a lamplit corner, putting aside the book that he had been reading, a man dressed in white slacks and a white shirt rose from an armchair.

The lamp base and shade gleamed, stainless steel or polished nickel. The vinyl upholstery on the armchair glistered like the flesh of an avocado drizzled with olive oil.

Everything in the room appeared to have a coat of lacquer or to be wet. The polished white-tile floor, the shiny blue top on the nightstand, the wall paint glimmering with a crushed-pearl glaze.

Even the shadows had a hard gloss, as if they were layers of smoky glass, and Ryan understood that this universal sheen was less real than it was an effect caused by the sedative that he had been given.

He felt that he had come fully awake, his wits sharp and his perceptions clearer and more penetrating than ever in his life, but the witchy luster of everything led him to the realization that he was narcotized. Sleep would take him again the moment he returned his head to the pillow.

He felt helpless and at risk.

At the windows pressed the murky and unwelcoming chrome-yellow darkness of any large city at night.

"Bad dream?" asked the male nurse.

Wally. Wally Dunnaman. A member of Dr. Hobb's team of eight. Earlier he had shaved Ryan's chest and abdomen.

"My throat's dry," Ryan said.

"Doctor doesn't want you having much to drink before surgery in the morning. But I can give you a few chips of ice to let melt in your mouth."

"All right."

At the nightstand, Wally removed the stopper from an insulated carafe. With a long-handled spoon, such a shiny spoon, he fished out a piece of ice, glimmering ice, and fed it to Ryan.

After allowing his patient three chips of ice, he stoppered the carafe and put down the spoon.

Studying his wristwatch, Wally Dunnaman timed Ryan's pulse.

In the yellow dream, neither the loving presence nor the hateful one had been this man. Nothing in this room, in this hospital, had inspired the dream.

Releasing Ryan's wrist, Wally said, "You need to sleep."

In some way that Ryan could not explain, the reality of the dream equaled the reality of this room, neither superior to the other. He knew the truth of that in his bones, although he did not understand it.

"Sleep now," Wally urged.

If sleep was a little death, as some poet had once written, this sleep would be more of a death than any other to which Ryan had given himself. He must resist it.

Yet he lowered his head again to the pillow, and he could not lift it.

Helpless and at risk.

He had made a mistake. He didn't know the nature of the mistake, but he felt the weight of it, holding him down.

As he strained to keep his eyes open, every surface with a sheen became a surface with a shine, every shine a glare, every glossiness a blinding brilliance.

Bells. The bells foretold, and now the bells.

Tolling, tolling, tolling, rolling, rolling, rolling, a solemn monody of bells shook Ryan out of sleep.

He first thought they were dream bells, but the clamor persisted as he strove to find the strength to pull himself upright, both hands gripping the bed railing.

Darkness still owned the world beyond the window, and the male nurse stood on this side of the glass, looking out, gazing down, into waves of rising sound.

Huge heavy bells shook the night, as though they meant to shake it down, such melancholy menace in their tone.

Ryan spoke more than once before Wally Dunnaman heard him and glanced toward the bed, raising his voice to say, "There's a church across the street."

When first conducted to the room, Ryan had seen that house of worship in the next block. The bell tower rose above this fourth-floor window.

"They shouldn't be ringing at this hour," Wally said. "And not this much. No lights in the place."

The strangely glossy shadows seemed to shiver with the tolling, such a moaning and a groaning, a hard insistent rolling.

The window-rattling, wall-strumming, bone-shivering clangor frightened Ryan, rang thickly in his blood, and made his heart pound like a hammer coming down. This swollen heart was still his own, so weak and so diseased, and he feared it might be tested to destruction by these thunderous peals.

He recalled his thought upon waking: *Bells. The bells foretold, and now the bells.*

Foretold when, by whom, and with what meaning?

If not for the sedative that fouled his blood and muddied his mind, he thought he would know the answer to at least two parts of that question.

But the drug not only lacquered every surface in the room, not only buffed a shine on every shadow, but also afflicted him with synesthesia, so he smelled the sound as well as heard it. The reek of ferric hydroxide, ferric oxide, call it rust, washed in bitter waves across the bed.

Interminable tolling, bells and bells and still more bells, knocked from Ryan all sense of time, and it seemed to him that soon it would knock sanity from him, as well.

Eventually raising his voice above the clangor, Wally Dunnaman said, "A police car down below. Ah, and another!"

Under the weight of the booming bells, Ryan fell back, his head once more upon the pillow.

He was helpless and at risk, risk, risk.

With a kind of fractured desperation that he could not focus to his benefit, he sorted through his broken thoughts, trying to piece them together like fragments of crockery. Something very wrong had happened that he still had time to rectify, if only he were able to understand what needed to be put right.

The bells began to toll less aggressively, their rage subsiding to anger, anger to sullenness, and sullenness to one final protracted groan that sounded like a great heavy door moaning closed on rusted hinges.

In the silence of the bells, as once more the sedative slowly drew over him its velvet thrall, Ryan felt tears on his cheeks and licked at the salt in the corner of his mouth. He did not have the strength to lift his hands and blot his face, and as he quietly wept his way into sleep, he no longer had the presence of mind either to be embarrassed by his tears or to wonder at them.

Shortly after dawn, when they rolled him on a gurney into the surgery, Ryan was alert, afraid, but resigned to the course that he had chosen.

The operating room, white porcelain tile and stainless steel, was drenched in light.

From the scrub room, Dr. Hobb arrived with his team, lacking only Wally Dunnaman, who had no role in the cutting. Besides Dougal Hobb, there were an anesthesiologist, three cardiology nurses, an assistant surgeon, and two others whose specialties and functions Ryan could not recall.

He had met them on the Medijet, and he had liked them all, so far as it was possible to like anyone who was going to saw you open and handle your internal organs as blithely as though they were the giblets in a Thanksgiving turkey. There was bound to be some social distance between the cutters and he who must be cut.

Except for Hobb, Ryan was not easily able to tell who was who in their hair-restraining caps, behind their masks, in their green scrubs. They might have all been ringers, the B team inserted after the A team had been approved and paid for.

As the anesthesiologist found a vein in Ryan's right arm and inserted a cannula, Dr. Hobb told him that the donor's heart had been successfully removed moments ago and waited now in a chilled saline solution.

Ryan had learned on the Medijet that he was to receive a woman's heart, which only briefly surprised him. She had been twenty-six, a schoolteacher who had suffered massive head trauma in an automobile accident.

Her heart had been deemed of suitable size for Ryan. And every criterion of an immune-system match had been met, greatly increasing the chances that all would go well not merely during surgery but also afterward, when his body would be less likely to aggressively reject the new organ.

Nevertheless, to prevent rejection and other complications, he would be taking a battery of twenty-eight drugs for a significant length of time following surgery, some for the rest of his life.

As they readied Ryan, Dr. Hobb explained to him the purpose of each procedure, but Ryan did not need to be gentled toward the moment. He could not turn back now. The wanted heart was free, the donor dead, and a single path to the future lay before him.

He closed his eyes, tuned out the murmured

conversations of the members of the team, and pictured Samantha Reach. Throughout his adolescence and adult life, he had sought perfection, and had found it only once—in her.

He hoped that she could be perfectly forgiving, too, although he knew he should start conceiving now his opening line for his first phone call to her, when he was strong and clearheaded enough to speak.

Closing his eyes, he saw her on the beach, blond hair and golden form, a quiver of light, an alluring oasis on the wide slope of sun-seared sand.

As the induced sleep came over him, he drifted down as if into a sea, and the darkness darkled into something darker than mere dark.

P
A
R
T

2

Now comes the evening of the mind.

Here are the fireflies twitching in the blood.

—*Donald Justice,* "The Evening of the Mind"

THIRTY-TWO

On the one-year anniversary of his heart transplant, Ryan Perry made no plans for a celebration. Being alive was celebration enough.

During the morning, he worked alone in the garage, performing routine maintenance on a fully sparkled '32 five-window deuce coupe that he had bought at auction.

In the afternoon, ensconced in an armchair with a footstool, in the smaller of the two living rooms, he continued reading Samantha's first book.

Styled as a solarium, the chamber provided an atmosphere to match that in the novel. Tall windows revealed a down sky, a limp pillow stuffed with the soft wet feathers of gray geese. Needles of rain knitted together scattered scarves of thin fog, which then unraveled through whatever tree or shrub next snagged them.

The room's collection of palms and ferns webbed the limestone floor with spidery shadows. The air had a green and fertile scent, for the most part pleasing, although from time to time there arose a faint fetid odor of what might have been decomposing moss or root rot, which seemed always, curiously, to be detectable only when he read passages that in particular disturbed him.

She had infused the novel with quiet humor, and one of her central subjects proved to be love, as he had intuited when he'd left the long message on her voice mail, before his transplant surgery. Yet in the weave of the narrative were solemn threads, somber threads, and the entire garment she had sewn seemed darker than the materials from which she had made it.

The story enthralled Ryan, and though the prose was luminous and swift, he resisted rushing through the pages, but instead savoured the sentences. This was his second reading of the novel in four days.

Winston Amory wheeled to Ryan's chair a serving cart on which stood a sterling-silver coffeepot with candle-burner to keep the contents warm, and a small plate of almond cookies.

"Sir, I took the liberty of assuming, as you are not at a table, you might prefer a mug to a cup."

"Perfect, Winston. Thank you."

After pouring a mug of coffee, Winston placed a coaster on the table beside the armchair, and then the mug upon the coaster.

Referring to his wife, Winston said, "Penelope wonders if you would like dinner at seven, as usual."

"A little later tonight. Eight would be ideal."

"Eight it is, sir." He nodded once, his customary abbreviated bow, before departing stiff-backed and straight-shouldered.

Although Winston managed the estate and marshaled the household staff to its duties with consummate grace and professionalism, Ryan suspected that he and Penelope exaggerated their Englishness, from their accents to their mannerisms, to their obsession with propriety and protocol, because they had learned, in previous positions, that this was what enchanted Americans who employed their services. This performance occasionally annoyed him, more often amused him, and in sum was worth enduring because they did a fine job and because he had complete trust in them.

Before returning home for further recuperation after receiving his new heart, he had dismissed Lee and Kay Ting, as well as their assistants. Each had been given two years of severance pay, about which none complained, plus a strong letter of recommendation, but no explanation.

He had no evidence of treachery in their case, but he had no proof that would exonerate them, either.

He had wanted to come home to a sense of security and peace.

Wilson Mott's report on Winston and Penelope Amory—and on the other new employees—was so exhaustive that Ryan felt as if he knew them all as well as he knew himself. He was not suspicious of them, and they gave him no reason to wonder about their loyalty; and the year had gone by without a single strange incident.

Now, with coffee and cookies at hand, Ryan again became so absorbed in Sam's novel that he lost track of the passage of time, and looked up from a chapter's end to find that the early-winter twilight had begun to drain from the day what light the rain and fog had not already drowned.

Had he raised his eyes only a few minutes later, he might not have been able to see the figure on the south lawn.

Initially he thought this visitor must be a shadow shaped by plumes of fog, because it appeared to be a monk in hooded habit far from any monastery.

A moment's consideration remade the habit into a black raincoat. The hood, the fading light, and a distance of forty feet hid all but the palest impression of a face.

The visitor—*intruder* began to seem a better word—appeared to be staring at that floor-to-ceiling window providing the most direct view of Ryan in his armchair.

As he put aside his book and rose to approach the window, the figure moved. By the time he reached the glass, he saw no sign of an intruder.

Through the drizzling rain, nothing moved on the broad south lawn except slowly writhing anacondas of fog.

After a year that had flowed by in the most ordinary currents, Ryan was prepared to dismiss the brief vision as a trick of twilight.

But the figure reappeared from among three deodar cedars that, with their drooping boughs, seemed themselves like giant monks in attendance at a solemn ceremony. Slowly the figure moved into view and then stopped, once again facing the solarium.

Dimming by the minute, the dying day exposed less of the face than before, although the intruder had ventured ten feet closer to the house.

Just as Ryan realized that it might not be wise to stand exposed at a lighted window, the figure turned and retreated across the lawn. It seemed not to step away but to glide, as if it too were merely fog, but of a dark variety.

The murk of dusk and mist and rain soon folded into night. The intruder did not reappear.

The landscaping staff received full pay for rain days but did not report to work; however, Henry Sorne, the head landscaper, might have paid a visit to check the lawn drains, a few of which, clogged with leaves, had overflowed in past storms.

Not Henry Sorne. The stature of the figure, the gracefulness with which it moved in the cumbersome coat, as well as something about the attitude in which it stood facing the window, convinced Ryan that this intruder had been a woman.

Penelope Amory and her assistant, Jordana, were the only women on the household staff. Neither of them had reason to be inspecting the lawns, and neither seemed to be the type to fancy a rainy-day walk.

The grounds were walled. The motorized bronze gates locked automatically when you passed through them and could not be left unlatched accidentally. Neither the walls nor the gates could be easily scaled.

Although the two walk-in gates featured electronic locks that could be released either from within the house or by the inputting of a code in the exterior keypads, the driveway gate could be opened also with a remote control. Only one person, other than staff, had ever possessed a remote.

Standing at the solarium window, now seeing nothing but his reflection painted on the night-blackened glass, Ryan whispered, *"Samantha?"*

▎

After dinner, Ryan took Sam's novel upstairs, intending to read another chapter or two in bed, perhaps until he fell asleep, although he doubted that even on a second reading her words would lull him into slumber.

As usual, Penelope had earlier removed the quilted spread and turned down the covers of his bed for the night. A lamp had been left on, as he liked.

Atop his stack of plumped pillows stood a small cellophane bag, the neck twisted shut and tied securely with a red ribbon. Penelope did not leave bedtime candy, which was what the bag contained.

This was not the traditional mint or the two-piece sample of Godiva often left on hotel pillows by the night maids. The bag held tiny white candy hearts with brief romantic declarations printed in red on one side of them, a confection sold only during the lead-up to Valentine's Day, which was less than a month away.

Bemused, Ryan turned the crackling bag over in his hand. He noticed that all of the candy messages visible to him were the same: BE MINE.

As he recalled from adolescence, in the original bags in which these treats were sold, several messages were included: LOVE YOU, TOO SWEET, KISS ME, and others.

To obtain a full collection that asked only BE MINE, you would have to purchase several bags and cull from them the hearts with the wanted message.

In the bathroom, sitting at the vanity, he untied the ribbon, opened the bag, and spilled the hearts on the black-granite counter. Those that were faceup revealed the identical message.

One by one, he turned over those that lay with their blank sides exposed, and in every case, the entreaty was the same: BE MINE.

Staring at the hearts, more than a hundred of them, he decided not to taste one.

He returned them to the bag, twisted shut the cellophane, and tied the ribbon tight.

The first anniversary of his transplant certainly must be the occasion for the gift, but he couldn't interpret the subtext of the two-word sentiment. He should not discount that the candy might have been given in all innocence and with good will.

Raising his gaze from the insistent red messages, he stared at himself in the mirror. He could not read his face.

THIRTY-THREE

Ryan sat in bed, reading until he finished Samantha's novel for the second time, shortly after two o'clock in the morning. He had not intended to stay up so late.

For a few minutes, he stared at the author's photo on the back of the book jacket. No camera could do her justice.

Putting the book aside, he leaned against the mounded pillows.

In the three months immediately after the transplant, the side effects of his twenty-eight medications stressed him and, in a couple of instances, considerably worried him. But dosages were adjusted, a few drugs were replaced with others, and thereafter his recovery went so well that Dr. Hobb called him "my superpatient."

At the one-year mark, no signs of organ rejection had appeared: no unexplained weakness, no fatigue, no fever, no chill or dizziness, no diarrhea or vomiting.

Myocardial biopsy remained the gold standard for identifying rejection. Twice in the past year, as an outpatient, Ryan submitted to the procedure. Both times, the pathologist found no indication of rejection in the tissue samples.

For exercise, he did a lot of walking, uncounted miles. In recent months, he began riding a stationary bike, as well, and lifting light weights.

He was trim, and he felt fit.

Judging by the evidence, he belonged to the fortunate and small minority in whom a stranger's heart might be received with negative consequences hardly greater than those of a blood transfusion. The most significant medical danger he faced was increased susceptibility to disease because of the immunosuppressant drugs he relied upon.

Yet he had been waiting for the turn, the change of tides, the rotation of the current light into an unknown dark. The events that had led up to the transplant seemed to be unfinished business.

Now came the candy hearts with their simple message, which was nonetheless cryptic for its simplicity. And the figure on the south lawn, in the rain.

He dimmed the bedside lamp. Even after a year of

comparative normalcy, he preferred not to sleep in absolute darkness.

Two decks served the master suite. The doors to both were three inches thick, with steel cores and two deadbolts. With the perimeter alarm set, they could not be opened without triggering a siren.

The main stairs ascended from the second floor to the penthouse landing, which was also served by the elevator. The door between that landing and the master suite was secured on this side by a blind deadbolt that had no keyway on the farther side.

Consequently, if intruders were secreted inside the house when the perimeter alarm was activated for the night, they could not gain entrance to the master suite.

In a hidden safe in his walk-in closet, Ryan had stored a 9-millimeter pistol and a box of ammunition. This evening, before bed, he loaded the pistol. It now lay in the half-open nightstand drawer.

He could make a good case against himself to the effect that his fears of conspiracy during the months leading to his transplant were not the result of mental confusion related to diminished circulation, were not caused by the side effects of prescription drugs, but were attributable to an unfortunate lifelong tendency to suspicion. When at an early age you learned not to trust your parents, distrust could become a key element of your life philosophy.

And if that self-indictment was the full truth of

things, he needed to resist another descent into paranoia. Perhaps a first step in that resistance ought to be returning the pistol to the safe at once, not in the morning.

He left it in the nightstand drawer.

No unexplained rapping arose. Lying on his right side, ear to the pillow, Ryan heard the slow steady beating of his good heart.

In time he slept, and did not dream.

▌

He woke in the late morning and, by intercom, advised Mrs. Amory that he would be taking lunch at one o'clock in the solarium.

After he showered, shaved, and dressed, he put both the pistol and the bag of candy hearts in the concealed safe.

The storm had passed the previous evening. But a new front was rolling in from the northwest, with rain expected by midafternoon.

When Penelope brought his lunch to the table in the solarium, Ryan asked if she had left candy on his pillow the evening before, though he did not describe the hearts.

In spite of whatever talent she might have for exaggerating her Englishness without once breaking character, she did not seem like a woman who could lie without a score of tics and other tells giving her away. She appeared confused by the question and then as baffled as was Ryan that someone should think it proper etiquette to treat him like a hotel guest in his own home.

After lunch, when she returned to clear the table, she said that she had mentioned the candy to Jordana and to Winston and that she was quite sure neither of them had been the party responsible for this perhaps well-meant but inexcusable occurrence. She had not spoken to Winston's assistant, Ricardo, as he had been off work the previous day and could not have been responsible.

A service representative with the firm that maintained their heating-cooling system had been inhouse and had changed filters on the third floor. And a repairman had worked on the under-counter refrigerator in the master-bedroom retreat. Mrs. Amory wished to know if she should contact them and ascertain if either had been the culprit.

The intensity of her gray-eyed stare and a certain set to her mouth suggested that she regarded this incident as a challenge to her authority and as a personal affront for which she would be pleased to pursue the miscreant to the gates of Hell, if necessary, and give him an upbraiding that he would find worse than the tortures that awaited him in the flames of damnation.

"It's commendable of you," Ryan said placatingly, "to be so committed to finding an explanation. But it's not all that important, Penelope. Let's not take this out of house. Someone must have meant it as a joke, that's all."

"You can rest assured, I'll keep my eye on those gentlemen when next they're on the premises," she said.

"I have no doubt of it," he said. "No doubt at all."

Alone in the solarium, he returned to his favorite armchair and opened Samantha's book to begin a third reading.

Rain began to fall at a quarter past two. As on the previous day, Nature was in an indolent mood, and the sky shed a languid drizzle.

From time to time, Ryan interrupted his reading to sweep the south lawn with his gaze.

He glanced up from the novel less often than he intended. Had the hooded figure returned, it could have watched him for half an hour or longer without his being aware of its presence.

The story, the characters, the prose still enchanted him, but from this third reading, he sought something more than any other work of fiction could have given him. Being in the story was being with Samantha, hearing her voice, which to him counted as both a joy and a sadness.

He also hoped to gain an understanding of why things were the way they were between them. Having completed the book the very day she learned of his transplant, Sam could not have written any part of it with the intention of explaining their estrangement to him, and anyway people didn't write entire novels to each other in the place of a letter or a phone chat. Yet on his first reading, in only three chapters, he had sensed that this book had something to reveal to him that would explain their current relationship.

Throughout, the novel sang with Samantha's voice, glowed with her grace, and reflected her sensibilities, but it also contained many scenes that Ryan would not have thought she could write, that sounded like Samantha... but like Samantha as she might have been if some of the experiences that shaped her life had never happened.

This made him feel that he had never fully known her. If he was to make things right between them, rounding out his understanding of Sam was a necessary first step, and the view into her heart provided by this novel seemed certain to help him.

Prior to twilight, Ryan put down the book to survey the lawn, the trees, and the south wall of the estate, on which bougainvillea flourished, providing a thorny obstacle to a quick exit by any intruder. No watcher in the wet.

He got up from the armchair, leaving the floor lamp lit to imply that he had stepped away for only a moment.

At a window near a corner of the room, from

between a pair of queen palms lush enough to shade him from the high ceiling lights, he studied the sodden landscape.

Whoever the woman might be, Ryan doubted she would return so soon to prowl the grounds, for she knew that she had been seen on her first visit. Yet stranger things had happened.

Beyond the rain, behind the clouds, the gentle hand of twilight dimmed the sky, and night soon threw the switch to black. The hooded figure did not appear.

After dinner, when Ryan retired to the third floor, he locked the door with the blind deadbolt. With some trepidation, he went directly from the suite foyer into the bedroom.

The bedspread had been removed, and the covers had been turned down, as they should have been. But nothing had been left on his stack of pillows.

As peculiar as the gift of candy hearts seemed, nevertheless Ryan felt foolish for expecting that it might represent the beginning of a new series of mysterious incidents that would send him spiraling into a whirlpool of irrationality like the one in which he had found himself more than a year ago. All of that bizarreness had proved to be coincidence that had seemed substantive only because of the effect

on his thinking of poorly oxygenated blood and subsequently because of the side effects of medications.

He checked the two doors to the decks. Each featured a standard deadbolt lock operated from inside
by a thumbturn and from outside by a key, and each
also had a blind deadbolt with a thumbturn on the
inside but nothing to mark its existence on the outside. Both locks on both doors were engaged.

After brushing his teeth, toileting, and changing
into pajamas, Ryan considered taking the pistol
from the safe. Counseling himself to maintain perspective and not to let his imagination overrule his
reason, he returned unarmed to the bedroom.

On his pillow lay a piece of jewelry, a gold heart
pendant on a gold chain.

THIRTY-FOUR

In the closet, Ryan pressed a hidden switch. A panel slid aside, revealing the eighteen-inch-square steel face of the wall safe.

Using the lighted keypad, he hurriedly entered the lock code. When the liquid-crystal display announced ACCESS, he opened the safe, snatched up the 9-millimeter pistol, closed the door, and stood for a moment thinking, the weapon gripped in both hands, muzzle pointed at the ceiling.

The checked grip felt rough against his palm. The weapon seemed too light for an instrument of mortal consequences.

He did not want to kill anyone, but he had not survived this far to die easily.

Barefoot, in pajamas, he left the closet, crossed the bedroom, and entered the retreat. He flipped up the light switch with one elbow as he crossed the threshold.

The amboina-wood Art Deco desk. Bookshelves. Entertainment center. Small bar with an under-counter refrigerator.

At the door to the first deck, he found the blind deadbolt still engaged from the inside. No one had left by this exit.

Two windows provided a view of the deck. He drew up the pleated shades on the first, then on the second, half expecting a pale and hooded face at the glass, a milky-eyed stare, a wicked grin, whoever had been circling toward him around the black lake. No presence awaited him, and both windows were locked from inside.

Off the retreat lay a windowless half bath. No one in there. His reflection in the mirror, his mouth pressed in a flat grim line, his eyes wild. The gun so huge.

Returning to the bedroom, at the door to the second deck, he found the blind deadbolt engaged. No one had departed by this exit, either.

Three windows, one inoperable. The other two locked. A gust of wind, a shatter of rain against the glass caused his heart to jump.

Nowhere to hide except under the bed. Although no one but an anorexic model could slip under a low-profile king-size job with sideboards, Ryan dropped to his knees anyway and peered into that space, where because of the superb housecleaning he found not even a ball of dust.

The foyer. The main door. Blind deadbolt locked.

Bathroom. A large open space. The marble floor cold under his bare feet. Nothing moved but Ryan's nervous reflections. A door led to a water closet, another to a walk-in linen storage. No one in either space.

His expansive personal closet had no open shelves, only drawers for folded items. Hanging clothes were behind cabinet doors.

By pushing the suits and shirts aside on the rods, a grown man could have hidden in any of a dozen different compartments. Ryan opened all the doors but confronted no intruder.

To have left the pendant on the pillow *after* Ryan had locked himself in the suite for the night, someone must have been in there with him. Yet no one remained; and no exit had been opened.

He returned to his bed, holding the pistol at his side, and stood staring at the pendant.

A patter like a pack of scurrying rats in the attic. He looked up. Not rats, rain. On the slate roof, rain.

If anyone had come into the suite from a deck, through a door or a window, they would have dripped on the carpet. Ryan would have felt the moisture under his bare feet.

No one had been here. Someone had been here. Unreason.

As if the pendant were bewitched and to touch it would ensure the transmission of a curse, Ryan hesitated to pick it up. But curiosity kills more than cats.

As it lay on the pillow, the gold heart revealed a single side, softly burnished. In his hand, dangling from the chain, the other side came into view. Two words, engraved: BE MINE.

The pendant was not a locket. He was relieved that it was not a locket. If it had been a locket, it would have contained something that he would not have wanted to see.

BE MINE.

As he wondered at those words, recalling the tiny candy hearts, a memory troubled him: the open wall safe as, in the grip of fear, he had snatched up the pistol.

Belatedly, what Ryan had seen in the safe registered with him. He stood listening to the rain rats and felt Fate gnawing at his bones.

If what he recalled was true, the normalcy of the past year was a trapdoor with a corroded spring, and the coils of the spring just now abruptly cracked and failed.

In denial of the memory, dropping the pendant on the nightstand, clutching the pistol, he returned to the closet, not hurriedly but at a death-row pace.

The sliding panel remained open, the safe revealed. When he slammed the door after grabbing the gun, the lock had automatically engaged. On the status display glowed the word SECURE.

Under the circumstances, that assurance seemed to mock him.

When he entered the lock code in the illuminated keypad, SECURE changed to ACCESS. After a hesitation, he opened the foot-square steel door.

The safe had contained four thousand dollars in cash, to be used in an emergency, two expensive watches, and a pair of diamond links for French cuffs, which he never wore. None of those items had been touched.

Also in the safe had been a small, hinged jewelry-display box containing the $85,000 engagement ring, already sized to Samantha's hand, that he had not been able to persuade her to accept. The box remained, and when Ryan opened it, the ring sparkled.

The previous night, he had also stowed the candy hearts in this safe. The ribbon-tied cellophane bag and all that it contained were gone.

This he had seen but not registered when, minutes before, he had been frantic to retrieve the pistol.

What he had not noticed earlier, but now discovered, was that the box of 9-mm cartridges had also been taken. He did not need to sort through the contents of the small compartment. The box could not be buried under the other items: They were follies and small; the box was full of mortality, big and heavy.

Ryan could not at first understand why an intruder, finding the safe, would take the bullets but not the delivery system, leaving him with ten rounds for defense.

Yes. Well. Of course.

He ejected the magazine from the pistol. The ten cartridges had been removed from it, as well.

Believing as he did in the necessity of action, Ryan had plunged into a search for an intruder, racing from room to room, tearing open doors, armed with a useless weapon, discovering no one to shoot, but now he had been pride-shot and humiliated by the metaphoric bullet of his adversary's mockery.

THIRTY-FIVE

A seven-digit access number opened the safe's programming to Ryan. He deleted his former lock combination and entered a new one based on a date important to him but meaningless to anyone else.

He suspected this was wasted effort. He alone had possessed the previous code, but someone had violated the safe anyway.

To open the panel that concealed the safe, he had used a hidden switch incorporated into the rheostat that controlled the closet lighting.

Although the trim plate that covered the junction box appeared to be fixed to the wall with two screws, they were only screw heads. They had no function except deception.

The control stick slid up for brighter, down for

dimmer. When the stick was all the way at the top of the slot, you could press up on the trim plate, moving it one click at a time on the hidden track to which it was attached. The combination that caused the panel to slide open, revealing the safe, was three clicks up, two clicks back, and two clicks up.

The pressure required to move the trim plate was sufficient that this secret function could not be accidentally discovered by a maid cleaning the closet.

A local alarm company, vetted and recommended by Wilson Mott, had installed both this small safe and a concealed walk-in model on the ground floor. They were bonded, with a long history of reliable service, and Ryan doubted that one of their employees was tormenting him.

Tormenting seemed to be the operative word, for if the immediate intention had been to harm him, he would already be dead.

Torment was a form of violence, however, and anyone who enjoyed inflicting it might be expected to move from psychological torment to physical, even to murder.

He put the useless pistol in the safe. In addition to removing the ammunition, the intruder might have tampered with the weapon. Ryan did not know enough about guns to trust his examination of the 9-mm to reveal any subtle but critical damage that had been done to it.

Before he bought another box of cartridges,

reloaded, and tested the pistol, he would have it examined by someone with the experience to certify its reliability. He didn't know if a tricked-up gun could explode in his hand when he pulled the trigger, but he wasn't going to find out the hard way.

Alternately, he could purchase a new pistol. The law required a waiting period for a handgun, however, and Ryan suspected that his tormentor had an agenda and a timetable that would bring them to a brink before the waiting period had passed.

As he closed the safe and watched the concealing panel slide into place, he realized that if the intruder had known about this wall safe, another secret of the house had most likely also been compromised.

In the bedroom once more, he plucked an electronic key from the nightstand drawer. He went to a six-foot-by-six-foot painting that was mounted tight to the south wall, and held the blunt end of the key to one of the eyes of a tiger in the painting. Behind that very spot, a lock-code reader triggered the release of the bolts that held in place the painting and the portion of the wall to which it was attached.

Most houses of this size and complexity featured a panic room in which the owners could take refuge in the event of a home-invasion robbery or a similar crisis. This one measured twelve by sixteen feet.

The door that was a painting swung inward. Ryan stepped over the raised threshold, into a fireproof space formed of poured-in-place concrete, lined with quarter-inch steel plate, and upholstered in the highest-quality soundproofing.

A land-line separate from the house phone system, dedicated electric service unrelated to the rest of the estate, dedicated incoming fresh-air and air-exhaust lines made the panic room self-sustaining. Invaders could cut the house services—or in a siege situation, they could be cut by authorities—and this haven would still function.

Packaged food, bottled water, a corner toilet, a backup chemical toilet, and other supplies would support those who took shelter here for several days. Two chairs and a bed were also provided.

On the bed lay the cellophane bag of candy hearts.

THIRTY-SIX

In slippers, with a bathrobe over his pajamas, turning on lights as he went, Ryan hurried down four
flights of stairs to the bottom floor of the house, directly to the service hall at the end of which lay the
laundry room.

One of the storage rooms off that hall, the one
that interested him now, always remained locked,
but he possessed a key. In a corner of this room
stood a wide, tall, black metal cabinet, also locked,
which for convenience could be opened with the
same key.

In the cabinet were racked recorders that stored
on magnetic disks the observations of the estate security cameras. Twenty cameras kept watch on the
exterior of the house and the grounds. Seven others
maintained surveillance of the interior hallways and

the penthouse landing, though no cameras intruded into any rooms.

He switched on a monitor that presented him with a menu from which he selected with a remote control. He was most interested in the camera that covered the penthouse landing, because it recorded everyone who, either by staircase or elevator, arrived in this area en route to the door of the master suite.

After he had specified the camera, the menu instructed him to enter the date, the hour, and the minute from which he wanted to begin viewing. He chose this date, this hour, thirty minutes earlier.

The twenty-by-fourteen-foot landing outside the master suite appeared on the screen. The date was noted on the lower left side. On the lower right, a digital clock kept a running count of the hour, minute, and second.

Intently focused on the recording, Ryan fast-forwarded to review in fifteen minutes the next thirty minutes' worth of images.

Near the beginning, he watched himself come off the stairs and proceed to the master-suite door, carrying Samantha's book, on his way to bed.

To conserve storage space, the camera didn't record fluid video but took a snapshot every half second. On screen, Ryan moved like a figure in an animation sequence drawn on stacks of flippable cards.

Earlier, when he entered the bedroom, he had first checked the bed to see if a second gift awaited.

Finding nothing on his pillow, he had spent some time brushing his teeth, preparing for the night.

Now, minute after minute, the camera failed to show anyone entering the locked master suite after him.

Here was proof that when he had gone into the suite, an intruder must have been there already, in the retreat off the bedroom.

While Ryan had gotten ready for bed, the unknown—but now soon to be seen—giver of gifts had placed the pendant and left the suite, somehow locking the blind deadbolt upon exiting.

But the video failed to support that theory. No one came out of the master suite until Ryan himself appeared again, this time wearing a bathrobe over his pajamas, hurrying to the stairs and ultimately to this room in which he now studied the security recording.

His search of the suite, following the discovery of the heart pendant, had been thorough. He had not missed any place where even a small child could have hidden.

Now he accessed the recording made by the camera that covered the third-floor deck outside the master-suite retreat, and studied the same time period. A single deck lamp provided enough light for the night-vision camera to present a picture nearly as bright as one taken during the day. No one departed by that door or by one of those two windows, either.

When he reviewed the recording of the other master-level deck, he saw no one come out of the door or out of the windows that opened directly off the bedroom.

No one had left the suite, but no one had been there when he searched every niche of the place.

Judging by the evidence, the gold pendant must have materialized magically on the pillow.

What appeared to be magical, however, must be always and only an ordinary event rendered enigmatic by the lack of one crucial fact.

Ryan racked his brain to think of what that fact might be, but both reason and imagination failed him.

Frustrated, about to switch off the monitor, he decided to have a look at the recordings made at twilight, the previous day, on the south lawn, when he had been reading in the solarium and had discovered he was under observation. Two cameras covered that area.

The system stored all of these recordings for thirty days, then dumped them unless otherwise instructed.

The first camera, mounted on the house, provided approximately the view that Ryan would have had from his armchair. It presented now the clotted gray goose-down sky, the drizzle, the solemn trees, the slithering fog, the saturated yard across which the hooded trespasser had glided.

He ran the scene beginning prior to the onset of twilight, and watched as the watery light drained from the day. Night came, but the intruder did not.

Disbelieving, having fast-forwarded through the recording, Ryan watched it again, but in real time, which seemed interminable. Sky, rain, trees, fog, inconstant light fading to darkness—but no visitor either ominous or otherwise.

The second south-lawn camera was mounted on a limb of an Indian laurel, covering some of the same ground from a different angle. The three deodar cedars, from the shadows of which the hooded figure had made its second appearance, were central to this view.

Through the fading light, into darkfall, no phantom glided forth from beneath the majestic drooping boughs of the cedars.

The previous evening, damn it, he had seen *something*. He had not merely hallucinated the figure. It was neither a trick of rain and fog nor a reflection on the window glass of some palm or fern in the solarium. He'd seen someone in a hooded raincoat, maybe a woman, moving and wet and *real*.

The watcher in the rain was as real as the candy hearts, as real as the gold heart pendant that lay now . . .

Where?

On the nightstand. Yes. After holding it by the chain and seeing the inscription, he put it on the nightstand. Later, after finding the cellophane bag of candy in the panic room, he had put that on the nightstand, as well.

Ryan switched off the monitor, locked the cabinet, left the storage room, locked the door, and returned to the master suite, overcome by a grim expectation.

On the nightstand stood only the lamp and the clock. The bag of candy and the pendant were gone.

A frantic but exhaustive search of the master suite turned up neither item.

When, last of all, he opened the safe with the new combination that he had recently programmed, the pendant and candy hearts were not in there, either. And like the ammunition before it, the pistol had been taken.

THIRTY-SEVEN

Because the master suite was not secure, Ryan could not assume that he would be safe when sleeping.

He considered spending the night in one of the guest quarters or bedding down in an unlikely place, such as the laundry. But if he was not safe in this third-floor redoubt, no haven existed anywhere within these walls.

Briefly he considered decamping to a hotel, but indignation at these violations of his privacy swiftly swelled into a righteous anger. He had not lived through a heart transplant only to run like a frightened child from a tormentor whose pranks were sophisticated in execution but insipid in concept, the kind of psycho-movie crap that made teenage girls scream in terror and delight.

Denied a gun, he went into the retreat to choose a knife.

The under-counter refrigerator contained not only soft drinks and bottled water, but also items on which he sometimes snacked: a variety of cheeses, a few pieces of fresh fruit.

A drawer in the bar cabinet contained utensils, including flatware and knives. There were a paring knife to peel the fruit, a standard kitchen knife with an eight-inch blade, and a more pointed knife with a serrated edge.

He chose the kitchen knife and returned with it to the bedroom. He placed it under the pillow beside his, on which Samantha had not rested her head in a long time.

Reclining against his mound of pillows, he switched on the TV but pressed MUTE. He watched a sitcom that was no funnier silent than it would have been with sound.

His mind relentlessly circled a disturbing corollary. If people were conspiring to torment and possibly to harm him now, then the conspiracy he had suspected *before* his transplant, which eventually he had pretty much dismissed as imaginary, had almost surely been real.

An element of that conspiracy had been the possibility that his cardiomyopathy had been the consequence of poisoning. So if he had been poisoned *then*, he should assume that he would be poisoned again, that his new heart would be destroyed like his first.

If that was true, he probably had been poisoned already. Trusting his new staff, he had eaten and drunk what they served.

He wondered how long after poisoning the heart-muscle damage manifested.

Of course the staff might be innocent. If some stranger could come and go from the house at will, undetected, the ingredients of Ryan's meals might have been poisoned without the involvement of the Amorys or their assistants.

An alternative assumption and corollary demanded consideration. If the perceived conspiracy and poisoning *before* his transplant had been imagined, then the current incidents might be imagined, too.

Indeed, he had nothing—not the raincoat-hooded presence on video, not the pendant, not the candy—to prove that any of these recent, taunting incidents had occurred.

Before his transplant, he had been on three medications that Dr. Gupta prescribed. Post-surgery, he took twenty-eight. If a drug or combination of drugs could, as a side effect, induce paranoid delusions and hallucinations, he was at greater risk now than he'd been a year previous.

But he knew that he was not delusional. He *knew* he was not.

Simmering anger instead of fear, determination to be the hunter instead of the prey, kept Ryan's mind circling around the puzzle in an alternately widening and shrinking gyre, circling in search of a single loose thread that when plucked would unravel the mystery into truth.

Bafflement hardened into frustration, until he wanted to scream to vent his exasperation. Instead, he picked up Samantha's book for distraction.

Earlier in the day, he had reached the twenty-seventh of sixty-six chapters in his third reading of the novel. Now, within a single paragraph, Sam's prose again bewitched him.

Once, while working on the book, she had spoken of subtext. He knew what that was—the underlying, implicit meaning of the story, which the writer never directly expressed. Not all works of fiction had subtext; perhaps most did not.

Samantha said that readers did not need to be consciously aware of the subtext to enjoy a story fully, because if the tale had been told well, they would subconsciously absorb the implicit meaning. In fact, the emotional effect of the subtext frequently could be more powerful when the reader was not able to put it into words, when it slammed him hard without his quite understanding by what he had been slammed.

Subtext could be layered, she said, implicit meanings spread one over another like the delicate layers in phyllo, that flaky pastry used in Greek and Middle Eastern desserts.

Ryan thought he understood her novel's primary subtext. But he sensed other layers, the meaning of which he could not infer.

More important, this mattered to him because in those depths of the tale, he sensed a waiting revelation that could explain why they remained apart although they loved each other. Why she had not at once accepted his proposal of marriage. And why she might never accept it.

The revelation was so elusive, however, that he might as well have been a fisherman casting a line without either a hook or bait, seeking a fish that never needed to eat.

Eventually he put the book aside and watched the muted TV, which he'd never turned off. Horsemen raced across desert plains, through purple sage, past weather-carved red rocks, under a vastness of sky, furiously firing guns, but without the clatter of hooves or the crack of shots, without a single savage human cry.

He listened to the house, waiting for a footfall, for the rustle of a garment, for the *snick* of his stolen pistol being cocked, for his name whispered by a voice that he would not recognize but that his heart would know.

He had lived too long with the fear of death to be kept awake by that alone. Eventually he grew sleepy.

He hoped to dream. He had not dreamed in a year. He welcomed even the bad dreams that had plagued him, for the texture they would give to sleep.

THIRTY-EIGHT

The poster in the bookstore window featured a photo of Samantha and the jacket of her novel. A headline announced that she would be signing copies from noon until two o'clock, this date.

Ryan had noticed the sign days ago. On seeing it, he thought he should not come here, but he knew he would.

Now he carried with him the copy that he purchased on the day the novel first appeared on store shelves. He wanted more than a signature.

Since he'd been here the last time, a smaller poster had been added beside the first: NEW YORK TIMES BESTSELLER!

He had not known that the book was such a success.

A sudden set of emotions swelled through him,

not one after another, but every wave at once. He was proud of her, so proud he felt like buttonholing passersby to assure them that she was unique and kind and worthy of success, but also pierced by regret that he had not been with her when she heard the news or when she got her first good review, and twisted by a guilt that he could not name, yet he also caught a wave that seemed more like happiness than anything he had felt in a long time.

Under the bestseller announcement, the smaller poster featured a reproduction of the most recent Sunday's *New York Times Book Review* hardcover bestseller list. Among fifteen titles, the ninth had been circled in red. In Sam's debut appearance on the list, she cracked the top ten.

"Sonofabitch," he said, "way to go," and he was grinning. "Way to go, you did it."

Excitement effervesced in Ryan, and he tried to think of a way—the *best* way—to memorialize this moment, this triumph. But then he realized that the bestseller list would not be news to Sam, as it was to him, that she had already celebrated this success and no doubt others.

He had come ten minutes before the scheduled conclusion of her signing. Through the store window, he saw a line of people waiting to get to the table at which Samantha sat, and he knew she would stay late, until she signed all their copies.

Even from a distance, the sight of Sam proved that

his new heart possessed all the capacity of the old one.

Suddenly concerned that she would glance up and see him with his face pressed to the window, that he would appear pathetic, he turned away from the bookstore.

He considered retreating to his car in the mall parking lot and waiting half an hour before returning. He worried he would miss her.

Here and there on the open-air promenade, benches provided weary shoppers with places to rest between bouts of spending. Enormous terra-cotta pots overflowing with red ivy geraniums flanked the bench on which Ryan sat.

For a few minutes, he tried to read Samantha's book, but with the prospect of meeting her, he grew too nervous to concentrate. And he had too much respect for her work, even on the third reading—especially because it *deserved* a third reading—to give it less than his full attention.

Here in the middle of California's four-month rainy season, with a new storm predicted to move in overnight, a temporary reprieve from miserable weather had been granted. A transparent sky, as bright and smooth as glass, cast reflections of silver sunshine on the southern coast.

Ryan watched small birds policing a restaurant patio for crumbs, numerous breeds of dogs on leashes and each one grinning with delight at every sight and scent, a tandem stroller with two pink babies in crocheted yellow tams and yellow-and-blue suits and yellow booties with blue pompons on the toes.

Putting aside for the moment the troubles of the last two days, he was glad for life, and he tried not to worry about how much more—or little—of it might be coming to him.

At 2:40, Samantha stepped out of the bookstore in the company of a cheerful-seeming woman in red shoes and a tartan-plaid dress, with jubilant masses of bouncing chestnut-brown curls and a way with extravagant gestures that, from a distance, made her appear to be declaiming Shakespeare.

Ryan's courage sank at the prospect of approaching Sam when she was in the company of a publicity agent or a publisher's rep. But evidently, the gesticulating woman was the bookstore manager, or at least a clerk, for after shaking Sam's hand, clapping her twice on the shoulder, and seeming to pretend for a moment to whirl a lasso above her head, she went back inside.

Not yet having seen Ryan, Sam walked in his direction, digging in her purse for something, perhaps car keys.

She wore an exquisitely tailored black pantsuit and white blouse with black piping. Trim, lithe, fashionable, she moved with the brisk confidence that would have identified her if he had unexpectedly seen her at a distance in the street.

Approaching her, he forgot every opening line he had practiced and could say only, "Sam," and she looked up as her right hand came out of the purse with a bristling bunch of keys.

They had not seen each other in more than ten months and had not spoken in seven.

He did not know what her reaction would be, and he was prepared for a strained smile or a pained grimace, a few impatient words and a brisk dismissal.

Instead, he saw something in her eyes that hurt him more deeply than would have anger or loathing. Although it might not quite be pity with which she regarded him, it was close.

He was grateful for her smile. As lovely as it was, however, it had an unmistakable melancholy aspect. "Ryan."

"Hello, Sam."

"Look at you. How are you doing?"

"I'm all right. I feel good."

She said, "You look like always."

"Not if you could see the humongous scar," he assured her, tapping his chest. He realized at once that he had said the wrong thing, so he quickly added, "Congratulations on the book."

She ducked her head almost shyly. "All I've proved so far is I'm at least a one-hit wonder."

"Not you. You've got the right stuff, Sam. You're working on a second, aren't you?"

"Sure. Yeah." She shrugged. "But you never know."

"Hey, number nine on the list."

"We've learned it rises to seven next week."

"That's wonderful. You'll go to the top."

She shook her head. "John Grisham doesn't have anything to worry about."

Holding up the copy he had brought with him, he said, "I've read it twice. I'm reading it again. I knew it would be good, Samantha, but I didn't expect it to be such—"

As he reached for words of praise, he discovered only surfing lingo would be adequate to express his admiration.

"—such a fully macking behemoth, pure rolling thunder."

The melancholy in her smile remained in her soft laugh. "We'll have to quote that on the paperback."

Although he yearned to put his arms around her, he restrained himself, unwilling to risk that she would stiffen in the embrace or shrink from him.

Trying for a smaller grace, indicating the bench flanked by ivy geraniums, he said, "Could we sit for a few minutes? I'd like to talk to you about it."

He expected her to plead an imminent appointment, but she said, "Sure. The sun is so nice."

On the bench, they sat angled toward each other and, riffling the pages of the novel, he said, "You never showed me this in progress, so I never could have anticipated . . ."

"I never share what I'm writing while I'm writing

it. Not with anyone. I wish I could. It's a lonely process."

"I've been thinking about subtext."

"Never think about it too much. The magic goes."

"This book is phyllo pastry," he said.

"You think so?"

"Totally. Implicit meanings. I'll never see them all."

"Feeling them's enough."

"Forget the phyllo."

"It's a flaky analogy anyway."

He said, "It's more like the sea. Thermal strata that descend forever, schooling sunfish in this one, and under the sunfish are clouds of luminescent plankton, under the plankton krill, and on and on, light playing down through the layers but shadows rising. And down there somewhere there's something of you, a mysterious other you. I mean . . . another side of you, a quality I never recognized."

She did not at once respond, and he thought that somehow he had offended her or had sounded so jejune that she was embarrassed for him, but then she said, "What quality?"

"I don't know. I can't get my mind around it yet. But I have this feeling that when I do, when I understand that part of you . . . I'll know why you couldn't accept my proposal."

She regarded him with such tenderness that he could hardly bear the weight of it.

"Sam," he pressed, "is what I feel possible? Is there something in this book that will tell me what it was I didn't have that you needed most?"

"I suppose there could be. There is. Though I didn't write it to enlighten you."

"I understand."

"But inevitably, I'm in it. All of me, down there under the luminescent plankton."

The melancholy of her smile was a deeper sorrow than before.

He glanced around, wondering if passersby were alert to the small drama on this bench. Sam was already something of a literary celebrity, and he did not want to discomfit her by making any kind of scene.

The shoppers hurried past unaware, self-amused children giggled, young couples hand-in-hand drifted by in mutual infatuation, and only an Irish setter on a leash looked alertly at Ryan and Sam as though catching the scent of distress, but it was pulled along by a man in khaki shorts and Birkenstocks.

"Sam, you know, I wish you'd just tell me what it was I didn't have."

"During all the time we were together, I tried to tell you."

He frowned. "Was I that dense?"

With the gentlest regret, she said, "It's not a thing you discuss like halitosis or table manners, Ryan. It's not a thing you can acquire overnight just because you know I need it. And the worst would be to fake it because you think it's wanted."

"So how was I supposed to know what it was, what you needed—by subtext?"

"Yes. By subtext. The implicit meaning of how I lived my life, what I felt, what mattered to me."

"Sam, I'm lost."

Revealing a pain at which her melancholy had only hinted, she said, "Sweetie, I know. I know you are, I know, and it breaks my heart."

He risked reaching out to her, and she took his hand, for which his gratitude was too great to be expressed.

"Sam, if I read the book enough to get it, to understand what you needed that I didn't have, and if I can be that for you, whatever it is, can we try again?"

She gripped his hand tightly, as though she wanted to hold fast to him forever. Nevertheless, she said, "It's too late, Ryan. I wish it weren't, but it is."

"Is there . . . someone else?"

"No. There hasn't been, not a single date this whole year, and I've been fine alone, I didn't want anything else. Maybe one day there will be someone. I don't know."

"But you loved me. I know you did. You can't just stop loving someone from one day to the next."

"I never stopped," she said.

Those three words, with such potential to exhilarate him, instead disheartened because her voice conveyed with them a quiet yet intense grief, an anguish, with which wives spoke of their recently deceased husbands, for whom their love would henceforth be unrequited.

"I love you," she said. "But I can't be in love with you."

Frustrated, he said, "You're parsing words."

"I'm not. There's a difference."

"Not enough to matter."

"Everything matters, Ryan. Everything."

"Please tell me what I've done."

She looked stricken. "No. Oh, God, no."

Her reaction seemed out of proportion to his question, which after all was just another way of asking what she needed that he had not recognized.

The sharp emotion of her response implied that they were at the hard point on which the lever of their relationship was balanced, the point on which it had turned from light to dark, from hope to hopelessness.

Designing software, running a business, you learned to recognize lever-point moments, to bear down on them and by bearing down to lift the whole enterprise over an impediment and swing it toward success.

"Please tell me," Ryan pressed. "Tell me what I've done."

Her hand tightened on his so fiercely that her grip

hurt him and her fingernails gouged almost to the point of drawing blood.

"Love you and yet talk about it? Face to face? Impossible."

"But if you love me, you want to get past this as much as I do."

"There is no getting past it."

"We will get past it," he insisted.

"I don't want to destroy everything."

"Destroy what? What's left if we don't try?"

"The year we had together when so much was right."

"That can't be destroyed, Sam."

"Oh, yes, it can. By talking about *this*."

"But if we just—"

"And nothing to be gained now. Nothing to be set right by words. Nothing to be *prevented*."

He opened his mouth to speak.

She stopped him before his inhalation escaped him as another breath of pleading words. "No. Let me keep loving you. And let me remember the time when I was in love with you, let me have that forever."

Because Ryan was so abashed at the purity of her passion, at the realization that she had loved him more entirely than he perhaps had the capacity to understand, and because still he did not know what need he had failed to fill, what mistake he had made, he could reply with only two words.

Once more, she stopped him before he could speak. "Don't say you're lost. Don't say it again." Her eyes were lustrous with grief and her voice tremulous. "It's true. I accept it's true, and that's why I can't bear to hear it again. I just can't, Winky."

She pulled her hand from his, not angrily but with a quiet desperation, got to her feet, hesitated as if she might change her mind and sit again, but then turned and walked away.

For fear of chasing after her, Ryan remained on the bench, in the glassy sunshine, the red ivy geraniums as colorful as a Tiffany lampshade, the shop windows a blur of glare, the arcs of water in a fountain shimmering like Steuben and splashing into the receiving pool with a bright, brittle, shattering sound.

Eventually he noticed the young Asian woman standing twenty feet away, in front of the bookstore. She appeared to be watching him, and must have seen him with Samantha.

She held in both hands perhaps half a dozen stems of pale-pink lilies rising from a cone of florist-shop cellophane tied with a blue ribbon.

Concerned that she might be an admirer of Samantha's book and, intrigued by his tête-à-tête with the author, might approach him to discuss the novel, Ryan rose from the bench. He could only tell this woman that he was lost, and she, too, would be unable to help him.

THIRTY-NINE

The winters of the past half decade had been among the chilliest on record for California, though temperatures that made a local reach for a sweater might seem like picnic weather to anyone in Maine or Michigan. With two hours of unseasonably balmy daylight remaining, Saturday crowds strolled the sprawling open-air mall, more to bask in the sun and to people-watch than to shop.

At one time, these multitudes would have energized Ryan, and he would have found the scene engaging. Now they made him edgy.

Recuperation from transplant surgery had required a period of calm and quiet. Thereafter, he avoided crowds, out of concern his immunosuppressant drugs would make him vulnerable to colds and flu that might be hard to shake. Eventually he spent more time at home not because of medical necessity but because he had come for the time being to prefer solitary pursuits.

This throng did not push or jostle, but wandered the mall maze at a relaxed pace. Yet these people seemed like crushing legions, a buzzing swarm, an alien species that would sweep him along to some inescapable hive. As he made his way toward the parking lot, he resisted a plein-air claustrophobia that, had he surrendered to it, would have sent him running pell-mell for open space.

Crammed with vehicles, the enormous parking lot was largely still and quiet. By this tail-end of the afternoon, most people who intended to come to the mall had already arrived; and with two hours of window-shopping weather remaining, few were ready to go home.

As he found the row in which he had parked, as he walked toward the farther end where he had left his deuce coupe, Ryan dwelt on the look in Samantha's eyes. He thought she pitied him, but now in his misery, he suspected it had been something even worse than pity.

Pity is pain felt at seeing the distress of others, joined with a desire to help. But Samantha could not help him; she made it clear that she could not. What he had seen in her eyes seemed more like commiseration, which might be as tender as pity, but was a compassion for the hopeless, for those who could not be reached or relieved.

The sun oppressed him, the glare of windshields, the heat rising from parked cars, the scent of tar wafting up from the hot blacktop, and he wanted to be home in the cool of the solarium.

"Hello," said a voice behind him. "Hello, hello."

He turned to discover the Asian woman with the bouquet of pale-pink lilies. She was in her twenties, petite, strikingly pretty, with long glossy black hair, not fully Asian but Eurasian, with celadon eyes.

"You know her, you know the author," she said, her English without accent.

If he was too short with her, his rudeness would reflect on Sam, so he said, "Yes. I know her. Used to know her."

"She is a very good writer, so talented."

"Yes, she certainly is. I wish I had her talent."

"So compassionate," the woman said, stepping closer and with her glance indicating the book he carried.

"I'm sorry," Ryan said, "but I'm afraid I have to be somewhere, I'm late."

"A remarkable book, full of such insights."

"Yes, it is, but I'm late."

Holding the lilies with both hands, she thrust them toward him. "Here. I can see the sorrow between you and her, you need these more than I do."

Startled, he said, "Oh, no, I can't take them."

"Please do, you must," she said, pushing them against his chest with such insistence that one heavy bloom broke off its stem and fell to the blacktop.

With pungent pollen from the stamens abrasive in his nostrils, nonplussed, Ryan said, "No, see, I'm not going anywhere that I'll be able to put them in water."

"Here, here, you must," she said, and if he had not taken the crackling cellophane cone in his free hand, she would have let the flowers fall to the ground.

Although he had accepted the lilies, he tried to pass them back to her.

He felt suddenly that he had been scorched, a line of fire searing along his left side. An instant later a sharper pain followed the hot shock of laceration—and only then he saw the switchblade knife.

As the lilies and the book dropped from Ryan's hands, the woman said, "I can kill you any time I want."

Stunned, clutching at his wound, Ryan collapsed back against a Ford Explorer.

She turned and walked away at a brisk pace toward the parallel row of cars, but she did not run.

The blade had been so sharp, it slit his shirt without pulling the threads, as cleanly as a straight razor slashing through one sheet of newspaper.

Reaching cross-body, right hand slick with blood, he frantically traced the wound. It was not ragged enough to be a laceration, more like an incision, about four inches long, too shallow to require stitches, not mortal, just a warning cut, but deep enough to have discernible lips.

He looked up and saw that, as petite as she was, she would swiftly disappear through the crowded rows of cars, perhaps in one of which she would escape.

Shock had silenced him. Now that he thought to shout for help, he could summon only a wheeze.

Looking for someone to call to his aid, Ryan surveyed the surrounding lot. In the distance, two cars moved away along the trunk road from which the rows of parking spaces branched. He saw three people on foot, but none nearby.

The woman with the knife vanished among the vehicles, as if she liquefied into the glass glare, into the heat rising off blacktop.

Ryan possessed his full voice now, but only cursed quietly, having had time for second thoughts about making a public spectacle of himself. Anyway, she was gone, beyond finding.

He crushed a few lilies underfoot, without intention, as he made his way to the dropped book, which he plucked off the pavement with his clean hand.

At his '32 Ford coupe, perspiration dripped off his brow onto the trunk lid as he fumbled in a pants pocket for his keys. He had broken out in a sweat that had nothing to do with the warm day.

In the trunk he kept a tool kit for road repairs.

With it were a moving blanket, a few clean chamois cloths, a roll of paper towels, and bottled water, among other items.

He stuffed a chamois through the tear in his shirt and pressed it to the wound, clutching his arm to his side to hold the cloth in place.

After he washed his bloody hand with bottled water, he half opened the folded moving blanket and draped it over the driver's seat.

A Chevy Tahoe cruised along the parking lane, but Ryan didn't hail the driver. He wanted only to get out of there and home.

He heard her voice in memory: *I can kill you any time I want.*

Having been excited by the drawing of his blood, maybe she would decide she needed to come back and kill him now.

The Ford single overhead cam 427, built solely for racing, had enough torque to rock the car as it idled. Behind the engine was a Ford C-6 transmission with 2,500-rpm stall converter.

Leaving the parking lot, Ryan was tempted to take the streets as if they were the race lanes of a Grand Prix, but he stayed at the posted speed limits, loath to be pulled over by the police.

The car was not a classic but a hot rod, totally customized, and Ryan had hands-free phone technology aboard. His cell rang, and even in his current state of mind, he automatically accepted the call. "Hello."

The woman who had slashed him said, "How is the pain?"

"What do you want?"

"Do you never listen?"

"What do you *want*?"

"How could I make it any clearer?"

"Who are you?"

"I am the voice of the lilies."

Angrily, he said, "Make sense."

"They toil not, neither do they spin."

"I said sense, not nonsense. Is Lee there? Is Kay?"

"The Tings?" She laughed softly. "Do you think this is about them?"

"You know them, huh? Yeah, you know them."

"I know everything about you, who you fire and who you use."

"I gave them two years' severance. I treated them well."

"You think this has to do with the Tings because my eyes are slanted like theirs? It has nothing to do with them."

"Then tell me what this is about."

"You know what it's about. You know."

"If I knew, you wouldn't have gotten close enough to cut me."

A red traffic light forced him to stop. The car rocked, and under the blood-soaked chamois, the stinging incision pulsed in time with the idling engine.

"Are you really so stupid?" she asked.

"I have a right to know."

"You have a right to die," she said.

He thought at once of Spencer Barghest in Las Vegas and the collection of preserved cadavers. But he had never found a connection between Dr. Death and anything that happened sixteen months previous.

"I'm not stupid," he said. "I know you want something. Everyone wants something. I have money, a lot of it. I can give you anything you want."

"If not stupid," she said, "then grotesquely ignorant. At best, grotesquely ignorant."

"Tell me what you want," he insisted.

"Your heart belongs to me. I want it back."

The irrationality of her demand left Ryan unable to respond.

"Your heart. Your heart belongs to me," the woman repeated, and she began to cry.

As he listened to her weeping, Ryan suspected that reason would not save him from her, that she was insane and driven by an obsession that he could never understand.

"Your heart belongs to me."

"All right," he replied softly, wanting to calm her.

"To me, to *me*. It is *my* heart, my precious heart, and I want it back."

She hung up.

A horn sounded behind him. The traffic light had changed from red to green.

Instead of pressing on, Ryan pulled to the side of the road and put the car in park.

Using the *69 function, he tried to ring back the weeping woman. Eventually the attempted call brought only a recorded phone-company message requesting that he either hang up or key in a number.

When he had a break in traffic, Ryan drove back into the street.

The sky was high and clear, an inverted empty bowl, but the forecast called for rain late Sunday morning, continuing until at least Monday afternoon. When the bowl was full and spilling, she would come. In the dark and rain, hooded, she would come, and like a ghost, she would not be kept out by locks.

FORTY

Ryan parked the deuce coupe and got out, relieved to find the garage deserted. Standing at the open car door, he withdrew the blood-soaked chamois from inside his shirt, dropped it on the quilted blanket that protected the driver's seat, and pressed a clean cloth over the wound.

Quickly, he folded the bloody chamois into the blanket, held the blanket under his left arm, against his side, and went into the house. He rode the elevator to the top floor and reached the refuge of the master suite without encountering anyone.

He put the blanket aside, intending to bag it later and throw it in the trash.

In the bathroom, he washed the wound with alcohol. Subsequently he applied iodine.

He almost relished the stinging. The pain cleared his head.

Because the cut was shallow, a thick styptic cream stopped the bleeding. After a while, he gently wiped the excess cream away and spread on Neosporin.

The rote task of dressing the wound both focused him on his peril and freed his mind to think through what must happen next.

To the Neosporin, he stuck thin gauze pads. Once he had applied adhesive tape at right angles to the incision, to help keep the lips of it together, he ran longer strips parallel to the wound, to secure the shorter lengths of tape.

The pain had diminished to a faint throbbing.

He changed into soft black jeans and a black sweater-shirt with a spread collar.

The master-retreat bar included a little wine storage. He opened a ten-year-old bottle of Opus One and filled a Riedel glass almost to the brim.

Employing the intercom, he informed Mrs. Amory that he would turn down the bed himself this evening and that he would take dinner in the master suite. He wanted steak, and he asked that the food-service cart be left on the penthouse landing at seven o'clock.

At a quarter till five, he called his best number for Dr. Dougal Hobb in Beverly Hills. On a weekend, he expected to get a physicians' service, which he did. He left his name and number and stressed that he was a transplant patient with an emergency situation.

Sitting at the amboina-wood desk, he switched on the plasma TV in the entertainment center and muted the sound, staring at 1930s gangsters firing noiseless machine guns from silent black cars that glided around sharp corners without the bark of brakes or rubber.

Having drunk a third of the wine in the glass, he held his right hand in front of his face. It hardly trembled anymore.

He changed channels and watched an uncharacteristically taciturn Russell Crowe captain a soundless sailing ship through a furious but silent storm.

Eleven minutes after Ryan had spoken to the physicians' service, Dr. Hobb returned his call.

"I'm sorry if I alarmed you, Doctor. There's no physical crisis. But it's no less important that you help me with something."

As concerned as ever, with no indication of ill temper, Hobb said, "I'm always on call, Ryan. Never hesitate if you need me. As I warned you, no matter how well the recovery goes, emotional problems can develop suddenly."

"I wish it were that simple."

"The phone numbers of the therapists I gave you a year ago are still current, but if you've misplaced them—"

"This isn't an emotional problem, Doctor. This is . . . I don't know what to call it."

"Then explain it to me."

"I'd rather not right now. But here's the thing—I've got to know who was the donor of my heart."

"But you do know, Ryan. A schoolteacher who suffered massive head trauma in an accident."

"Yeah, I know that much. She was twenty-six, would be twenty-seven now, going on twenty-eight. But I need a good photograph of her."

For a beat, Hobb was as silent as Russell Crowe's ship when it plowed through hushed seas so terrible that sailors were lashed to their duty stations to avoid being washed overboard.

Then the surgeon said, "Ryan, the best man on that list of therapists is Sidney—"

"No therapist, Dr. Hobb. A photo."

"But really—"

"A photo and a name, Dr. Hobb. Please. This is so important."

"Ryan, some families prefer the recipients of their loved one's organs to know who gave them the gift of life."

"That's all I want."

"*But* many other families prefer that they—and the donor—remain anonymous. They want no thanks, and their grief is private."

"I understand, Doctor. And in most cases I would respect that position. But this is an extraordinary situation."

"With all due respect, it's unreasonable to—"

"I'm in a position where I can't take no for an answer. I really can't. I just can't."

"Ryan, I'm the surgeon who removed her heart and transplanted it to you, and even I'm not privy to her name. The family wants its privacy."

"Somebody in the medical system knows her name and can find her next of kin. I just want a chance to ask the family to change their minds."

"Perhaps it was the donor's explicit condition that her name not be revealed. The family may feel morally powerless to override the wishes of the deceased."

Ryan took a deep breath. "Not to be indelicate, Doctor, but with the jet fees and medical expenses, I've spent a million six hundred thousand, and I'll need expensive follow-up care all my life."

"Ryan, this is awkward. And not like you."

"No, wait. Please understand. Every penny this cost me was well spent, no charge was excessive. I'm *alive*, after all. I'm just trying to put this in perspective. With all the costs, no insurance, I'd still like to offer five hundred thousand to her family if they'll provide her photo and her name."

"My God," Hobb said.

"They may be offended," Ryan said. "I think you are. They may tell me to go to hell. Or you will. But it's not that I think I can buy anything I want. It's just . . . I'm in a corner. I'll be grateful to anyone who can help me, who has the decency and mercy to help me."

Dougal Hobb, the storm-tossed sailing ship, and Ryan shared a long silence, as if the surgeon were mentally cutting open the situation to explore it further.

Then Hobb said, "I could try to help you, Ryan. But I can't fly blind. If I knew at least *something* about your problem..."

Ryan reached for an explanation with which the physician might not be able to sympathize but to which he might accord a higher value than the absolute privacy of the donor's family.

"Call it a spiritual crisis, Doctor. That she died and I lived, though she was certainly a better person than I am. I know myself well enough to be sure of that. And so it haunts me. I'm not able to sleep. I'm exhausted. I need to... to be able to properly honor her."

After another incisive silence, the surgeon said, "You don't mean to honor her in a public way."

"No, sir. I don't. The media never got wind of my illness, the transplant. I don't want my health problems to be public knowledge."

"You mean honor her... say, as a Catholic might honor someone by having a Mass said for her."

"Yes. That's what I mean."

"Are you a Catholic, Ryan?"

"No, Doctor. But that's the kind of thing I mean."

"There's someone I could talk to," Hobb acknowledged. "He has the full file on the donor. He could put the question before them. Before the family."

"I would be grateful. You can't know how grateful."

"They might be willing to provide a photograph. Even a first name. But if the family doesn't want you to have her last name or contact information for them, would you be satisfied?"

"The photo would be enormously . . . comforting. Anything they can do for me. I'd be grateful for anything."

"This is highly unusual," Hobb said. "But I must admit it's happened before. And we resolved it that time. It all depends on the family."

The woman with the lilies wanted to torment Ryan, to carve his nerves to ribbons before she put a sharp blade through his heart. Before further violence, she would most likely give him at least a day to consider the shallow incision in his side, to anticipate his next wound.

Night and rain were her allies. Twenty-four hours from now, she would have the collaboration of both.

"One more thing, Doctor. The photo and whatever else the family will share—I need it as soon as possible. Twelve hours or sooner would be ideal."

If Dougal Hobb whetted his scalpel on those words, he decided not to cut with it. After a silence, he said only, "Spiritual crises often last years, even a lifetime. There's usually not an urgency about them."

"This one is different," Ryan said. "Thank you for your help and your thoughtfulness, Doctor."

FORTY-ONE

The filet mignon cut like butter.

As he ate, Ryan wondered about the woman's expertise with the switchblade. She maneuvered him with the lilies, inflicting precisely the wound she intended.

Had she cut deeper, he would have needed medical assistance. She sliced shallow enough to leave him with the option of treating the wound himself—and evidently expected that he would.

Although she might prove herself a killer when the time came, she remained for now a death tease. She wanted this game to last, inflicting the maximum psychological torture before gutting him—if gutting was the only thing she had in mind.

The confidence and delicacy with which she wielded the knife might have been learned on the street, but Ryan suspected she was not anything as common as a gang girl. The bloody business in the shopping-mall parking lot had been not butchery but switchblade ballet.

Unsettling as the encounter had been, he was glad for it.

As recently as the previous evening, he had required himself to consider the possibility that these new incidents—the hooded watcher in the rain of whom no security-camera proof existed, the tiny candy hearts and the inscribed gold heart pendant, which were no longer in his possession—were delusional, as the strange events more than a year earlier had evidently been delusional, and were related to his current battery of twenty-eight medications.

He had rejected that possibility, which of course had been his subjective and perhaps unreliable opinion. The wound in his left side counted as objective proof sufficient to settle the issue.

After dinner, he returned the food-service cart, with the dirty dishes, to the landing, and buzzed Mrs. Amory to retrieve it.

For an hour, he nursed a second glass of Opus One and paged through Samantha's novel, spot-reading passages, as other men in a crisis might open the Bible at random and read verses in the hope of receiving divine guidance.

At nine o'clock, he went to the Crestron panel embedded in the wall of the master-suite foyer and accessed the security cameras. He toured all the interior hallways, and when he found every one of them dark, he assumed the Amorys had retired to their private quarters for the night.

On the lowest floor of the house, in the service hall that led to the laundry, he unlocked the storage room that he had visited the previous evening, and quietly closed the door behind him. He unlocked the tall metal cabinet that contained the security-camera recorders, and he switched on the monitor.

Back then, when he had first reviewed the recording that should have captured the hooded figure in the rain, the phantom's absence rattled him. At that time, of course, he had not yet been confronted by a switchblade diva, and still had reason to wonder if his outré experiences owed anything to pharmaceuticals.

In that frame of mind, he had not been a sufficiently analytical observer of the video. He'd been looking for what was manifestly not there, when perhaps he should have been studying what *was* to be seen.

Now he selected the first south-lawn camera recording taken at twilight, more than forty-eight hours earlier. He watched it in real time, because a lot of details flew past unnoticed in a fast-forward replay.

Again the drizzle, the slithering shapes of fog, the deodars, and the fading light provided an atmospheric backdrop against which no hooded figure appeared, though Ryan had seen it twice that night.

Something about the lazy coiling and twining of the serpentine bands of fog struck him as curious. When he reversed the twilight to watch it be imposed again upon the day, a moment came when the fog *twitched*. Following the twitch, the meandering mist repeated the exact movement it had made moments earlier.

He reversed a minute, pushed PLAY, and saw that a piece of the recording had been cloned to fill in for something deleted. Further in the twilight, a second piece of cloned video occurred—when the hooded intruder should have walked out of the deodars.

In the lower-right corner of the screen, accompanying the duplicated video, the timer flashed the seconds in continuous sequence, without repeating the count that went with the original segment. The hacker who had done this was a wizard with the system and a demon for detail.

For a while, Ryan reran the cloned bits—the first forty-nine seconds long, the second thirty-one seconds—thinking through the implications of this discovery.

A day had passed between the time he saw the hooded intruder and when he first reviewed the security-camera video. Someone could have tampered with it in the interim.

But last night, before reviewing the recording of this twilight, he had raced down here in pajamas and bathrobe to see who might have entered and departed the master suite to put the heart pendant on his pillow. The deletion of that person from the penthouse-landing video and the replacement of the incriminating segment with cloned images had to have been done immediately in the wake of action, as the intruder was still on the move.

This suggested that the woman with the lilies worked with at least one partner. Assuming she was the one who repeatedly violated the master suite, her backup had been tied in by computer to the security system—most likely from somewhere inside the house—busily deleting her image from video as soon as she passed out of frame.

She could no longer be considered a psycho loner. The conspiracy theory, previously a sieve, suddenly held water.

More important, the capabilities of those aligned against Ryan were impressive, and suggested depth of support.

Finally he possessed evidence. Without witnesses to the attack, he was unable to prove that the cut in his side hadn't happened in an accident. But cloned images on a security recording couldn't be accidental.

This was not much evidence by police standards. But he had no intention of turning to the police until he knew the motives of the conspirators—and perhaps not even then.

The woman with the switchblade claimed to want him dead, and he believed that her intention was indeed eventually to kill him. Her motive, however, remained a mystery.

The Wilson Mott operative, Cathy Sienna, had listed five roots of violence: lust, envy, anger, avarice, vengeance. She had referred to them as failings rather than motives, but they were motives all right. As with anyone intent on murder, more than one might apply.

As Ryan was about to switch off the monitor, the image on the screen flickered and changed. Instead of a view from any security camera inside or outside the house, there appeared a glistening, viscous mass, red and marbled and blue-veined and throbbing, like a menace discovered inside a cracked-open meteor in an old science-fiction movie.

For an instant Ryan had no idea what the thing might be, and then he realized this was video of a beating human heart and its attendant structures, inside an open human chest.

Although he did not touch the remote control, the screen divided into quadrants representing cameras at different locations around the estate—presenting the same gruesome video. A moment later, four other camera views flashed on the screen, all featuring the throbbing heart, and then four more, and four more. . . .

This was not a real-time event, not a mutilation occurring on the estate, but instead an educational film of open-heart surgery. The surgeon's hands entered the shot, and the camera pulled back to show the surgical team.

The security system cycled through all the cameras, and then again, faster and still faster, until the images passed in such a frenzy that the action in the documentary could not be followed. The monitor went dark.

From the racked array of magnetic-disk recorders in the cabinet arose the distress cries of electronics in death throes. Then silence—and on every piece of equipment, the indicator lights went dark.

Ryan didn't need to call in tech support to know that the system had crashed, that the standard thirty days of preserved recordings had been wiped, and that he no longer possessed evidence of security-video tampering.

FORTY-TWO

In the master retreat, Ryan pulled open a desk drawer, fingered through folders in a hanging file, and located the one containing the photo of Teresa Reach, which he had removed from the album in Spencer Barghest's study.

Prior to the diagnosis of cardiomyopathy that he had received from Dr. Gupta almost sixteen months earlier, he had been convinced that in this photograph he would discover a clue that would lead him to an explanation of the strange events occurring at that time.

Ultimately his obsessive analysis of the photo revealed nothing useful. Eventually he decided there had been no conspiracy against him, no poisoning, only innocent coincidences that seemed mysterious and meaningful because of his suspicious nature and because ill health affected his clarity of mind.

Perhaps the time had come to look at Teresa again.

He no longer had the workstation that Mott had provided for the enhancement and analysis of the photograph. His unassisted eyes would have to be enough.

As he sat at the desk, the phone rang: his most private line. Caller ID provided no identity.

When he picked up the handset, the woman with the lilies said, "Review the activity in your checking account. You'll discover you made a hundred-thousand-dollar wire transfer as a donation for cardiovascular research. I imagine a financial loss is to you more painful than a knife wound."

Instead of playing her game, he said, "Who are you people?"

"There are not people. There is me."

"Liar. You have institutional capabilities. Big backup."

"Whoever I am, you're dead."

"Not yet," he said, and hung up.

※

Be to do. Not: Be to be done to. Seize the moment. Act, don't react. Catch the wave, shoot the curl, skeg it, nail it, don't be nailed, exist to *live,* never exist to exist. Existence is an entrance, not an exit. To be or not to be is not the question.

Ryan toured the great house, turning lights on as he went, turning them off in his wake, seeing little of the rooms through which he roamed, seeing instead the place that he had come from: the roaches crawling and the roaches of another kind pinched in an ashtray, the posters of Katmandu and Khartoum, journeys never made because Dad's daily head trips to more exotic realms take the travel money, take the rent money, so sometimes a trip to Vegas in the van, with Mom and the man, whatever man at the moment might be the man that her main man can never be, the high spirits on the eastward drive, the hard light of the vast desert and the light talk of big money, betting systems and card-counting schemes, bottles of Dos Equis to pass the miles, the groping in the front seat while in the back of the van you pretend deafness, pretend sleep, pretend death, pretend never to have been born; sometimes being left alone in casino parking lots at night, hiding in the back of the van because when you sit up front where you can be seen, strange people rap on the window and sweet-talk you—vampires, you figure— and try to get you to unlock the door, and then the cheap motel, always the same cheap motel, where you wait in the van while Mom and the man of the moment spend "quality time" together; a day later or two, the drive westward, the desperate talk about money, the bitter accusations, the rest stop where one of them hits her and she hits back, and you try to stop it, but you're small and weak, and then he does something to her right there in the open, and you have to walk away, away into the hot dry land, walk toward home, you can't watch, but you can't walk hundreds of miles, so when they pull up beside you in the van, you have to get in the back, and they're up front *laughing*, like nothing happened, and then it's all the way home, the desert without beauty in this direction, the Mojave a vast dirty ashtray, Mom and the man talking about the next time, scoring big the next time, refine the system, practice the card count-ing, all the way home to Dad and Katmandu and Khartoum and the roaches and the roaches and the next man of the moment.

When he had walked the house twice, Ryan re-turned to the master suite, where he did not bother to lock the door.

Certain that he would be tormented considerably more before the next attack came, he did not put a knife under his pillow.

Dr. Hobb had advised him to drink only sparingly because alcohol might interfere with the absorption and diminish the effectiveness of some of his twenty-eight medications. He poured a third glass of Opus One.

Ryan sat in bed with Samantha's book. He fell

asleep while reading, and he dreamed of the events of her novel, relived vivid moments of the story.

These were strange dreams because he never appeared in the cast, and because all through the night he expected each scene to shimmer as if it were a reflection on water, to shimmer and to part as a previously hidden presence rose out of the depths of subtext and turned upon him a blank and pitiless stare.

At 8:14 he was awakened by a call from Dr. Dougal Hobb. The surgeon had already received from the family an e-mailed photograph of their daughter, whose heart now beat in Ryan's breast.

"As I foresaw, they were willing to give you her first name, as well, but not the family name," Hobb said. "And after I explained that you were anguished, having what you described as a spiritual crisis, they refused compensation."

"That's . . . unexpected," Ryan said. "I'm grateful."

"They're good people, Ryan. Good, decent people. Which is why you have to swear to me you will not write or speak publicly about this poor girl, using either the photo or her name. As good as these people are, I would nevertheless not be surprised—and wouldn't blame them—if they sued you for violation of their privacy."

"The photo, her name—they're just for me," Ryan assured him.

"I am e-mailing everything to you as we speak."

"And, Doctor...thank you for taking my request to heart and acting on it so quickly."

Instead of going down to his study on the second floor, Ryan used the laptop and the compact printer in the master suite to open and print out the surgeon's e-mail.

Except for a slightly different hair style, the heart donor proved to be a dead ringer for the woman with the switchblade.

Her name had been Lily.

FORTY-THREE

Her raised chin, her set mouth, her forthright gaze suggested more than mere confidence, perhaps defiance.

Sitting at the desk in the retreat, studying the photo of Lily, Ryan knew this must be the twin of the woman who assaulted him.

I am the voice of the lilies.

He put the photo of Lily X beside the picture of Teresa Reach. The black-haired Eurasian beauty, the golden-haired beauty, the first vibrantly alive in the photo but dead now, the second dead even when photographed, both victims of automobile accidents, both having been diagnosed as brain-dead, one assisted into death by Spencer Barghest, the other by Dr. Hobb when he harvested her heart, each with a twin who survived her.

The longer Ryan considered the two photos, the more uneasy he grew, because it seemed that before him lay a terrible truth that continued to elude him and that in time, when he least expected, would hit him with the power of a tsunami.

Not long after meeting Samantha, Ryan had read a great deal about identical twins. In particular, he recalled that the survivor, separated from an identical by tragedy, often felt unjustified guilt as well as grief.

He wondered if Lily's twin had been driving the car in which she had suffered the catastrophic head trauma. Her guilt would then be to a degree justified, and her grief intensified.

The longer he compared the photos, the more clearly he recalled how certain he had been, sixteen months ago, that the image of Teresa held the answer to the mysteries then plaguing him. That intuition began to prickle his spine again, the apprehension that she was the key not only to what had happened to him sixteen months earlier but also to everything that was happening now.

Ryan had exhaustively analyzed Teresa's photo and had found no detail that could be called a clue. Laboriously repeating that analysis was not likely to lead him to any eureka moment.

But perhaps the photo itself did not contain the revelation. Maybe the importance of the photo was who had taken it or where he had found it, or *how* she had been assisted out of life, by what means and under exactly what circumstances—details that might be contained in Barghest's written accounts, if they could be found, of the suicides that he had made possible.

At 9:45, Ryan placed a call to Wilson Mott, who as always was pleased to hear from him.

"I'll be flying to Las Vegas this afternoon," Ryan said. "The people who worked with me there last year—George Zane and Cathy Sienna—are they available now?"

"Yes, they're available. But neither of them is based in Nevada. They work out of our Los Angeles office."

"They can fly with me," Ryan said.

"I think it's more appropriate if they don't use your Learjet. We have our own transport. Besides, if they have to make appointments and preparations for you, they need to be there at least a few hours in advance."

"Yes, more appropriate. All right. If you recall, the last time I had two appointments."

"I've got the file in front of me," said Mott. "You had business with two individuals at separate locations."

"It's the gentleman that I'll need to repeat," Ryan said. "And rather urgently."

"We'll do our best," Mott said.

Ryan hung up.

He put the photos of the two dead women in the manila envelope.

Unbidden, an image came into his mind's eye: the hospital room in which he had stayed the night before the transplant, the floor and walls and furniture polished not by anyone's hand but by the effect of the sedative he had been given, even the shadows glossy, Wally Dunnaman at the window, the chrome-yellow night of the city beyond, and the air shivering with the crash of bells.

Standing in the warm master retreat, beside the elegant amboina desk, Ryan Perry began to tremble, then to shake, and dread overtook him. He asked himself *what* he dreaded, and he did not know, although he suspected that soon he would be provided with the answer.

P
A
R
T

3

A dirge for her the doubly dead
in that she died so young.

—*Edgar Allan Poe*, "Lenore"

FORTY-FOUR

Late Sunday afternoon in Las Vegas, the low sky looked as gray as the face of a degenerate gambler standing up from a baccarat table after being busted to bankruptcy.

The high Mojave lay in the grip of a chill. Down from the bald faces of the mountains, down from the abandoned iron and lead mines long forgotten, off the broken slopes of pyrite canyons and feldspar ravines, across desiccated desert flats, through the bright barrens of the casinos came a damp wind, not yet strong enough to whip clouds of dust off sere and empty lots or to shake nesting rats out of the lush crowns of phoenix palms, but sure to swell stronger as the day waned.

At the private-plane terminal, George Zane waited

with a twelve-cylinder black Mercedes sedan. The man looked even more powerful than the muscle car.

As he opened the rear door for Ryan, he said, "Good afternoon, Mr. Perry."

"Good to see you again, George. Got some bad weather coming."

"Whether we need it or not," the big man replied.

In the car, as they turned onto the airport-exit road, Ryan said, "Do you know if Barghest is going to be out tonight? Will we be able to get into his place?"

"We're headed straight there," Zane said. "Turns out he drove to Reno for some kook conference, won't be back until Wednesday."

"Kook conference?"

"That's what I call it. Bunch of our best and brightest getting together to talk about the benefits of reducing human population to five hundred million."

"What's that—six billion people gone? How do they figure to make that happen?"

"Oh," Zane said, "from what I read, they've got a slew of ways figured out to get the job done. Their problem is selling the program to the rest of us."

At an intersection, a few sheets of a newspaper were airborne on the breeze, billowing to full spreads, gliding slowly in a wide spiral, their flight as ponderous as that of albatrosses circling in search of doomed ships.

"Shouldn't we wait a couple hours, until after dark?" Ryan wondered.

"Always looks less suspicious to go in during daylight if you can," Zane said. "Straight on and bold is better."

The neighborhood appeared even more conventional in daylight than it had been at night: simple ranch houses, gliders and swings on the porches, well-kept yards, basketball hoops above garage doors, an American flag here and there.

Dr. Death's house looked as ordinary as any residence on the street—which made Ryan wonder what might be in some of the other houses.

As Zane swung the Mercedes into the driveway, the garage door rose. He drove inside, where earlier he had dropped off Cathy Sienna and where now she stood at the connecting door to the house.

As the garage door rolled down, she greeted Ryan with a professional smile and a handshake. He had forgotten how direct her stare was: granite-gray eyes so steady that she seemed to challenge the world to show her anything that could make her flinch.

She said, "I didn't realize you enjoyed yourself so much the last time."

"It wasn't as much fun as Disneyland, but it was memorable."

"This Barghest," George Zane said, "gives crazy a bad name."

In the kitchen, Ryan explained that he wanted them to look for places in which Dr. Death might have taken special pains to hide his files of assisted suicides. Trapdoors under carpets, false backs in cabinets, that sort of thing.

Meanwhile, he would be once more reviewing the ring binders full of photographs of dead faces.

Judging by the portion of the house that Ryan passed through, the connoisseur had not added to his macabre collection; it was a relief to discover the home office still contained no cadaver art.

Evidently, even Barghest needed a refuge where dead eyes were not fixed upon him.

A third ring binder stood on the bookshelf beside the two that had been there sixteen months earlier. Ryan took it down first and stood paging quickly through it, half expecting to be startled by a familiar face.

Of the eleven recent photographs in the new album, the oldest appeared to be of a man in his seventies. The youngest showed a fair-haired boy with delicate features, his blue eyes taped open, no older than seven or eight.

A windowpane rattled softly and rising wind soughed in the eaves. Something fluttered in the attic, perhaps a roosting bird.

Eleven assisted deaths in sixteen months. This ferrier had poled across the Styx with some regularity.

Ryan returned the album to the bookshelf, retrieved the original two ring binders, and carried them to the desk.

Having gone directly to the shelves on entering the room, he had not noticed the familiar book on the desk. A copy of Samantha's novel lay facedown.

Staring at Sam's jacket photo, Ryan settled in the office chair. He hesitated to inspect the book.

When finally he picked it up, he turned to the half-title page, then to the full-title. He was relieved to find no inscription from the author, no signature.

Paging through, he discovered notations in the margins, petty criticisms, some of them vulgar enough to sicken him. He read only a few before closing the book in disgust.

Understandably, Spencer Barghest would have been interested enough in the novel to buy a copy. He'd been in a relationship with Sam's mother for at least six years. And he had in some way assisted her twin sister, Teresa, out of this world, which was either a noble act of compassion or cold-blooded murder, depending on your point of view.

The point of view that mattered most was Teresa's, but given the shortage of reliable mediums these days, the authorities were not likely to obtain a deposition from her.

Putting the book aside, Ryan turned next to the first ring binder. Sixteen months earlier, none of these faces in this album had meant anything to him. He was curious to see if that would be the case again or if he might have overlooked something the first time.

Perhaps his personal journey over the past year had sharpened his sensitivity to suffering, because these faces affected him more profoundly than before. They remained death portraits, but on this second viewing, he was more poignantly aware that they were *people*, even in death each of their faces alive with character.

If he had missed anything important the first time through the binder, he missed it again—and did not have the courage to review it a third time.

The second album was the one from which he had extracted the photo of Teresa that had obsessed him. He had sat here, mesmerized by the reflections in her eyes—until Cathy Sienna had stepped in from the hall to say the house was giving her the creeps.

Ryan had agreed and, assuming that the discovery of Teresa's death portrait was the lodestone that had drawn him here, he had closed the ring binder and returned it to the shelf.

Now he found the third plastic sleeve still empty. Perhaps Barghest had not discovered that Teresa's photo was missing.

Twelve sleeves farther into the album, he came across someone he knew. He closed his eyes in disbelief.

If it belonged in this sick collection at all, surely this face should be in the third ring binder, the new one, among the portraits of the people to whom Barghest had evidently ministered since Ryan's previous visit. *Impossible* that it belonged with the faces of those who had been unfortunate enough to come under his care *years* ago.

Heart knocking harder than it had when Lily's sister had cut him in the parking lot, Ryan opened his eyes and found that he had not mistakenly identified the woman in the photograph.

I'm here. I'm watchin' over you. You'll be just fine.

The smooth dark skin.

Don't hold your breath, honey.

The emerald-green eyes.

You hear him, don't you, child?

Twelve sleeves after Teresa, who had been dead six years, was Ismay Clemm, one of the two cardiology nurses who had assisted Dr. Gupta with the myocardial biopsy.

FORTY-FIVE

The rising wind choked and wheezed in the eaves, as if words were caught in its throat, and in frustration thrashed the branches of the melaleucas beyond the study window.

Sixteen months ago, sitting in this room, Ryan had been certain he stood at the threshold of a discovery that would strip bare the lurid details of the conspiracy against him. Now the same conviction gripped him.

The first time around, upon finding Teresa's photo, he thought he had before him the essential piece of the puzzle. Already half obsessed with the perfection of Samantha's face, he was at once riveted by its perfect duplicate. Seeing the six-year-old death portrait mere hours after having risen from the bed of a lover whose countenance, as she slept, matched the dead face detail for detail, Ryan had been struck by an intense awareness of the eternal presence of death in life that at first disoriented him and then led him to focus on Teresa as the hub from which all the recent weirdness had radiated.

Teresa Reach, however, could neither complete the puzzle nor even contribute to its solution. She was not part of the web that unknown others seemed to be spinning around Ryan.

He couldn't properly call her a red herring, because no one had planted her photograph in the ring binder with the intention of misdirecting him. In his eagerness to seize the moment, to act, he had raced to the conclusion that her presence in this collection of faces was the illuminating thing he had come to Las Vegas to discover.

But here, sixteen months and twelve pages later in the album, a greater astonishment and the true key lay before him: Ismay Clemm, the fiftysomething cardiology nurse, who had not only assisted with the myocardial biopsy but also had checked on him repeatedly, after the procedure, when he had been on the bed in the prep room, sleeping off the lingering effects of the sedative.

There, he had for the first time experienced the dreams that for a while plagued him: the black lake, the haunted palace, the city in the sea. As much as anything, those repetitive nightmares—and the paranoia that they reinforced, the suspicion of being drugged or poisoned that they enflamed—had motivated him to make that first trip to Vegas while waiting for Dr. Gupta to report the results of the biopsy.

Although Ryan now knew beyond doubt that Ismay Clemm was the pivot point on which he could turn from confusion to clarity, he paged through the rest of the ring binder, studying faces. He needed to be certain he did not make the same mistake now that he had made when he leaped to the conclusion that Teresa would be the key to the door of truth.

The remaining faces were those of strangers. He returned to the nurse. Not Ismay, surely. Ismay's other.

If these events had a theme, it was identical twins. Samantha and Teresa. Lily and her deranged sister with the switchblade.

Ryan heard a rapping, but it was Zane or Sienna in another room, sounding out a wall for indications of a hidden cache.

He had no idea in what town Ismay Clemm lived. Because her name was unusual, Ryan used his cell to avail himself of a new information service that searched for listings not by city but by area code. He could find no number for Ismay in either the 949 or 714 areas, which might only mean that her phone was unlisted.

At four o'clock on a Sunday afternoon, reaching Dr. Gupta to ask after Nurse Clemm would be difficult. Getting to him on a weekday would be no easier.

A year ago, after discovering that his patient had been under the care of Dr. Dougal Hobb for more than a month, Dr. Gupta had sent Ryan's records to Hobb, and a curt note to Ryan expressing dismay that he had not been informed sooner of this decision. He was not likely to take or return a call.

As a consequence of all this, Ryan had changed internists, as well. He moved from Forry Stafford to Dr. Larry Kleinman, who offered a concierge medical practice.

He considered calling Kleinman's 24/7 contact number to ask if the doctor would be willing to seek from the hospital the name of the other cardiology nurse who had assisted Gupta in the biopsy that day. But as he stared at the death portrait of Ismay's twin, he remembered the lean nurse whose body fat was less than a cricket's. Whippit. No. Whipset. First name Kara or Karla.

Of the Whipsets that he found in the 949 area code, one had a first name similar to what he recalled. He recognized it at once: Kyra.

He placed the call, and she answered on the third ring.

After he identified himself and apologized for intruding on her privacy and on her Sunday, Ryan said, "I'm hoping you might know how I can get in touch with Ismay Clemm."

"I'm sorry. Who?"

"The other nurse who assisted in the procedure that day."

"Other nurse?" Kyra Whipset said.

"Ismay Clemm. I very much need to talk to her."

"I don't know anyone by that name."

"But she assisted during the biopsy."

"I was the only nurse on the procedure, Mr. Perry."

"A black woman. Very pleasant face. Unusual dark-green eyes."

"I don't know anyone like that."

"Could she have been . . . assisting unofficially?"

"I think I would remember. Anyway, it's not done."

"But she was there," he insisted.

His conviction made Nurse Whipset uncertain. "But how did she assist, what did she do?"

"When the first tissue sample was taken, she told me not to hold my breath."

"That's it? That's the extent of it?"

"No. She also . . . she monitored my pulse."

"How do you mean?"

"Well, she stood beside the examination table, holding my wrist, checking on my pulse."

With a note of bewilderment, Kyra Whipset said, "But throughout the procedure, you were hooked up to an electrocardiograph."

He tried to recall. The memory wouldn't clarify.

Nurse Whipset said, "An electrocardiograph with

a video display. A machine monitored your heart activity, Mr. Perry."

Ryan remembered the fluoroscope on which he had watched the tedious progress of the catheter as it followed his jugular vein into his heart.

He could not recall an electrocardiograph. He could not say for certain that she was wrong, and he had no reason to suspect that she might lie to him. But what he remembered instead of the ECG was Ismay Clemm.

"After the procedure, I had to lie down on the bed in the prep room, to let the sedative wear off. She checked in on me a few times. She was very kind."

"I looked in on you a few times, Mr. Perry. You were dozing."

Staring at the death portrait in the ring binder, he said, "But I remember her clearly. Ismay Clemm. I can see her face now."

"Can you spell the name for me?" Nurse Whipset asked.

After he spelled it, she spelled it back to him to make sure she had gotten it right.

"Listen," she said, "I suppose it's possible for some reason she briefly visited the diagnostics lab during the procedure, and I was too busy to pay much attention to her, but she made an impression on you."

"She made an impression," he assured Kyra Whipset.

"Because of the sedative, you might not recall it

clearly. Your memory might have exaggerated her time in the room, the level of her involvement."

He did not disagree with her, but he knew it had not been that way, not that way at all.

"So," she said, "give me a number where I can reach you. I'll make a couple of calls to people at the hospital, see who knows this woman. Maybe I can get contact information for you."

"I'd appreciate that. Very kind of you," he said, and gave her his cell number.

▌

Rap-rap-rapping: George Zane and Cathy Sienna testing walls, testing cabinets.

Ryan removed Ismay Clemm's death portrait from the plastic sleeve in the ring binder and put it on the desk.

The sharpening wind was a scalpel now, stripping the skin off every tract of bare land it found. Beyond the window, trees shuddered in clouds of yellow dust, in the acid-yellow light of late afternoon.

From the manila envelope that he had brought with him, Ryan took the photos of Teresa Reach and Lily X. He lined them up with the death portrait of the woman who looked like Ismay Clemm.

He knew now a disquiet that was different in character from any he had known before.

This journey had taken him from dead-center in the realm of reason, where he had lived his entire life, to the outer precincts, where the air was thinner and the light less revealing. He stood on the borderline between everything he had been and a new way of being that he dared not contemplate.

He had half a mind to return two photos to the ring binders and leave at once with just the picture of Lily.

The problem with that was—he had nowhere to go except home, where sooner or later he would be slit open and have his heart cut out of him again, this time without anesthetics.

After a while, the air acquired a faint alkaline taste from the dust-choked wind that relentlessly groaned and snuffled at the windows.

When eventually Ryan's cell phone rang, the caller was not Kyra Whipset, but a woman named Wanda June Siedel, who said that she was calling on Nurse Whipset's behalf.

"She says you want to know about Ismay Clemm."

"Yes," Ryan said. "She was . . . very kind to me at a difficult time in my life."

"That sounds like Ismay, all right. Sure does. She and me were eight years best friends, and I don't expect ever to know somebody sweeter."

"Ms. Siedel, I'd very much like to talk with Nurse Clemm."

"You call me Wanda June, son. I would sure like to talk to Ismay myself, but I'm sorry to tell you, she's passed on."

Gazing at the nurse's photo on the desk, Ryan avoided for the moment his most important question. Instead he said, "What happened?"

"To be blunt, she married wrong. Her first husband, Reggie, he was a saint to hear Ismay tell it, and I expect he must have been if half her stories about him were true. But Reggie, he died when Ismay was forty. She married again seven years later, that was to Alvin, which is why she came here and I ever met her. She loved Alvin in spite of himself, but he never set well with me. They made it eight and a half years, then she fell backwards off a convenient stepladder and smashed the back of her skull bad on some convenient concrete."

When Wanda June did not continue, Ryan said, "Convenient, huh?"

"Son, don't take me wrong on this. I'm making no accusations, have no intention to smirch anyone's reputation. Lord knows, I'm no policeman, never even watched them CSI shows, and there was plenty of policemen on Ismay's case, so it's got to be that they knew what they were doing when they called it an accident. Can't be but crazed with grief and loneliness why Alvin took up with another woman just a month after Ismay's gone. Crazed with grief and loneliness, crazed by the estate money and the insurance money, poor crazed and lonely Alvin."

"She died in the fall, Wanda June?"

"No, no, son, they did some powerful surgery on

her, and she had brain swelling bad for a time, didn't know who she was, but she came around, she had fortitude and the Lord. No memory of the convenient stepladder or the convenient concrete, but she was getting back all the rest of herself, she got to be Ismay again. She was in a rehab hospital, working on some left-arm paralysis, which she was nearly shed of, when she was slammed by a convenient massive heart attack, while poor Alvin was visiting her with some friend of his, them alone in the room with Ismay and the door shut, and that was just one convenience too many for Ismay, God bless and keep her."

"I'm sorry for your loss, Wanda June. I can hear in your voice how close you were to her." He asked the most important question: "When did Ismay die?"

"It was three years ago this past Christmas Eve. Alvin, he was bringing her a gift, this beautiful silk scarf, which I guess was so beautiful it gave her a heart attack, which is comforting to think that beauty was what did her in, 'cause it wouldn't have been anyway convenient if the heart attack didn't happen and somebody then had to strangle her accidentally with the scarf."

If Wanda June Siedel could be believed, Ismay Clemm had died twenty-one months prior to the myocardial biopsy during which Ryan had met her.

He sat listening to the angry yellow wind, the gears of his mind having ground to a halt on the thought-obstructing fact that had just been thrown into them.

Wanda June didn't need encouragement to continue: "Ismay, she met Alvin on a Christian Internet site, which right there is some contradiction, the Internet being the devil's playground. If Ismay hadn't gone on the Internet, she wouldn't ever met Alvin, she would still be out there in Denver with her sister, which means she and me never would have been friends, but I'd rather never known her than her be dead before her time."

"Denver," Ryan said.

"That's where she was born, lived as a girl, and then married to Reggie. She moved here to Newport, to Costa Mesa actually, she was forty-seven, because Alvin had a job here, such as it was, and so she got on with the hospital."

"And her sister—she's still alive?"

"The sister, Ismena, she didn't marry Alvin, she doesn't do e-mail let alone Internet, so she's still not fallen off a stepladder or swallowed a silk scarf or anything, she's doing fine, she's a sweetheart like Ismay."

Reason might have returned to the universe. If there was a sister, an explanation might exist that would comport with the world of laws and logic with which Ryan was comfortable.

"So you've stayed in touch with Ismena," he said.

"Ismena Moon, that's the maiden name, Alvin was

a Clemm. Ismena and me write each other, talk on the phone some."

"She still lives in Denver?"

"She does, she lives in the very house Ismay and Reggie owned, bought it away from Ismay once Ismay up and married the supposedly Christian Alvin, not that it's my place to question anyone's faith, stepladder or no stepladder."

"Wanda June, what did Kyra Whipset tell you about me?"

"Didn't even talk to her. She just knew somebody who knew me and knew I was friends with Ismay. They said you'd been impressed by her or something, would I call you."

"As I said earlier, Ismay was very kind to me at a terrible time in my life. I wanted to . . . to repay that kindness. But I didn't know she had passed on."

"Son, I would love to hear that story, her kindness, what she did for you, put it in my Ismay-memory book."

"I'll tell you sometime, Wanda June. I promise. But right now, I was hoping you might put me in touch with her sister, Ismena."

"Ismena misses Ismay so terrible, she would enjoy a polite young man like you with something good to say about the late lamented. I'll give you her number."

FORTY-SIX

In the Mercedes sedan, on the return trip to the airport, George Zane drove, Cathy Sienna rode shotgun, and Ryan slouched in the back, slowly shuffling again and again through the photographs of the three women—Teresa, Lily, Ismay—each of them having been one half of a set of identical twins, each of them with a living sister.

According to Samantha, good stories had deep texture. They acquired texture in numerous ways. The texture of character faults and virtues, of intentions contrasted with actions, of personal philosophy shaped by backstory, of mannerisms and habits, of contrasts and contradictions, of mundanities and eccentricities, of points of view and styles of speech. The texture of vivid visual images, of smells that came off the page, of sounds that resonated in the mind's ear, of metaphor and simile. She could list dozens of sources for narrative texture. Ryan couldn't remember them all.

In the texture, you began to see patterns. Some were patterns of plot, which you could think of as like the center lines on a highway and the guardrails at its extremes, there to be sure that you got to your destination without getting lost in byways of meaningless event. Others were patterns of the obvious theme, to give the story purpose that made it meaningful, in part just as the rules of construction for a sonnet gave it meaning, in part just as the truth of human suffering in a blues song made it worth singing.

The most difficult patterns of all to understand, the most intriguing, and usually the most ominous were those that arose from subtext, not from the surface theme but from the implicit meaning of the tale. The less you thought about those patterns, the more you understood them, for they were the patterns of primal truths, some of which the modern mind rejected on a conscious level.

Studying the photos of the three dead women, brooding about their living sisters, Ryan suspected that this pattern of twins, though seemingly the key to the plot, rose more from subtext and that the more intently he focused on it, the farther he traveled from the revelation he sought.

The yellow wind made pendulums of the traffic

lights suspended over intersections, tore dead fronds off tall palm trees, harried tumbleweed out of vacant lots and along busy streets, buffeted the car, hissed at the windows, and in general made such an exhibition of its power that a pagan might have cast basketfuls of flower petals into it as an offering, to solicit exemption from the miseries of the coming storm.

Returning the photographs to the envelope, he said, "George, Cathy, I'm flying out to Denver from here. I don't know that I'll really need anyone with me, but there's a longshot that I may have a security issue. I'd feel a lot more comfortable with someone who had a license to carry."

"We're both cool to carry in Colorado," Zane said, "and Cathy has all the gun training that I have. Fact is, she may be the better shot."

"I'll lay twenty to one on that," she said.

Ryan asked, "Are you up for Colorado, Cathy?"

"I only brought one change of clothes in my overnight bag."

"That's all you'll need. We'll be going back to California tomorrow."

In truth, it didn't seem likely that Ismena Moon, a fifty-eight-year-old woman described as a sweetheart, would prove to be a threat to Ryan's physical safety.

He wanted someone with him more for company

than protection. He had been something of a loner the past year, and solitude had taken its toll.

Denver in particular seemed to be a dangerous place for him to be alone. On his previous visit, he had arrived confused, as he would be arriving this time, and he had departed confounded, in a condition close to despair.

Besides, since he had first seen Cathy this afternoon in Spencer Barghest's garage, Ryan had felt there was a question he wanted to ask her. Needed to ask her. A question of considerable importance. He just didn't know what it might be. He sensed the question half-formed in the back of his mind. Perhaps it would fully coalesce in Denver.

Forty minutes out of Las Vegas, high over Utah, above the weather and bound for Colorado, Ryan excused himself and went to the lavatory.

He dropped to his knees and threw up in the toilet. He had developed a nervous stomach awaiting takeoff, and it had grown worse in flight.

At the sink, he rinsed out his mouth twice and washed his hands. He was struck by the paleness of his fingers, as white as bone.

When he looked at his face in the mirror, he found that it was paler than his hands, his lips without color.

Reluctantly he met his eyes and for some reason

thought of Alvin Clemm and the convenient step-ladder, the convenient concrete, the silk scarf and the convenient heart attack.

His legs grew weak, and he sat on the toilet. His hands were shaking. He clasped them, hoping one would steady the other.

He didn't know when he had gotten up to wash his hands again. He found himself at the sink, scrubbing.

He was sitting on the toilet again when he heard a rapping, which quickened his heart until he realized this really was a hand upon a door.

"Are you all right?" asked Cathy Sienna.

"I'm sorry," he said. "Yes. I'm sorry."

"You're okay?"

"A little airsickness," he explained.

"Do you need anything?"

"Just a minute. Give me a minute."

She went away.

Airsickness wasn't the correct diagnosis. He was sick with fear about what he would find on the ground, in Denver, in the house of Ismena Moon, which had once been the house of Ismay.

FORTY-SEVEN

Leaving stars behind, and moon, they descended through deep clouds, a white boil at the portholes, and then Denver appeared below, sparkling in the clear night air.

In flight, Ryan had phoned Ismena, telling her only that her late sister had done a kindness for him that he'd never forgotten and, as he was in Denver, he would like to stop by and find out more about Ismay. After Ismena welcomed their visit, Ryan had arranged for a Cadillac Escalade, which awaited them at the airport.

The January night was so bleak that his cold hands felt warm by comparison. His breath plumed from him, curls of vapor lingering for brief moments before deliquescing into the still air.

His stomach was settled, but not his nerves, and

after they put their two small pieces of luggage in the back of the Escalade, he asked Cathy Sienna to drive. In the passenger seat, he read Ismena's address from a notepad on which he had written it, and Cathy keyed it into the navigator.

She drove well, handling the big SUV as if she had put fifty thousand miles on it before this. Ryan suspected that she was good not merely with a gun and a car but also with just about any machine or tool, good with things because she preferred them to people.

The very act of driving brought a slight unconscious smile to her. Although she usually guarded her expressions closely, her face was not a mask at this moment, but relaxed as Ryan had not before seen it.

"Do I need to know who this woman is, why we're here?" she asked.

He told her only about Ismay Clemm's kindness to him during the myocardial biopsy—and then that he had this day learned the nurse had died twenty-one months before he met her.

Of the reactions he expected from Cathy, she exhibited none. The faint smile remained, and she kept her eyes on the road, as if he had said nothing more surprising than that, judging by the lowering sky, snow would soon fall.

"Twenty-one months. What do you make of that?" she asked.

"Ismena and Ismay are identical twins."

"So you—what?—think it was Ismena at the biopsy?"

"Maybe. Probably."

"But she was using Ismay's name? Why would she?"

"That's one thing I want to find out."

"I guess you would."

He waited for her to say something more. She drove in silence, and only spoke to say "Yes, ma'am," each time the computerized voice of the navigation system gave her an instruction.

For her line of work, Cathy had been trained to listen carefully to what a client needed to tell her about his problems and to have no curiosity about any portion of his story that he failed to disclose. But her ability to feign disinterest in this case seemed almost superhuman.

As the navigator announced a final turn to the left coming in three hundred yards, Ryan recognized the park with the aspen trees and the church beside it.

"Pull over," he said. "I know this place. If her house is just around the corner, we can walk from here."

Their jackets were not heavy enough for the weather, but the air remained still, with no wind-chill factor. Hands in their pockets, they walked first into the park.

The aspens had shed their leaves for winter. The

smooth bare limbs described pale geometries against the night sky.

A recent snow, not yet despoiled by children's boots, mantled the grass, and the brick walkways wound like channels of dark water through the whiteness.

"I was here once," he told Cathy, "sixteen months ago."

She walked with him and waited.

"That time, I had the most powerful experience of deja vu. The air was as still then as now, but the aspens were whispering, as they always do when they're leafed out. And I thought how much I'd always loved that sound—and then realized I'd never heard it before."

A lamppost spilled light upon an iron bench. Icicles depended from the front skirt of the bench, and ice glazed the bricks directly under them.

"Sitting on this bench, I became convinced I'd sat here many times in the past, in all seasons and kinds of weather. And I felt the most powerful nostalgic sense of . . . of love for this place. Strange, don't you think?"

Again surprising him, she said, "Not really."

Ryan looked at her. Aware of his stare, she did not return it.

"Are you experiencing any of that now?" she asked, gazing up into the aspen architecture.

Shivering, Ryan surveyed the park. "No. It's just a place this time."

They walked to the front steps of St. Gemma's Church, where a bronze lamp in the shape of a bell brightened the oak doors.

"I knew what the church would look like before I went inside. And when I went in . . . I felt I'd returned to a much-loved place."

"Should we pay a visit?"

Although he knew he could not have been located and followed to Colorado so quickly, Ryan imagined that if he went into the church, he would find waiting for him the woman with the lilies and the knife, this time without the lilies.

"No," he said. "It won't feel special now. It'll be like the park—just a place."

His ear lobes began to sting with cold, his eyes watered, and the icy air had a faint ammonia scent that burned in his nostrils.

On the opposite side of the church from the aspen grove lay an expansive cemetery. No fence encircled it, and lampposts flanked a central walk.

"I didn't see this before," he said. "I didn't come this far. When I left the church, I was so . . . spooked, I guess, I just wanted to get back to the hotel. I thought I'd been poisoned."

This statement seemed to strike Cathy Sienna as more peculiar than anything else that he had revealed. As they walked past the cemetery toward the corner, she was first silent, but then said, "Poisoned?"

"Poisoned or drugged with hallucinogenics. It's a long story."

"No matter how long it is, seems to me poisoned-and-drugged is a bigger leap than some other explanation."

"What other explanation?"

She shrugged. "Whatever other explanation you didn't want to consider."

Her answer disturbed Ryan, and suddenly so did the graveyard.

"I'll bet she's buried here," he said.

"You mean Ismay Clemm?"

"Yeah."

"You want to look for her?"

Grimacing at the gravestones in the snow, Ryan said, "No. Not in the dark."

On the first block of the next cross street, houses stood on only one side, facing the cemetery.

The sixth house, a Victorian place with elaborate cornices and window-surround moldings, belonged to Ismena Moon. The porch light welcomed them.

Lace curtains on the mullioned windows and a brass door knocker in the form of a wreathed cherub holding a diadem in both hands suggested the interior style.

A slim handsome woman in her mid-sixties answered the door. She had white hair, a light café-au-lait complexion, and large clear brown eyes. Her sensible black dress shoes with block heels, blue rayon dress with high round neckline and narrow white collar, white cuffs, and gathered sleeves suggested she had recently returned from vespers or another service.

"Good evening, ma'am. I'm Ryan Perry, and this is my associate, Cathy Sienna. We have an appointment to see Ismena Moon."

"That would be me," the woman said. "So pleased to meet you. Come in, come in, you're dressed to catch pneumonia in this weather."

Ismena and Ismay were not identical twins, or twins of any kind.

FORTY-EIGHT

The parlor was high Victorian: floral wallpaper; deep maroon velvet drapes, trimmed and tasseled; lace curtains serving as sheers between the velvet panels; a cast-iron fireplace complete with kettle stand, with a black-and-gold marble surround and mantel; an étagère filled with collectible glass, two Chesterfield sofas, plant stands with ferns, sculpture on pedestals; a side table draped with a maroon cloth covered by a crocheted overlay; and everywhere a fabulous and precisely arranged clutter of porcelain busts, porcelain birds, groupings of ornately framed photographs, and knickknacks of all kinds.

Ismena Moon prepared coffee, which she poured from a Victorian-silver pot, and with which she served a generous selection of exotic cookies that she called biscuits.

While Ryan had been expecting a fifteen-minute meeting in which he might get to the truth of events on the day Dr. Gupta performed a myocardial biopsy, Ismena imagined their visit to be an occasion for socializing, with one of her favorite subjects—her sister, Ismay—as the inspiration for the get-together. She was such a charming woman, and so gracious, that Ryan could not disappoint her.

Besides, his identical-twin theory had deflated as completely as a hot-air balloon lanced by a church steeple. He needed a rational explanation for how a woman dead twenty-one months could have spoken with him on that day. For a moment, when he discovered there was a third sister, Ismana, his hope revived that *she* was Ismay's twin, but she was the oldest of the three, and had died before Ismay.

"I can see how the similarity of the names would lead you to think twins," Ismena said. "But they're all just forms of *Amy*, you see, which was quite a popular name in the Victorian era, with many derivatives. Amia, Amice, Esmee, on and on."

Victoriana, Ismena explained, had fascinated the Moon family going back to their grandfather, Dr. Willard Moon, who had been one of the first black dentists west of the Mississippi, with a patient list of mostly white folks. Ismay had been somewhat less infatuated with all things Victorian than was

Ismena, but like everyone in the Moon family, she had been a great reader, and her favorite books and writers were mostly from the nineteenth century, primarily from the Victorian part of it.

Ismena indicated a book-lined alcove off the parlor, which featured two leather armchairs and reading lamps. "She was never happier than when she was in one of those chairs with a book."

As Ismena had been talking, Ryan had stepped to the alcove to look over the titles on the bookshelves, which included complete collections of Dickens and Wilkie Collins.

Moving along the shelves, he stepped around a white marble bust displayed on a pedestal.

Ismena said, "That was a favorite thing of hers. Of course, she had to have it fixed above the parlor door, exactly as in the poem, but I am definitely not comfortable with a thing that heavy hanging over my head."

"Like in what poem?" Cathy asked.

"'The Raven,'" Ismena said. "Poe was her very favorite, though the poetry more than the stories."

While she spoke, Ryan came to the Poe collection.

Ismena recited the verse from memory: "'And the Raven, never flitting, still is sitting, *still* is sitting / On the pallid bust of Pallas just above my chamber door.'"

The meter of the verse, the compelling repetitions, the rhymes, the alliteration conspired to catch

Ryan's breath for a moment, not because the poem was new to him—it wasn't—and not only because it was lyrical and brilliant, but also because the unmistakable style of Poe, his essential voice, seemed of a piece with the strange events of the past sixteen months.

As he withdrew a volume of Poe's collected poetry from a shelf, a yet more powerful sense of the uncanny overtook Ryan when he heard Cathy, in the spirit of the moment, recite: "'Once upon a midnight dreary, while I pondered, weak and weary, / Over many a quaint and curious volume of forgotten lore—'"

"'—While I nodded, nearly napping, suddenly there came a tapping,'" Ismena continued with delight, "'As of someone gently rapping, rapping at my chamber door.'"

"Not sure I remember," Cathy said, "but maybe . . . ' "'Tis some visitor," I muttered, "tapping at my chamber door—/ Only this and nothing more."' "

"But it wouldn't be only a visitor, would it?" Ismena asked. "Not in one of Mr. Poe's creations."

The rapping.

Ismay had known about the rapping.

After the biopsy, as he dozed in the prep room, she had said to Ryan, *You hear him, don't you, child? Yes, you hear him.*

He didn't understand how she could have known about the rapping, but of course that was not as much of a stumper as how she could have been there almost two years after dying.

You must not listen, child.

Now he opened the volume of verse to a random page—and saw a poem titled "The City in the Sea."

"Ismay knew all of Mr. Poe's verses by heart—except for 'Al Aaraaf.' She just couldn't make herself like that one."

Ryan scanned the early lines of "The City in the Sea," and found something that he felt compelled to read aloud: " 'But light from out the lurid sea / Streams up the turrets silently / Gleams up the pinnacles far and free / Up domes, up spires, up kingly halls / Up fanes, up Babylon-like walls...'"

His voice must have trembled or otherwise betrayed his fear, for Ismena Moon said, "Are you all right, Mr. Perry?"

"I had a dream like this," he said. "More than once."

After scanning more lines, he looked up, realizing that the two women were waiting for him to explain himself.

Rather than elucidate, he said, "Ms. Moon, I see that you have half a dozen copies of Poe's collected poetry."

"Ismay bought it over and over again every time she found a new edition with different illustrations."

"May I pay you for one of them? I'd like it as a...as a memento of Ismay."

"I wouldn't think of accepting a dime," she said. "You take whichever one you like. But you still haven't told me what kindness she did for you that impressed you so much."

Carrying the book, he returned to the Chesterfield on which Cathy sat, and settled there to spin a story peppered with a little of the truth. He set the date of this tale before Ismay's death, did not mention a heart transplant, but instead gave himself a multiple bypass. He told of how afraid he'd been that he was going to die, of how Ismay counseled him so wisely for an hour in the hospital one night, two hours the next night, and how she stayed in touch with him after his release, keeping his spirits up at a time when he would otherwise have fallen into depression.

He must have told the story well, because Ismena was moved to tears. "That's her, all right, that's how Ismay was, always giving."

Cathy Sienna watched him dry-eyed.

Ismena pulled on calf-high boots and a coat, and walked with Ryan and Cathy across the street to the cemetery. She led them to Ismay's grave and focused her flashlight on the headstone.

Ryan thought about how things would have been different from the way they were now if he had found this cemetery and this grave on his previous visit to Denver, before his transplant.

FORTY-NINE

In the Escalade, Ryan was neither in a mood to talk nor capable of thinking of anything to say. Cathy remained professional and uninquisitive.

Painted with reflected city light, mottled black and chrome-yellow, the low sky seemed to be smouldering. Like drifting ashes, snow flurries fluttered across the windshield.

At the hotel, her room was four floors below his. Getting off the elevator, she said, "Dream well," as the doors slid shut between them.

Because he had only an overnight bag, Ryan had not wanted the assistance of a bellman. When Cathy left him alone in the elevator, his stomach turned over, and he felt as if the cab would plunge to the bottom of the shaft.

Instead, it took him to his floor, and he found his suite.

Beyond the windows, Denver rose in a lurid light, as if Ryan had brought the city in the sea with him out of a dream.

Sitting at a desk, he took his medications with a bottle of beer from the honor bar.

When he swallowed the last of two tablets and five capsules, he opened the book of poetry and paged through it from the beginning.

He found a poem titled "The Lake," and it was the wild lake of his dream, lovely in its loneliness, bound all around with black rocks and tall pines.

When he came again upon "The City in the Sea," he read it silently twice, and the final four lines a third time, aloud: " 'And when, amid no earthly moans, / Down, down that town shall settle hence, / Hell, rising from a thousand thrones, / Shall do it reverence.' "

Farther into the volume, he found his third dream in a poem titled "The Haunted Palace."

He could think of no chain of sound reasoning that would explain Ismay Clemm or those dreams that had been inspired by the work of her favorite writer.

As for diving into unreason and conjuring some supernatural explanation, Ryan had no practice swimming in seas of superstition. This seemed to be a dangerous time to take the plunge.

He did not believe in ghosts, but if Ismay had been a ghost with a message to impart, he could not puzzle out her meaning.

He almost put the book down without paging to the end, but he remembered how he had put aside the ring binder in Barghest's study after finding Teresa's photo—delaying for sixteen months the discovery of Ismay Clemm's photo, twelve sleeves later.

The next-to-last poem in the book, titled "The Bells," called to mind something else Ismay had said to him. He heard her admonition now almost as clearly as if she had been here in the hotel room with him.

If you hear the iron bells, you come to me.

Poe's "The Bells" had four sections, and Ryan read them with growing disquiet. The first celebrated the merry bells on Christmas sleighs. The second dealt with the harmony of wedding bells. The third part took a dark turn, describing fire-alarm bells and the human tragedy they could foretell.

The fourth part spoke of iron bells rung by ghouls high in a church, the melancholy menace of their tone.

"'For every sound that floats,'" he read aloud, "'From the rust within their throats / Is a groan.'"

Hearing the words spoken disturbed him more than reading them from the page, and he fell silent.

The extraordinary rhythms, rhymes, and repetitions of the rest of the poem brought back to him the cacophony and the chaos of the ringing bells that had awakened him in the hospital bed on the night before his transplant.

He could see, he could smell, he could hear the room again, Wally at the window, looking down, down, down, into waves of rising sound, a gloss on every surface, even shadows with a shine, and the shiver of the bells in his bones, in his blood, ringing thickly in his blood, and the smell of rust, a red and bitter dust, washing wave after wave, after heavy warning wave.

Finally he put the book aside.

He did not know what to make of any of this. He did not *want* to know what to make of it.

He knew that he would not sleep. Not in his current condition.

But he was desperate for sleep, for dreamless sleep. He could not tolerate being awake.

He did something then of which Dr. Hobb would not have approved, not for him or for any heart-transplant recipient. He raided the honor bar and hammered himself into sleep with a series of gin-and-tonics.

FIFTY

In the Learjet, Ryan at first sat apart from Cathy Sienna. Because he had awakened with a hangover and had needed time to chase off his headache, to settle his stomach with bland food, and to pull himself together, they were late leaving Denver. The runway rush, the lift-off, and the big banking turn across the Rockies had the potential to bring up his breakfast, and he preferred to ride out the start of the trip by himself.

Safely airborne, he went to her. The jet had conference-style seating. He sat facing her, and after concluding a paragraph, she looked up from a magazine.

"You have exceptional self-control," he said.

"Why? Just because I made you wait ten seconds while I finished reading?"

"No. You're self-controlled in every sense. Your pretense of being without curiosity is particularly impressive."

"Mr. Perry, each day, life presents us with much more than we can understand. If I chased after everything that makes me curious, I'd have no time for the part of life I *do* understand."

The flight attendant arrived to ask if they would like a snack or anything to drink. Ryan ordered a bit of the hair of the dog in the form of a Bloody Mary, and Cathy asked for black coffee.

"Anyway," she continued, after the attendant went away, "an understanding of what's important comes to you if you're patient."

"And what's important to you, Cathy?"

She had been holding the magazine, one finger marking her page, as if she expected to return to it in a moment. Now she put it aside.

"No offense, but of the things that are the most important to me, there aren't any that I just talk about with a stranger on a plane to pass the time."

"Are we strangers?"

"Not entirely," was the most that she would give him.

He studied her forthrightly: her lustrous dark hair, her high brow, wide-set and deep eye sockets, nose with a slight endearing crook, that sensuous mouth, proud chin, strong but feminine jaw, and back to her granite-gray eyes that made you feel as if she had rolled you out as thin as phyllo on a cold slab of baker's granite. Although attractive, she lacked the physical perfection of Samantha, yet something about her convinced him that, in profound ways, she was enough like Sam to be her twin, which made him feel comfortable with her.

"A year ago, I had a heart transplant," he said.

She waited.

"I'm glad to be alive. I'm grateful. But . . ."

He hesitated to continue for so long that before he spoke, the flight attendant returned with the Bloody Mary and the coffee.

Once he had the cocktail in hand, he didn't want it. He nestled the glass in a drink holder in the arm of his chair.

As Cathy sipped her coffee, Ryan said, "The heart I received was from a young woman who sustained major head trauma in a car crash."

Cathy knew dead Ismay—or someone pretending to be her—appeared to him prior to the transplant, and she knew that he had experienced one dream, maybe others, related to the nurse. Now Ryan could see her fitting those pieces of knowledge together with smaller bits she knew and others that she might infer, but still she asked no questions.

"Her name was Lily," he continued. "Turns out, she has a sister, an identical twin."

"You were sure Ismay must be a twin."

"I thought identical twins were a theme, I needed

to figure out the meaning of the theme. But maybe twins are just a motif."

His terminology clearly puzzled her, but she said nothing.

"Anyway," he said, "Lily's sister—I think she was driving the car when the accident happened."

"We could find out easily enough. But why does it matter?"

"I think she's eaten with guilt. Guilt that she can't endure. So she's resorting to what psychiatrists call transference."

"Shifting her guilt to you."

"Yes. Because I received Lily's heart, the sister blames me for Lily being dead."

"Is she dangerous?"

"Yes."

"This isn't an issue for private security alone. Call the authorities."

"I'm reluctant to do that."

Her gray eyes now seemed to be the shade of the snow-cloud layer above which they flew, and he could no more see below the surface of her gaze than he could see the land below the storm.

Into her silence, he said, "You're wondering why I'm reluctant. I'm wondering, too."

He looked out the porthole beside him.

Eventually, he said, "I think it's because I'm at least a little bit sympathetic to her, to the way she feels."

And after a further passage between the winter clouds and the fierce blind sun, he said, "Going into this, I didn't realize the emotional weight that accompanies...living with someone else's heart. It's this great gift but...it's a terrible burden, too."

All the time he had been looking out the porthole, she continued to watch him. Now as he turned to her again, she said, "Why should it be a burden?"

"It just is. It's like...you have an obligation to live not just for yourself but also for the one who gave you her heart."

Cathy was silent for so long, her gaze fixed on her mug, that Ryan thought she would pick up the magazine again when she had drunk the last of the coffee.

He said, "The first time we met in Vegas, sixteen months ago, do you remember telling me that I was haunted by my own death, that I felt an ax falling but couldn't figure out who was swinging it?"

"I remember."

"Do you remember helping me to consider my possible enemies by listing the roots of violence?"

"Of course."

"Lust, envy, anger, avarice, and vengeance. The dictionary says avarice is an insatiable greed for riches."

She finished her coffee, put the cup aside, but did not return to the magazine. Instead she met his stare.

Ryan said, "Do you think avarice can be a greed for something other than money?"

"A synonym for *avaricious* is *covetous*. A man can covet anything belonging to another, not just money."

The flight attendant arrived to ask if Cathy wanted more coffee and whether something was wrong with Ryan's Bloody Mary. She took the mug and the glass away.

Following the attendant's departure, Cathy Sienna broke a mutual silence. "Mr. Perry, I need to ask a terrible question. Blunt and direct. Do you want to die?"

"Why would I want to die?"

"Do you?"

"No. Hell no. I'm only thirty-five."

"You do not want to die?" she asked again.

"I'm terrified of dying."

"Then there are steps you've got to take, and you know them. But in addition to going to the authorities, you've got to do more. I think you must make . . . the heroic act."

"What do you mean?"

Instead of answering, she turned to the porthole beside her and stared down upon the field of winter clouds, the barren furrows under which seeded snow was harvested by a hidden world below.

Her skin seemed translucent in the high-altitude light, and when Cathy pressed a few fingers to the glass, Ryan had the strangest notion that, if she wanted, she could reach through that barrier as if it were less substantial than a gauzy membrane, even less solid than the surface tension on a pond.

He did not repeat his question, because he recognized that this withdrawal was different from her other silences, more contemplative and yet more urgent.

When she turned to him again, she said, "You may not have time for the heroic act. To be effective for you, it requires a future of satisfactory works."

The directness of her stare, the tone of her voice, and her earnestness implied that she believed she was speaking plainly to him, her meaning unmistakable.

Confused, Ryan did not at once ask her to clarify, because he recalled what she had said earlier—that understanding comes with patience—and he suspected that any question he asked would be met with the same advice.

"What you need to do," she continued, "is offer yourself as a victim." Perhaps she saw bafflement in his face, for she elaborated. "Suffer for the intentions of others, Mr. Perry. If you have the courage and the stamina, offer yourself as a victim all the rest of your life."

If he'd been required to put into words the course of action that she had just suggested, he could not have made much sense of it. Yet on some deep level of his mind, in some profound recess of his heart, he knew that she had planted a truth in him and that in time he would understand it fully, and only in time.

Without another word, he returned to the seat in which he had been sitting before joining Cathy, and they completed the flight apart from each other.

Crossing Arizona into California, Ryan considered that he did not have to go home, where Lily's sister must be waiting. He could go anywhere, to Rome or Paris, or Tokyo. He could spend the rest of his life on the run in high style and never exhaust his fortune.

Nevertheless, he rode the plane down to southern California, where the day was overcast and the sea choppy in the distance.

On the Tarmac, before going to the limo that Ryan had arranged to transport Cathy back to Los Angeles, she came to him and said, "You remembered what I said about the roots of violence. Do you remember the taproot—always the ultimate and truest motivation?"

"The hatred of truth," he said. "And the enthusiasm for disorder that comes from it."

To his surprise, she put down her small suitcase and hugged him, not in the manner of a woman embracing a man, but with a fierceness that expressed more than affection. She whispered in his ear and then picked up her suitcase and went to the car that waited for her.

In his own limo, leaving the airport, Ryan thought again of escape. They could drive to San Francisco. He could get a new car there and drive himself, next to Portland then east to Boise, down to Salt Lake, to Albuquerque and Amarillo. Spending a night or two in each place, on a perpetual road trip.

His cell phone rang.

He checked the screen. His father was calling.

When Ryan answered, the old man said, "What the shit is going on, kid?"

"Dad?"

"How deep is the shit you're in? Are you gonna drown in it? Am I going down with you, what the *hell*?"

"Dad, take it easy. Calm down. What's happening?"

"Violet is happening, right here, right now, get your ass over here."

For a moment, Ryan thought his father had said *violence* was happening, but when the word registered properly, he repeated it: "Violet."

"What're you doing with a psycho bitch like this, kid? Are you out of your freakin' mind? You get her out of here. You get her out of here now."

Lily and Violet, sisters in life, sisters forever.

FIFTY-ONE

Nearly nine years earlier, Ryan had bought houses for his mother and father—Janice and Jimmy—and put them on monthly allowances. Considering the general indifference with which they raised him and the number of times the indifference was punctuated with craziness and cruelty, he didn't feel that he owed them anything. But he was famous, at least in the business world; the media lived to make a goat of a guy like him, which would be inevitable if they found his parents living in near destitution. Besides, there was a kind of satisfaction in treating them better than they had treated him.

Because Janice and Jimmy divorced when Ryan was nineteen, he put his mother in a view house on the hills of Laguna Beach, and settled his father closer, in a place half a block from the beach in

Corona del Mar. Janice liked glitz and square footage, but his father wanted a cozy bungalow with "attitude and funk."

Corona del Mar, which was a part of Newport Beach, didn't have a reputation for funk. Ryan found a 2,200-square-foot cottage-style bungalow with enormous charm, confident that Jimmy would bring plenty of attitude and funkiness with him.

Unsure of the situation he would find, he had his limo driver park a block away, and he walked to the house.

Step by step, he considered backing off until Wilson Mott could get armed escorts here.

The United States was one of the few places in the world where a wealthy man could safely live without being parenthesized by bodyguards. In the interest of leading a normal life, with as much liberty as he could keep, Ryan used Mott's armed escorts only when absolutely necessary.

In this instance, while prudence argued for backup, instinct said he must go in alone. Instinct and a belated acknowledgment of the truth also told him that by his actions, he had narrowed his many possible futures to this one aneurysm in the time stream, and Fate would either end him here or give him another chance. Only he could save himself.

He opened a white gate in a white picket fence and walked under a trellis draped with bougainvillea in its less flamboyant winter dress but still with an impressive spray of red petals as bright as blood. A brick walkway led to a porch with side trellises up which climbed trumpet vines.

A gardening service maintained the landscape. Left to Jimmy, the lawn would be dead, and everything else would have rioted into a tangle reminiscent of a third-act set for *Little Shop of Horrors*.

The front door stood ajar. He did not ring the bell, but pushed the door open and stepped inside.

He seldom came here, so the time warp always surprised him, just as it always depressed him. The Age of Aquarius had passed in most of the rest of the world, but here the clocks had stopped in 1968. The psychedelic posters, the Grateful Dead memorabilia, here Sly and the Family Stone, there Hendrix and Joplin, here the Jefferson Airplane, the Day-Glo peace signs, the portrait of Chairman Mao, bamboo window shades flanked by tie-dyed drapes, and of course the hookah on the coffee table.

Jimmy sat on the sofa, and Lily's sister, Violet, stood over him with a silencer-equipped pistol.

Seeing Ryan, his father said, "Shit, man, you took long enough. We have a situation here. Whatever you did to make it, you unmake it right now, 'cause this bitch is a stone-serious psycho."

At sixty-three, Jimmy had no hair on the top of his head but a sufficient crop at the back to make a ponytail. He wore a headband like one that Pigpen had worn, a mustache like David Crosby's, beads purportedly worn by Grace Slick. The only thing about him that was not copied after someone else were his eyes like burnt holes into which had drained water and ashes, the aftermath of a fire, full of childlike calculation and need and quiet desperation, restless eyes that Ryan could bear to meet only when his old man was sufficiently stoned that the fear and resentment and bitterness were for the moment drowned in chemical bliss.

"Bamping," Violet said.

Hearing movement, he turned to see a man step into the living room from the hallway. He was Asian, Ryan's size, and had a pistol of his own.

Indicating Jimmy, she said to Bamping, "Take him to his bedroom and keep him quiet until this is done."

"I don't want to go back there," Jimmy said. "I don't want to go with him."

Violet put the muzzle of the silencer against Jimmy's forehead.

"Dad," Ryan said. "Do what they want."

"Screw 'em," Jimmy said. "Fascist shits."

"She'll blow your brains out, Dad. What can he do to you that would be more final?"

Licking his lips and the fringe of mustache that overhung them, Jimmy rose unsteadily from the sofa. He was a skinny wreck. The seat of his jeans sagged, he had no butt left, and sticking out of his

T-shirt, his elbows looked almost as big as his fore-arms.

"She's making this worse for me," Jimmy said to Ryan. "Bitch won't let me have a joint. Make her let me have one."

"I don't set the rules here, Dad."

"It's your house, isn't it?"

"Dad, go with Bamping."

"Go with what?"

"Bamping. That's his name. Go with him now."

"What kind of name is Bamping?"

"Don't do this anymore, Dad."

"When they bought your company, did they buy your balls?"

"Yes, they did, Dad. They bought them. Now go with him."

"This sucks. This whole situation sucks."

"It's no tangerine dream, that's for sure," Ryan said.

"What's that supposed to mean?"

"Nothing."

"It means something, all right. Wise-ass."

At last Jimmy allowed Bamping to escort him back the hall to the bedroom. A door closed.

"Very carefully," Violet said, "take off your jacket."

"I'm not carrying a weapon."

"Very carefully," she repeated.

He took off the jacket and draped it over the sofa, where she could examine it if she wished. At her command, he took off his shirt and placed that beside his jacket, and then he turned in a circle with his arms extended like the wings of a bird.

Satisfied that he wasn't armed, she pointed to a La-Z-Boy recliner and said, "Sit there."

Obeying, Ryan said, "Funny."

"You are amused?"

"I wouldn't go that far. But it's funny how the warriors of the Greatest Generation and washouts of the next both like their La-Z-Boys."

He did not recline but sat straight up, leaning forward.

"Where have you been?" she asked.

"Denver."

She kept at a distance from him, not willing to get as near as she had been to Jimmy. "Were you running away?"

"I thought about it," he admitted.

"I didn't expect you to come here."

"If I didn't, you would have killed him."

"Yes."

"I guess you still might."

"I might," she said. "I will certainly kill you."

"Maybe I didn't come alone."

"You came in a limousine, which is parked a block away. There is only the driver. He is in the car, listening to very bad music and reading an obscene magazine."

Although Ryan's fear was not diminished, a peculiar calm came over him, as well. He wanted not a single day more that was alike to the days of the past sixteen months. He had been saved from certain death, but he had lost Samantha, he had lost a sense of purpose, and he had lost the capacity for pure joy. His lifelong conviction that the future was worth the travails of the day, while not broken, had been shaken. He had arrived at a lever-point moment. Here he must pivot to a better future or give up the game.

"If you're going to kill me," he said, "may I have the courtesy of knowing fully why?"

FIFTY-TWO

The bamboo shades, dropped to sills, were dimly backlit by the overcast day but admitted no light to the living room or to the dining room that lay beyond a wide archway. Illumination came from two table lamps turned low, from the luminous shapes ever-changing in a lava lamp, from three candles glimmering in colored glasses on the fireplace mantel, and from two glass vessels on the coffee table, in which floating wicks burned scented oils.

More than light, shadows shaped the room, smoothing every sharp corner into a radius, layering velvet folds of faux draperies over flat surfaces, and conspiring with the pulsating candlelight to suggest that the ceiling had an undulant form.

The woman roamed ceaselessly through orderless patterns of pale light and masking shadow, through shimmering nimbuses and quivering penumbras. Her languid movements might have seemed lethargic to some, but not to Ryan, who saw in her the measured restlessness and the lethal power of a tiger.

"Who is this?" she asked, pointing with the pistol to a poster.

"Country Joe and the Fish," Ryan said.

"I don't see fish."

"It's the name of the band. They changed the world."

"How did they change the world?"

"I don't know. That's what my father told me."

Lamplight uplit her face and, with illusory powder and mascara, painted her features into a stark kabuki mask.

"What is the stink?" she asked.

"Scented candles, scented oils."

"The other odor, under that."

"You're probably smelling the pot."

"Marijuana?"

"Yeah. The smoke saturates things. That's why he burns scented candles, to mask it."

"Why does he smoke pot?"

"I don't know. Because he always has."

"He is addicted?"

"They say it's not addictive."

"Doesn't marijuana make you mellow?"

"I don't use it. I don't know. That's what they say."

"He isn't mellow," she said.

"No. He never has been."

Dressed in black slacks, black sweater, and black jacket, she was a shadow moving through shadows. For the most part, the various lamps and candles confirmed her presence only as their light found her hands and her face. Whatever the denomination of the light that paid on her skin, it was given back as gold.

Ryan knew he should be alert for an opportunity to rush her and struggle for the weapon. Often, she pointed the gun away from him and seemed to be distracted by Jimmy's nostalgic collection.

He suspected, however, that her distraction was more apparent than real, that any opening he saw was only an opportunity to be gut-shot.

Indicating another poster, she asked, "Who is this?"

"Another band. The Grateful Dead. They changed the world."

"How did they change it?"

"I don't know. Maybe Dad can tell you."

"I know where your mother lives, but I have not met her yet."

"You're in for a treat," Ryan said.

"Is she like him?"

"Like but different. With her it's alcohol and men, especially men who like alcohol."

"I am thinking about killing all three of you."

Ryan said nothing.

At another poster, she said, "Who is this?"

"Jim Morrison and the Doors."

"Did they change the world?"

"That's what I hear."

As Violet moved past him into the portion of the room that lay behind his La-Z-Boy, Ryan turned his head and started to turn in his seat to follow her.

"Face forward," she said, pointing the pistol at the bridge of his nose.

He did as he was told.

"If you turn your head to look back, I will shoot you. The people in these posters—where are they now?"

"I don't know. A lot of them are dead."

"So the world changed them," she said.

He could barely hear her soft steps. She must have picked up something to have a look at it, for it knocked slightly against a table when she put it down.

In the lengthening silence, he searched his mind for a question or a comment that would begin to give him some control of their conversation.

From so close that her voice startled him, from just behind his right ear, she said, "I told your father my name. Do you know the name of my sister?"

The difference of intonation between the statement and the question was the difference between

an emotionless declaration and the apparently innocent but entrapping query of a police detective.
Her last eight words were a bottled accusation, and
the wrong reply would pull the stopper, releasing her
anger.

After a hesitation that he realized might be dangerous, he said, "Yes. Her name was Lily."

"How did you learn her name? Did you deduce it
from my flowers, from something that I said?"

"No. I asked the family for it, and for a photo,
which is how I know you're identical twins."

"You were given a photo by the family?"

"Yes."

"But I am the family."

"Well, I guess it came from your parents."

"Liar," she said.

She slammed the side of his head with what might
have been the butt of the pistol, and blood burst
from his crushed ear.

As he tried to push up from the chair, the next
blow landed on the top of his skull, so swiftly delivered after the first that the agony in his ear had just
begun to bloom.

A scintillation of pain followed the natural sutures
between the frontal bone of his skull and the two
parietals. Behind his eyes, which had squinched
shut with the pain, he saw the squiggly line of those
sutures picked out in the darkness by sputters of
coppery sparks.

Defensively, frantically, he clasped the top of his head with his hands, so the third blow cracked his fingers. He cried out, or thought he did, but even if he screamed, the fourth blow cut it short, and knocked him unconscious.

FIFTY-THREE

He regained consciousness in stages defined by an increasing tolerance for light. At first, rising from oblivion, he found the oil lamps unendurably bright, their flames so sharp that it seemed each flicker lacerated his eyes. He didn't know where he was or to whom the lamps belonged, and his head was such a mass of pain that he could not think of the words to ask that the wicks be snuffed. He sank back into senselessness, returned, sank again, and by degrees adapted to light and recovered his memory.

When he knew who he was and where and in what circumstances, he raised his chin from his breast and focused on Violet, who sat in an armchair, across the coffee table from him.

"Do you know your name?" she asked.

He could hear her clearly with his left ear, but her

words came to his right as though water flooded the canal. Perhaps the torn ear was only pooled with blood and he was not to any degree deaf.

"Do you know your name?" she asked again.

His answer cracked unspoken in his dry throat. He worked up some saliva, swallowed, and said shakily, "Yes."

"What is your name?"

"Ryan Perry."

He sensed that she possessed the skill to administer a pistol-whipping without risking a concussion, but that she lost control this time and was concerned that she would be able to have less fun with him than she originally intended.

"What is the date?"

He thought for a moment, remembered, told her.

From ear to ear and nose to nape, his head ached, not in a way that mere aspirin could address. In addition to the ache were more intense paroxysms, recurring and receding waves radiating from the right side around to the back of the skull, and trailing these stronger tides of pain were quick but even sharper pangs, six and eight and ten at a time, tattooing a line from his right temple, across the orbit of that eye, and down the bridge of his nose.

When he lifted his left hand off the arm of the chair, intending to put it to his head, he inhaled with a hiss through clenched teeth, because it seemed that broken glass must be embedded in his knuckles.

The index finger was bent immovably at an unnatural angle, and the little finger appeared to have been crushed beyond repair. His hand dripped blood, and the leather upholstery glistered with a slickness of it.

Half of Violet's face lay in soft shadows, half shone gold in lamplight, but both celadon eyes were bright with interest.

"Once more I ask—who gave you a photograph of Lily?"

"Supposedly the family. It came through my surgeon."

"Dr. Hobb."

"Yes."

"When did you receive the photo?"

"Yesterday morning."

"Sunday morning?"

"Yes. And I saw she was your twin."

"And then you fled to Denver."

"First to Las Vegas. Then to Denver."

"Why there?"

He could not explain Ismay Clemm to himself, let alone to this woman. He said, "You cut me in the parking lot. You invaded my house and covered every trace of how you got in and out. You screwed with the security recordings, opened blind deadbolts—"

"Electromagnets can open blind deadbolts. Did it seem like sorcery?"

"I was scared. I had to go somewhere you couldn't find me, somewhere I could think."

"What thoughts did you have in Denver to bring you home again?"

He shook his head, and that was a mistake. A liquid pain sloshed through his cranium.

When the agony passed, he said, "There's no way to put it into words. You wouldn't understand."

"Try."

"You wouldn't understand," he repeated.

Ryan began to contemplate using the coffee table to turn this situation around. The two glass vessels, if overturned and shattered, might splash burning oil not only on the floor and furniture but also on Violet.

She said, "I didn't expect you to come here."

"Yeah. You already said."

"I thought you would let me kill your father."

"I didn't come here just for him."

"What else did you come here for?"

He did not answer. He didn't have to answer everything. She would eventually kill him whether he replied to all her questions or not.

Violet said, "Do you wonder who I am—besides being her sister?"

"I'm pretty sure you're not a schoolteacher."

"What does that mean?"

"A schoolteacher like she was."

"Lily was not a schoolteacher."

Because space had been allowed for the La-Z-Boy to expand to its full length as a recliner, the chair stood farther from the coffee table than Ryan would have liked. If he had been closer, he could have thrust out his legs, kicking the table, tumbling the lamps to shatter on the floor.

"Lily was a seamstress."

"Why would they lie about what she did?" he asked.

Instead of answering the question, Violet said, "I am a security agent. Government security. But different from the FBI, the CIA. Oh, very different, Mr. Perry. You have never heard of this bureau, and you never will."

"Secret police."

"Yes. Essentially. Your bad luck to take the heart of someone with a sister capable of taking it back."

"I didn't take anything. You feel the way you feel. I understand why you might feel that way. I really do. But I was on a recipient list, and she was on a donor list, and we matched. If not me, someone else."

"The list you were on—the United Network for Organ Sharing."

"Yeah. That's right."

"How long did you wait for a heart, Mr. Perry?"

If she pointed the pistol away from him or if she started to get up from the armchair, or if she was distracted for any reason, he might be able to throw himself off the chair, overturn the table, spill the lamps, and in the flare of flames and chaos somehow avoid being shot. The scene played in his mind, admittedly a Hollywood moment of stuntman choreography, but it might work, just might, because there were moments when life imitated movies. He had to play along with her, keep her talking, and hope she gave him an opportunity.

"Dr. Gupta—he gave me a year to live. A year at the most. But I might have been dead in six months, even less. They didn't find a match for almost four months."

"Some people wait a year, two years," she said. "Many never find a match. You had a perfect match . . . in one month."

"No. Four. Four months."

"One month after coming under Dr. Hobb's care."

"Because Dr. Hobb is an exceptional surgeon with a worldwide reputation, licensed to practice in several countries. He can get his patients on the list of the *International* Network for Organ Sharing."

Her pale-green eyes widened as if he had told her something she did not know, information that she must now factor into the equation. "The *International* Network for Organ Sharing." She nodded thoughtfully, as if absorbing this news, but then her eyes narrowed. "There is no such list, Mr. Perry."

"Of course there is. I was on it. Your sister was on

it. After her accident, they matched us, and Dr. Hobb got the call."

She rose from the armchair, but because the pistol remained trained on Ryan, he had no clear chance to get from the recliner to the coffee table.

"What accident do you refer to?" she asked.

"The car crash. Her head trauma."

In the flat, uninflected voice of someone in a trance, Violet said, "Lily was in a car crash."

Her celadon eyes were hard and cold and glazed. She moved slowly around the coffee table, diminutive but no less the predatory tiger.

"Listen...things happen," Ryan said. "They just happen. It's nobody's fault."

"Things happen," she said flatly. "Nobody's fault."

"If maybe..."

"If maybe?" she asked, pausing by the fireplace.

"If maybe you were driving, you can't blame yourself."

"You think I was driving."

Anything he said could be the wrong thing to say, but silence might itself inspire her to shoot him.

"I don't know. I just thought maybe that explains...explains the intensity of your feelings. Explains why...we're here like this."

If eyes revealed intentions, hers told him that he was a dead man. Her stare felt as sharp as shards of porcelain, shatters of her insane rage borne on her gaze.

"I was not driving, Mr. Perry, because there was no accident. No car crash, no head trauma, no *international* list. Fully alive, perfectly healthy, Lily was matched to you and *then* put to death so you could have her heart."

FIFTY-FOUR

Shaking his battered head made the throbbing pains swell stronger, striking up an internal sound like the repeated hard plucking of the bottom-note string on a bass fiddle, and fired off sharper pangs by the quiverful. Yet he shook his head, shook it, denying what Violet had said.

"Why did you fly to Shanghai for a transplant, Mr. Perry? Why all the way to Shanghai?"

"That's where the car crash happened. She was on life support, brain-dead, they kept her alive until I could get there with Dr. Hobb and his surgical team."

"Do you know what Falun Gong is, Mr. Perry?"

He shook his head. He didn't know. She made it sound like he should, but he didn't.

"Falun Gong is a spiritual practice expressed through certain exercises and meditations."

"I never heard of it. Why should I?"

"It was founded in 1992 and banned in 1999 after ten thousand Falun Gong practitioners silently protested the government's arrest and beating of many people in the city of Tianjin."

Shaking his head not only exacerbated the pain but also cast his thoughts into a junkshop jumble, as an earthquake dumps the orderly contents of supermarket shelves onto the floor in a seismic potluck. Yet he continually shook his head, as though he didn't want either the pain to stop or his thoughts to clear.

"A spiritual life is not an approved life. Half the people in my country's labor-camp prisons are Falun Gong," she continued. "They are beaten, worked to death, and tortured."

Judging by the sound of her voice, Violet had moved around the La-Z-Boy, in back of him. He raised his head, and though his vision brightened and dimmed somewhat with the ebb and flow of the pain, he could see well enough to confirm that she was not in the part of the room that lay before him.

"Face forward," she commanded. "Do not turn."

Ryan did not think that she would shoot him in the back of the head. She would first want to hurt him more, and when the time came to finish it, she would want him to be staring down the muzzle of the gun when she squeezed the trigger.

"Lily was Falun Gong. A poor, sweet dreamer of a

girl. My twin but nothing like me. My mind is darker, and my heart."

As if she knew what he had thought, Violet pressed the muzzle of the pistol to the back of his skull, which forced him to stop shaking his head.

"Oh, God, don't. You're making a mistake."

The round muzzle seemed to imprint a third eye in the back of his head, for when he closed the pair with which he had been born, he could see down the barrel to the bullet.

"Lily was a seamstress living on subsistence wages, seeking something to brighten and give meaning to her existence. Falun Gong."

On his face, on his hands, on the chair, his spilled blood issued a faint odor that perhaps only he could smell, and nausea threatened.

She said, "They arrested Lily two years ago. I spent a year trying to get her freed, trying so cautiously, so surreptitiously."

His darkness yawed like the deck of a ship, and he opened his eyes, fixing his stare on the armchair where previously she had been seated, forcing stillness on the room to stave off nausea.

"Forced labor, beatings, torture, rape—not all the Falun Gong prisoners are subjected to those things. Some are kept in good health to be harvested."

A sob escaped Ryan, and he struggled to control himself, for he intuited that instead of earning sympathy for him, his tears would inspire only a murderous contempt. His best hope was steadiness, the exercise of restraint, and an appeal to reason.

"I never heard of Falun Gong," he insisted. "Never."

"There is a hospital in Shanghai that exists for two purposes only. First for certain . . . experiments. Second, to provide transplant procedures for exalted state officials in ill health and for wealthy foreigners who can meet the very high cost."

To his surprise, the woman stepped into view again on his left side. She had pressed the muzzle so hard against the back of his skull that he felt the impression of it even after the pistol had been taken away.

"I learned three days before your surgery that Lily had been transferred from the labor camp to that hospital."

She held the pistol in a two-hand grip, five feet from him, aimed at his throat but no doubt allowing for the barrel to pull up with the shot, to shatter his teeth with the bullet and to punch out the back of his head.

"My sweet Lily's kidneys were needed by two comrades, her liver by another, corneas by a fourth, and her heart by some lord of the Internet, one of the hundred most eligible bachelors."

He learned now a new thing: Fear could take such a grip on a man's emotions that he could experience no other sentiment, on his intellect that he could think of nothing but dying, on his spirit that he could not hope, on his body that he could suddenly not feel the pain of terrible wounds, but could feel only terror with every fiber of his being.

"I didn't know," he groaned, but the words came from him without premeditation, like a chant or litany that had been repeated on ten thousand other occasions and was now, with thought denied him, the only thing he knew how to say.

"You knew," she insisted.

"I swear I didn't." More litany. "I swear I didn't. I swear I didn't. I couldn't have done this if I'd known."

"Dr. Hobb brings patients from around the world. Over the years, a hundred sixty of Dr. Hobb's patients have been matched in a month or less. Dr. Hobb knows."

"Maybe he does, I can't speak for him, I can't defend him. *But I didn't know.*"

"They say so many have been harvested that where their bodies are buried, the ground grows red bamboo. Groves of red bamboo."

"I didn't know."

She lowered the muzzle from his face, and the sound-suppressor on the pistol allowed only a soft and surprisingly biological sound when she shot him in the left foot.

FIFTY-FIVE

Terror could not anesthetize against a bullet wound, at least not entirely, and it could not staunch the blood. But the wound proved less debilitating than Ryan would have imagined, producing not violent and thrilling throes of pain, not agony, but suffering of a kind that cleared his fogged thinking, that broke him out instantly in a head-to-foot sweat even as a chill settled through his stomach and his bowels, racking him with shudders that rattled his teeth.

He didn't scream because he didn't have the wind for it, but the woman said, "If you scream, I'll make you stop the hard way, and then what follows will be even worse for you than it would have been."

The sounds he made were sometimes low and choked-off, sometimes thin and tremulous and pathetic, but they would not carry beyond the walls of the house.

Instead of sliding to the floor, he withdrew into the commodious recliner, holding in his right hand the soft shoe that encased his wounded foot, because he found that gentle pressure eased the pain.

"After losing my Lily, I lived to find you."

With that singular languid restlessness, Violet circled the room again, like some black bird that had flown in through an open door, a winged messenger of merciless intent, seeking now a permanent roost.

"I needed ten months to escape China. Three of us defected on a mission. Then two more months to get to this country, to study you and plan."

Behind the brightness of his pain, a dark incoming tide washed through Ryan's mind, rising above all the sea walls of his defenses, and from beneath his fear of death welled a worse fear that until now he had neither experienced nor imagined to exist.

"Hobb knew," she said as she roamed.

And now all that Ryan could say was, "He didn't tell me."

"Of course he didn't say, 'Let's go to Shanghai and tear open a perfectly healthy girl for you.'"

"If he didn't tell me, how could I have known?" he pleaded, but the plea sounded weak to him. "How could I have known?"

"By what he implied."

To this he could say nothing.

She would not relent: "And by what you inferred."

The dark tide breaching his long-defended sea walls was a tide of truth.

She said, "By the implicit meaning of an *international* donor's list, by the implicit meaning of only a one-month wait for a match, by the implicit meaning of the astronomical cost, by the implicit meaning of an emergency flight to Shanghai, by the implicit meaning of the thousand winks and nods you must have witnessed."

The word shuddered from him: "Subtext."

Actions had consequences. Having always understood this, he had largely lived by the rules in business and in his personal relationships.

The new and most devastating fear welling in him, which he had never known before in thirty-five years, was the fear that actions also had consequences beyond this life.

Her anger having given way to a calm determination to have justice, the woman approached him, with a grave and stern decorum.

"I was groomed to pass for American. To come here one day and form a secret cell."

A note of profound resignation informed her voice, her green eyes seeming to be dreaming.

"*My* secret plan was to bring Lily, disappear into new identities and truly become Americans. Now this country is ruined for me. And China. And I have nowhere."

She stared at him along the barrel of the gun.

Thick blood oozed slowly from the bullet hole in Ryan's shoe, his broken left hand curled into a claw, his head ached as if it were held together by tightly pulled barbed wire, but none of his pains squeezed the tears out of him. They were pressed from him by the recognition of the willful blindness with which he had committed himself to Dr. Hobb, with which in fact he had led his entire life.

Less to Violet than to himself, in response to a confessional impulse, he said, "That night Samantha told me I had to be careful. 'You especially,' she said. 'You, being you, have to be careful.'"

Violet asked, "The author?"

"She said I should just let it happen, I shouldn't *handle* it, just accept, let it happen the way it should."

Again his pain entirely receded, as previously it had been for a while suppressed by terror that crowded out all other feelings.

"My God, she knew what I was capable of. She knew when I didn't. When I didn't know, she knew . . . but loved me."

This time terror, too, was extinguished with the pain, and he had the capacity for only one sentiment, which ruled his emotions, his intellect, his body, a feeling that was new to him but at once familiar: shame.

Ryan Perry had not known until this moment that something in him was broken.

The roots of violence included avarice. Greed.

He said, "My blind greed killed your sister."

"Greed? You've got all the money in the world."

"A greed for life."

He had coveted her heart, any healthy heart, and had lied to himself, had hid himself from himself.

Violet looked at him along the barrel of the pistol.

Now, too late, he realized that sixteen months earlier, in the early hours of his crisis, he had been given an extraordinary grace, a chance to achieve the insight Samantha needed to see in him if they were to marry: an awareness that life and the world have subtext, implicit meaning, that this meaning has consequences. Ismay Clemm, a victim of her husband's greed and of Spencer Barghest's lust for death, had traveled farther than from Denver to California, to warn him away from one path and to lead him toward another. In urgent dreams, Ismay revealed to him three Hells, but he saw them only as three puzzles.

"Nine rounds left," said the voice of the lilies. "Eight to wound and one to finish."

By whatever office Ismay held in death, she had revealed the simple truth. Ryan saw now that he had turned that truth inside out, twisted and knotted it, until he made a mare's-nest of it. Instead of wonder, he reacted with suspicion. He saw dark conspiracy where he should have seen grace. He reasoned his way to explanations that required sinister poisoners, hallucinogenics slipped into his food, conniving employees, a whole world turned mysteriously against him. Only one conspirator had existed: He had conspired against himself to avoid facing the reality of a deeply layered world and eternity.

Looking up at Violet, he said, "The taproot of violence is the hatred of truth."

Dead Lily's living twin shot Ryan high on the left side, just under the shoulder blade.

He was still of this room but not entirely, in part transported and removed from his pain, his body so weak that it no longer had the capacity to share with him the symptoms of its suffering. But this time he entertained no illusion that anyone had secretly slipped drugs to him.

"Ismay gave me . . . one last chance. The bells."

He met Violet's eyes because he felt he owed her the right to see life fade from his.

"Bells?" she said.

"Months before the transplant. Ismay said, if I heard bells . . . come for her. I didn't."

"Ismay. Who is she?"

Lacking both the strength and the clarity of mind to explain, he said merely, "My guardian."

"I rang the bells," Violet said.

He did not understand.

"In the old days, they left some churches standing. Only to hold events in them that would mock their purpose."

"Iron bells."

"The day Lily died, I got a message to her. Said . . . I'd be with her in spirit. I'd ring the bells to testify."

Ryan recalled the ominous tolling, tolling, tolling. And the terrible feeling that he had made a grave mistake of which the bells were warning him.

"Told her I'd ring bells to promise justice," Violet continued. "Told her, when she heard the bells, to know she'll live forever in my heart."

Although afraid of death, Ryan did not think he could take much more of life. He assured her, "It's all right. It's justice."

While talking, she had lowered the pistol. She raised it again.

He said, "Fulfill the promise of the bells."

She shot him high on the right side, under the shoulder blade.

Jolted by the shot, ripped, with the stink of blood now seeming to him like the lovely scent of sacrifice, he saw shadows throughout the room moving toward him.

Little more than an hour earlier, at the airport, before Cathy Sienna had boarded her limo for Los Angeles, she had hugged Ryan fiercely and had whispered in his ear four words no one had ever said to him before. Now for the first time in his life, he spoke those same words to another, with a humility and a sincerity that he was grateful to find within himself: "I'll pray for you."

Because he had one foot outside of time, Ryan could no longer accurately gauge the passage of seconds, but it seemed to him that Violet regarded him for a full minute or more between shots. He was summoning the strength to reassure her again when she turned away from him and fired at one of the posters.

Six shots remained in the magazine, and she used them on dead celebrities, on Chairman Mao, on the lava lamp, which burst brightly.

Without another look at Ryan, she walked out of the room and left him to die.

FIFTY-SIX

Whether he was weak from loss of blood or loss of motive, Ryan made no attempt to move from the La-Z-Boy, where he curled like a dog seeking sleep, both legs drawn up, his head resting upon one arm of the chair.

When the lava lamp had exploded, one of the two table lamps was knocked over and extinguished by flying debris. Now largely lit by candles and by two wicks floating in pools of scented oil, the room, though little damaged, seemed strangely like a ruin brightened only by the last residual flames of a great fire.

Whether long after Violet had gone or immediately in her wake—Ryan could not be certain—a hunched and scampering figure entered, muttering worriedly, cursing angrily. It hovered over him, touching and poking, its breath sour enough to be the exhalations of a troll that ate whatever might wander under its bridge, and then it went to a tall sapphire-blue cabinet painted with stars and moons.

When the figure had been bent over him, Ryan hadn't been able to focus his failing vision; but from a distance, he now identified his father.

The cabinet of stars and moons featured doors on top and drawers below. Jimmy pulled out one of the drawers and emptied its contents onto the floor.

"Dad."

"All right, I know, all right."

"Call 911."

Carrying the drawer, he hustled back to Ryan. Reflected oil-lamp light made lanterns of his eyes.

"Can't let the sonofabitch cops find my stash."

He released the false bottom of the drawer, plucked it out, threw it aside. Next he removed a four-inch-deep, rectangular metal lockbox of the kind in which small businesses secured their folding cash at the end of the day.

"I'm shot."

Fumbling with the lockbox latches, Jimmy said, "Minute, minute, minute." From the metal box he took plastic bags of pot and hashish. "Gotta flush, then I'll call."

"Call *then* flush."

"Too much shit going down here, too much shit. Can't get caught with this stuff, too."

"Dad. Please. Call."

As Jimmy scuttled away through the baleful light, muttering to himself—"Gotta flush, gotta flush, gotta flush"—he was reminiscent of no one so much as Rumpelstiltskin, except more demented.

Ryan tried to get up from the chair. He passed out.

Approaching sirens woke him.

Jimmy was bent over the La-Z-Boy, pressing a rag to Ryan's head.

"What're you doing?"

"Gotta stop the bleeding."

The damp rag smelled like dishwater, but Ryan didn't have the strength to push it away. He spoke through it as it fluttered against his face: "Dad, listen."

"They're almost here."

"Wore masks."

"Who did?"

"Broke in wearing masks."

"Like shit they did."

"We never saw faces."

"I saw their faces."

The tail of the rag flicked into his mouth, and he spat it out. "They had . . . wrong address."

"Be quiet. Keep your strength."

"They wanted Curtis someone."

"Shit they did. No Curtis here."

"Shot me before they realized."

As the sirens died, Jimmy said, "Pullin' up in front."

Rallying himself, Ryan grabbed the rag and tore it away from his face. "*Listen.* That's the story."

Confused, his father said, "We need a story?"

Ryan would not finger Violet and her two associates. He didn't want the old man to do it, either.

"Deep shit, Dad. We need a story."

"Masks, wrong address, Curtis someone," Jimmy said.

"Can you do it?"

"Bullshit cops? Been doing it all my life."

A moment later, paramedics were in the room.

So recently willing to die, Ryan was surprised, as the medics bent to him, how much he wanted to live.

FIFTY-SEVEN

Three years and five months after the release of her first novel, Samantha published her third. Lexington, Kentucky, at the end of her twenty-one-city publicity tour, was not a standard stop on authors' promotional schedules. She had asked her publisher to include it after Atlanta, to bring her close to St. Christopher's Ranch, which would give her an excuse to phone him.

She thought he might feel less comfortable agreeing to see her if she came across the country just for that purpose, and might be more relaxed if he thought she happened to be in the neighborhood. Two weeks earlier, when she called him, he seemed pleased to hear from her, and she secured an invitation without pressing for it.

That morning, she rented a car and drove deep

into the Bluegrass region, taking back roads where she could, in no hurry, enchanted by the rolling rural landscape, the miles on miles of black plank fences, white plank fences, and limestone walls, beyond which magnificent Thoroughbreds grazed in pristine meadows.

St. Christopher's Ranch sat on seventy acres. Its meadows were as lush as any in the area, and the horses at pasture were beautiful though not Thoroughbreds. The main house stood far back from the county route, at the end of a driveway overhung by ancient oaks.

Encircled by a deep veranda, this enormous but elegant Kentucky manor house, white with black trim, was shaded from the worst of the June sunshine by the largest willow trees that Sam had ever seen.

Both ramps and steps rose from walkways to the veranda. She took the wide steps.

This spacious porch was furnished with gliders and large padded wicker chairs, in one of which sat a tow-headed and freckled boy of about thirteen, tanned and barefoot, in blue-jean shorts and a DOGS ROCK T-shirt. He was reading a book and, because he had no arms, he turned the pages with his toes.

"Hey," he said, looking up from his book, "you ever been told you sure are pretty?"

"Heard it a couple times," she said.

"What's your name?"

"Sam."

"With a name like that, a girl better be pretty. If I was ten years older, you'd be toast."

"You ever been told you're a terrible flirt?"

"Heard it a couple times," he said, and grinned.

As instructed by phone, she went through a screen door into a front hall with a lovely old walnut floor. Here the ranch offices were situated in an atmosphere so relaxed, all the doors stood open.

Father Timothy was in his office, at his desk, where she had been told he would be when she arrived. Tall, stoop-shouldered, with a face weathered by sun and wind, he could have passed for any ranch hand or experienced horseman if he had not been in a monk's habit.

"Because this is a dog-wash day, Binny had a lot to do this morning, and since he wasn't sure exactly when you'd get here, he asked me to take you to him."

"Binny," she said.

"Oh, you wouldn't know, we call him that around here. His name being well known, and him wanting a low profile. It's just what we call him instead, for privacy's sake."

In her first novel, there had been a character nick-named Binny.

Father Tim led her through the main house to what he called the park, which was rather like a quadrangle on a college campus. Three other houses, similar to the original manor house but newer, embraced this large paved area, which was shaded by a grove of oaks.

The park bustled with festive activities. Children in wheelchairs sat at low tables, working on all manner of craft projects. A group of ambulatory kids in karate pajamas took instruction in martial arts. A storybook hour was under way, with children seated on pillows, in a semicircle around an animated nun evoking a rabbit's surprise and fright with flamboyant gestures. And everywhere dogs lazed or frolicked, golden retrievers and Labradors, all vigorous and well-groomed and happy.

"The brothers live in the expanded main house," Father Timothy explained as Sam accompanied him through the oak-shaded park, "and the sisters have a convent farther back on the property. These three other houses are dormitories, but we need to build a fourth. We don't segregate the children by types of disability, Down syndrome rooms with paraplegic, so they can learn to appreciate one another's special strengths."

St. Christopher's accepted orphans and abandoned children with special needs of all kinds. The younger ones eventually might be adopted, but those over six, who were harder to place, most likely could expect to live at the ranch until they were adults.

The brothers' several enterprises included the

breeding and raising of show-quality dogs. Although this work produced a profit, the unsold dogs ranked as important as those who went on to show-prize glory or to happy homes, because these remained on the ranch and were not merely companions to the children but were also trained to socialize them and to help them learn confidence.

Beyond the park, wide paved pathways led to stables and riding rings, to more fenced pastures, to the convent, and to service buildings, one of which contained the on-site veterinary office and the dog-grooming facility.

Father Tim escorted Sam to the dog-wash, opened the door, and said, "I'll not intrude upon your reunion. You'll recognize Binny—as the kids say, if he had one more floppy ear, he would be just like the dogs."

The big room included bath sinks, grooming tables, and dog dryers. One golden retriever sat in a dryer, gazing out mournfully, as if imprisoned. Ryan, assisted by a Down syndrome boy of about fifteen, administered astringent gel to the ears of a black Lab who had already been dried.

Not having noticed Samantha yet, Ryan said to the boy, "Find his collar there, Rudy, and take him back to Sister Josephine."

Rudy said he would, then saw Sam and smiled. Ryan knew the meaning of the smile, and turned.

He wore rubber boots and a rubber apron over

khakis and a green knit shirt. Sam had never seen him dressed with such disregard for style—nor had he ever looked more elegant.

Because she had not been sure how this would unfold, she was moved and happy to see that at the sight of her, his face brightened with unmistakable delight.

"There you are," he said. "My God, there you are."

The way he looked at her brought tears to her eyes, and seeing this, Ryan busied her with an introduction to Rudy and then to Ham, the Labrador who needed to be returned to Sister Josephine.

"Rudy here," Ryan said, "is going to be a great dog groomer." The boy ducked his head shyly. "He's already pretty good except he doesn't like the part where you have to express their anal glands."

"Yuch," the boy said.

As Rudy left with Ham, Ryan said, "Let me get out of this gear, wash up. We'll have lunch. I made it. The lunch, I mean." He shook his head. "You're actually here. Don't go anywhere. Let Tinker out of the dryer, she's done. She's mine. She'll be going to lunch with us."

The retriever was grateful to be paroled and doubly grateful for an ear massage and a chin scratch.

Ryan took off the apron, hung it up, took off the boots, laced on a pair of running shoes, and then scrubbed his hands and forearms at one of the long, deep dog-wash sinks.

"Tinker is wonderful," Sam said.

"She's the best. She wonders why she's stuck with me instead of with a kid who'll throw the ball all day for her."

"I'm sure she adores you."

"Well, yes, 'cause I'm the one with the cookies."

Ryan took her hand so naturally that it seemed they had never been apart, and Tinker led them outside, around the building, and up a set of exterior stairs to a second-floor porch.

His apartment was smaller than the one that she'd had on Balboa Peninsula: kitchen and living room in a cramped space, the bedroom positively tiny.

Lunch consisted of cold chicken, cheese, potato salad—"I make a killer potato salad"—fresh tomatoes and cucumbers. Together Ryan and Sam prepared the table on the porch.

Unlike the porch she'd had on Balboa, this one enjoyed no all-embracing pepper tree, but it had a roof. The view was of a baseball diamond and fenced pastures beyond.

"How's the book doing?" he asked.

"Fastest-selling yet."

"Fantastic. I told you. Didn't I tell you? You're no one-hit wonder."

They talked about the book business, about what she was writing now, and about St. Christopher's, of which it seemed he might be able to talk for days and never exhaust his supply of charming stories.

She had come to see if he was well and happy, for it mattered very much to her that he should be both. When a man went to the extraordinary length of giving away his entire fortune, you had to worry that he had done so under the misguided romantic notion that he would find his problems lifted from him with the weight of the wealth, only to discover that the world was a harder place without a bottomless bank account. But he seemed happier than she had dared to hope, and she knew he was not putting on a show for her, because he was still as easy to read as any book by Dr. Seuss.

"The days, the weeks, the years are so full here, Sam. There are always dogs to wash, stables to paint, lawns to mow, and always kids who think only I can solve their problems because I've got one dog-ear. I love the kids, Sam. God, they're great, they struggle with such limitations, but they never complain."

He could have had the ear repaired with cosmetic surgery, but for reasons she could only guess at, he had chosen to live with it. Likewise the scars on his head: Tufts of hair bristled at odds with all the hair around them or didn't grow at all. Poor nerve response in his left foot caused it to drag a little, but he didn't limp; he moved with his usual grace, adapting to the foot as if he had been born with the problem. He remained the handsomest man she had ever known, and now he possessed a sweet beauty that had not been his before, that had nothing to do with looks.

They talked through the afternoon, and although Samantha had no intention of asking him what had happened back in the day, when his life had changed so radically, he eventually came to talk of it, and for the first time she heard about all that he had withheld from her—Ismay Clemm, the dreams, the paranoid pursuit of conspiracies that for a while he believed extended to her mother, even to her. He spoke of his blindness and of his mistakes with an ease and humility—even with a slightly melancholy humor—that made this the most riveting narrative to which she had ever listened, no less because of the way these events had so profoundly changed him than because of the events themselves.

She questioned none of the supernatural elements of his story, for though she had never seen a spirit herself, the world had always been to her a place of infinite layers, and all its flawed people a community of saints potential. And most of the time, as Ryan now knew, grace is offered not in the form of a visitation like that of Ismay, but in the form of people just like us. People like Cathy Sienna, who had known Ryan needed to be told the roots of violence, even if he would not consider them until too late, and who later, on that flight back from Denver, had told him that he should offer his suffering and his achievements for the intentions of others, which was now in fact how he lived, with no expectation of ultimate mercy but with the hope that others might receive it.

She had been in love with him once, and still she loved him. This was a different love, emotional and intellectual and spiritual, as before, but not sensual. Through his suffering, he learned to love truth, and on this afternoon she saw that his love of truth led him to an understanding of her that he had never possessed before, an understanding of her so complete that perhaps he alone in the world really knew her. During this astonishing afternoon, her love for him had grown deeper, and she wondered if in her life she would know anything again quite like it.

In late afternoon, when the time came to part, they both knew it and rose together from the table. He and Tinker escorted Sam back across the ranch, past the stables and the riding rings, through the quadrangle, to her car in front of the original manor house.

As they walked, he said, "One more thing I need to say to you, Sam, and I know you'll want to argue, but I ask you up front to cut me some slack. No argument. No comment. Just listen. I'm a fan of your books, after all, so that ought to earn me a big measure of courtesy. A writer needs to keep her fans happy."

She perceived in his calculated light tone that what he needed next to say to her was more important to him than anything else they had talked about throughout the afternoon. By her silence, she assented.

He took her hand again, and they walked a few steps before he said, "Looking back on it all, for the longest time, I couldn't see why a guy like me was so important to the universe that I would be sent Ismay Clemm or be given all the signs that could have prevented me from being a user who now lives with a dead girl's heart and with her life on my conscience. Why would *I* be given so many chances when I was so clearly not a guy who would take them or even recognize them? And then one day not long ago, I knew. Reading this third book of yours, I knew. It was you, Sam. I was given all those chances because of you."

"Ryan—"

"You promised no comment. See, here's how it is. You're a fine person, more than fine, you're grace personified. And what you're doing with your life is important. It's necessary that you're happy, because in your happiness, you're going to show so many other people the way, through your books. Be happy, Sam. Find someone. Marry. Have kids. What an incredible mother you will be. Have kids, Sam, embrace life, and write your brilliant books. Because if there's any hope for me, when my time comes, it's not because I gave everything away, and it's not because I live here among monks, not one myself and never can be. No, if there's any ultimate redemption, it will be because I passed through your life without scarring you, and did not diminish who you are. No comment, now, not a one."

They had reached her car, and she did not know that she could drive or that she could talk. But she knew what he wanted of her, what he needed. So she found within herself the depth of courage to make no comment on what he had said, and instead to smile at him and find something to say that might end this on a lighter note.

"You never did tell me . . . what was the William Holden film that you kept waking to and thinking had a message for you?"

By his smile and then his soft laugh, she knew that she had found a right question.

"God must have a sense of humor, Sam. And for sure He became so exasperated with me that He tried to hammer me over the head with a sign only less obvious than a burning bush. It's not what the movie is about that matters. It's the title that might have made me think—if I'd taken the clue and bothered to research it." He paused for effect. "*Satan Never Sleeps.*"

She found a laugh in that, though of the kind that bruises.

He held her for a moment, and she held him, and she kissed his cheek, and he kissed her brow.

Driving away, she looked once in the mirror and

saw him standing in the lane, watching her leave, and she could not look back again.

Along the county road, when she found a widening of the shoulder where she could park, she stopped the car.

An unfenced meadow sloped up toward a trio of oaks. She climbed the meadow to the trees and sat with her back against the largest of them, hidden from traffic on the road below.

For a long time, she wept, not so much for him and not at all for herself, but for the condition of all things and for the way the world could be but is not.

In time, she found herself thinking about nothing more than the birds and their songs, the sound of the breeze in the high branches of the oaks, and the shafts of sunlight, clear and pure, that fell through the trees and found the grass and caressed it.

She rose then and returned to the car. She needed to go home. She had a new book to write. And a life to find.

ABOUT THE AUTHOR

DEAN KOONTZ is the author of many #1 *New York Times* bestsellers. He lives in Southern California with his wife, Gerda, their golden retriever, Anna, and the enduring spirit of their golden, Trixie.

Correspondence for the author should be addressed to:

Dean Koontz
P.O. Box 9529
Newport Beach, California 92658